Copyright © 2024 by Ken Lozito

All rights reserved.

No part of this book may be reproduced in any form or by any electronic or mechanical means, including information storage and retrieval systems, without written permission from the author, except for the use of brief quotations in a book review.

Published by Acoustical Books, LLC

KenLozito.com

Cover design by Tom Edwards

**IF YOU WOULD LIKE TO BE NOTIFIED WHEN MY NEXT BOOK IS RELEASED VISIT**

WWW.KENLOZITO.COM

Paperback ISBN: 978-1-945223-73-0

Hardback ISBN: 978-1-945223-74-7

# RESURGENCE

**KEN LOZITO**

ACOUSTICAL BOOKS LLC

# CHAPTER 1

Connor walked down a quiet corridor, peacefully dim and silent but for the small background sounds of environmental recordings. The ambient lighting of the pale walls was akin to that of a yellow main sequence star. It was the middle of the afternoon, and he'd taken a circuitous route to the conference room near the *Reliant's* main bridge.

It had been almost a year since the *Reliant* and its exploratory fleet had left New Earth's star system, and over three years since they'd re-established contact with Old Earth.

He rounded a corner, and two junior officers stepped aside.

"General Gates," they said.

Connor gave them a nod as he passed them.

He'd served on—and later commanded—more than a few warships during his military career. The *Reliant* was technically a heavy cruiser class warship for service in the Colonial Defense Force Fleet, but its design had been changed. The superstructure was that of a warship, but the interior had been reconfigured to accommodate both a civilian and military crew, which meant it had lost some of its teeth so they could afford certain luxuries required for long deployments far from home.

No one would ever mistake life aboard a ship for anything but what it was. A ship would never be the same as living on a planet, but Connor had to admit that they'd come a long way from the spartan and spatially challenged ships he'd served on.

Connor walked inside the conference room, and the CDF officers stood up and saluted him. There were several civilians seated at a table, along with holoscreens that displayed others from various ships in the task force. His gaze flicked toward the video feed from the *Challenger,* and he spotted his son Ethan seated next to Major Caleb Arvad.

"Good afternoon," Connor said as he strode toward his seat. "Director Grayson," he said to his neighbor seated next to him.

A deep, sonorous chuckle bubbled up from Dennis Grayson's stocky chest, and he gave Connor a lopsided smile. "No Lenora?"

Connor frowned and glanced around the room. It wasn't like his wife to miss one of these meetings, even if the long deployment was wearing on her patience. "Must be running late."

Dennis nodded. "I'm looking forward to tonight's game. Tell her I won't fall for the same tricks twice."

Connor chuckled. "I'll convey the message, but I doubt it'll help."

What had started out as a friendly poker game among friends one evening had turned into a regular weekly gathering. Fortune hadn't favored Connor at last week's game, nor had it Dennis, who had been successfully bluffed by Lenora.

"Reminds me of my beautiful niece. Bright blue eyes that exude innocence, and then they strike!" He barked out a laugh and then sighed.

Connor nodded and saw Martinez looking at him. "Colonel Martinez, why don't we get started."

Martinez nodded and tapped a button on his holo-interface to record the meeting. He arched an eyebrow, smiling. "Colonial Expeditionary Force, I hereby begin the meeting as we start the final leg of our mission." There were several muffled cheers and more than a few chuckles around the conference room. "One last sector and one last chance to increase our knowledge of these star systems. One last chance to put our mark on the historical record."

Oliver Martinez had served with Connor for the past four years, ever since the first expedition that had taken them back to Earth. He was an outstanding officer, knew how to read the room, and was decisive when the situation required it.

These all-hands meetings were part of the protocol that had been agreed upon. They needed to involve both the military and civilian leaders of the task force, who would then provide updates to their subordinates. It was necessary for cohesion in a mixed crew like this.

"COMCENT, along with the Earth Coalition, is requesting a review of the effectiveness of the exploratory task force ships to assist with forming the strategy for future exploration initiatives," Martinez said, and paused for a moment to look at Connor.

"These missions are relatively new," Connor said, "and like many governmental programs, there are a lot of opinions as to the best way to explore star systems near both Earth and New Earth. We're on the edge of this effort, and we have the unique opportunity to influence these explorations beyond the immediate future."

Dennis leaned forward. "Why do I feel like that was directed at me?"

Connor smiled, and flicked his eyebrows once.

Dennis spread his hands palms up. "We need a balanced

approach to exploration that accurately weighs the risks involved but doesn't hinder the progress of the overall mission."

"We're not under any time constraints, so we can take as long as we like."

"True," Dennis said, pausing for a moment before looking at the others. "Decisions made in a vacuum are sometimes necessary, but this isn't one of those instances. Therefore, I urge each of you—commanding officers of your respective ships and civilian administrators—to consider this mission and future missions. Make your thoughts known as to how you think these missions should be conducted. General Gates is a proponent of a multi-ship task force to ease the risk of being so far from home. However, there are proposals for singular ship missions that are equipped for longer voyages."

Martinez cleared his throat. "There are no guarantees out here. We will eventually encounter other alien civilizations. Hopefully, they won't be as hostile as others we've met. I, for one, believe in a multi-ship task force like this, with a heavy cruiser class and three destroyer class ships. We'd still have the option of short deployments for single ships while not straying far from backup."

The holoscreen for Major Caleb Arvad brightened, indicating he'd like to speak. "This becomes a logistical issue, and many of the risks can be overcome with the protocols we use while exploring. Infinity drives are improving all the time, so if a ship were to suffer mechanical issues, help might not be that long in coming. As for hostile alien encounters, that's why we take a measured approach to star systems."

Connor nodded. "You make a good point, Major Arvad. We're not charging blindly into a star system, hoping for the best. Reliance on established protocols and how we remain agile is important, and we need to allow for improvements along the way. We're not going to decide anything here. In fact, this is a measured approach that will take into account all of our opinions, using them as data points to assist in designing a way forward."

Dennis tipped his head toward Connor. "Well said, my friend."

The meeting progressed with status updates for the entire task force. One undeniable fact was that longer deployments had increased wear and tear, even with the best of alloys. Equipment had a shelf life and must be maintained.

"Excuse me, sirs, I have an additional item to bring up if there's time," Major Arvad said.

Martinez glanced at the meeting timer for a second and nodded. "There's time. Go ahead, Major."

"Long-range scans show a lone planetary body in the expanse, about the size of a moon. Ordinarily, we'd tag the rogue moon to avoid as we transition into hyperspace, but there are strong indicators of rich mineral deposits and ice. I'd like to propose a salvage mission before we move on in the sector."

Martinez pursed his lips for a moment and then brought up a new data feed in the holotank, which showed the scan data. He looked at Connor. "What do you think, General Gates?"

Connor peered at the data. He considered tossing the question back at Oliver, since he was going to allow him to take the lead on exploration of this sector. "I think it's a good idea. Give our people a chance to stretch their legs. Set a course. And Major Arvad, I'll expect a detailed mission proposal from you by tomorrow morning."

"Yes, General Gates," Arvad said and smiled a little. "I have the perfect candidate already working on it," he said, tilting his head a little toward Ethan.

Connor's eyebrows twitched as he smiled. His son was

among the most enthusiastic about the exploration initiative and had good reasons for his position. Connor lowered his chin a little. "I look forward to reviewing it."

The meeting wrapped up, and the holoscreens winked offline.

"Do you have a moment, General?" Martinez asked.

The others filed out of the room, and it was just the two of them. Connor had been checking his messages to see if Lenora had sent him something. He closed his personal holoscreen and stood. "Sure, what is it?"

"Just something I've noticed. Before the meeting, I was reviewing the personnel records and applications for promotions."

"Okay."

Martinez looked as if he was considering how to articulate a sensitive subject.

Connor rolled his eyes. "Come on, Ollie. Say what's on your mind."

Martinez sighed. "It's not so much the applications but the lack of a certain application I was expecting. Not only me but also Caleb."

Connor nodded slowly in understanding. "Then Ethan will miss this round."

Martinez grimaced. "Ethan has got the time in grade, sir. Caleb's review of his performance is glowing. I don't know why he'd put this off."

"Have you asked him?"

"I'd planned on it, but..." Martinez said, giving Connor a meaningful look.

"Want me to do your recruiting for you?"

Martinez grinned. "Not a chance, sir, but I know you've got some insight."

"Of course *I* do, but what do *you* think?"

Martinez considered it for a moment. "He's done well with that team he's built. The hybrids are excellent spacers. He's already doing the job of a major."

"That he has. Promoting Ethan to captain was the right thing to do, but he's got his own goals. He could also be in the process of putting his application forward."

"Does he really think he'll be assigned somewhere else? He's become a specialist when it comes to exploration."

"I'm sure Major Arvad will give him a kick to get him in gear."

Martinez chuckled. "I've been on the receiving end of those a time or two in my career."

Connor laughed. "It happens to the best of us. Sometimes more than a few times."

# CHAPTER 2

Connor left the conference room and headed for the dining lounge, shaking his head at the thought. He'd spent most of his life in the military and had eaten in mess halls and galleys alike. After spending nearly a year on the *Reliant*, where the traditional mess hall had been renamed to a more civilian friendly "dining lounge," he realized the designation had penetrated even his own habitual references to such things. But while the dining lounges on the *Reliant* were nicer than any galley he'd ever taken his meals on, the food wasn't much different.

Lenora's locater reported she was inside.

Connor entered the lounge and walked up the stairs to the upper level. There were booths along the wall where giant wallscreens showed images of the region of space they happened to be in. The distant stars that filled the expanse didn't claim his attention, nor the rather impressive red nebula that stretched across the way; rather, it was Lenora that captivated him. She sat with her back toward him, and her shoulders shook a little, drawing up tightly. He slowed his pace. They'd been married for nearly three decades, and he knew something had upset her.

Connor stopped and Lenora blew out a breath, shoulders slumping a little as she quickly wiped her eyes. She must've heard him.

He gently placed his hand on her shoulder, rubbing it. The muscles were tight, almost sharp under his touch. She looked up at him with misty eyes, and her cheeks were blotched with red.

"What's wrong? What happened?"

She closed her eyes and shook her head. Then she reached for his hand and squeezed it for a second, gesturing for him to sit.

"Connor," she said with a sad smile, "it's Lauren. She's pregnant."

Connor blinked, and his thoughts flatlined for a few long moments. Then the edges of his lips lifted, and he smiled. "Really? When?"

Lauren and Isaac had been married for almost three years and had returned to New Earth over a year ago.

Lenora swallowed and lifted her eyes toward his. "She's six months along." The statement was borderline scathing, with hints of pain.

Connor's eyes widened. "Six months? Are you sure she didn't mean weeks?"

Lenora shook her head irritably. "I'll forward you the video message. She said she delayed telling us because we were away."

A small knot settled in the pit of his stomach, and he winced. He reached across the table and held Lenora's hand. Being away this long had been hard enough on Lenora. It would have been a lot worse if they'd known Lauren was pregnant.

His heart rate spiked. Lauren was pregnant! His chest filled with pride at the thought of his baby girl becoming a mother. Lauren had grown into a loving and mature woman. She was going to be a wonderful mother. A lopsided smile appeared on his face, and Lenora glowered a little. "We're going to be grandparents!"

Lenora winced with a sad smile. Her cheeks reddened as more tears came. Connor leaned over and hugged his wife. They shared the moment, their hearts swollen, even if it was a little bittersweet.

"Connor, we should be there," Lenora whispered. "We need to be there."

He rubbed her back soothingly and nodded. "We will. We'll be back in time for the baby to be born. Might be a little close."

Lenora stiffened and leaned away, staring at him for a long moment. "I should be there for her. We both should."

"We didn't know, Lenora."

"I didn't know they were trying to have a baby. She never mentioned it."

"She must've had her reasons."

Lenora leveled an accusing look at him. "I must've begun to open a comlink a half a dozen times, but the damn relay between us and New Earth is down for some reason. Regardless, she should've told us. Why would she wait so long?"

Connor arched an eyebrow. "Technically, she's an adult and doesn't have to tell us anything she doesn't choose to."

"Don't give me that. She managed me—us—like we're one of her patients. Why aren't you angry about this?"

Connor knew a thing or two about managing relationships, especially with family. He considered his reply for a few moments before answering. "Because she's having a baby. Our baby is having a baby." He grinned. "If that doesn't put a smile on your face, I don't know what will."

A wide range of emotions showed in Lenora's gaze, going

from irritation to love as her heart softened. Then her gaze narrowed playfully. "When did you become such a sap?"

He laughed. "That's on you." Her eyes gleamed. "We know our daughter. Lauren was looking out for us."

"By lying to us."

He sighed. "Yeah, she did by omission."

"I don't like being lied to. We're all adults here. How dare she treat us like we're the child!"

"You're right. She should've told us. Good intentions aside, is this really something you want to go to war over?"

Lenora pressed her lips together for a second and then shook her head. "No, of course not. But that doesn't mean I'm not going to give her a piece of my mind. I thought we were all past keeping secrets and the like."

Connor felt a tiny pang of guilt at that. He'd been the one to keep a few secrets early in their marriage, believing he was protecting Lenora. Sometimes he was, but he'd be lying to himself if he thought that was all there was to it. Maybe Lauren had inherited some of his old habits.

She sagged in her chair and stared at the table. "You know, when I agreed to come on this trip, I knew it was going to be long, but I hadn't expected it to be so…" she trailed off.

Connor waited a few seconds until Lenora lifted her gaze toward his, then said, "That life would go on in our absence. I know what that's like."

Lenora blinked at him a few times. "How did you deal with it?"

"You ought to know. It was you and the kids I was coming back to. I dealt with it by giving you all my full attention when I came back. The by-product was making it more difficult to leave. Not necessarily a bad thing when you think about it."

Lenora smiled fondly in remembrance and sighed. "I can't wait to go back home."

He chuckled. "No, really?"

She rolled her eyes. "I can now say that ship living isn't for me. Planet-side is where I'd rather be." She arched an eyebrow. "Just in case there were any doubts."

Connor pursed his lips for a moment. "What if the ship was bigger?"

Lenora shook her head emphatically. "It could never be big enough."

"Not even if it was the size of a small moon or something like that?"

"Keep dreaming. How would we even build a ship that big? Probably a moot point anyway, at least until there are more people."

Connor nodded. "You're probably right about that."

Lenora's gaze narrowed, and a playful glint came to her eyes, lips curving. "Speaking of which."

He snorted, knowing that look. It came sometimes whenever the subject of having more kids came up. "Really? *Now* you want to talk about this?"

She nodded, her expression becoming serious. "We've been putting this off for a long time."

He frowned. "Yeah, but with Lauren starting a family, I figured that—"

"That what? We'd stop having children? We're not that old, Connor."

He blinked. "Are you trying to catch up to Diaz?"

Lenora laughed and shook her head. "He's got a colony of his own." She shrugged. "Maybe."

They stared at each other for a long moment. The subject had come up over the years, and they'd decided to keep putting it off. With prolonging capable of expanding the human lifespan to well over two hundred years, it wasn't uncommon for generations of children to overlap. It did make for peculiar aunt/uncle and niece/nephew relationships, but those were easily overcome.

Connor leaned toward her and smiled. "Do you mean right now?"

She laughed and pushed him away. "Fiend."

"I just figured if we're going to catch up to Diaz, we better get started." He was tempted to scoop her up out of that chair, dining lounge or not, and carry her all the way back to their quarters.

They were both silent for a few minutes, enjoying some quiet time.

She smiled and her eyes drew him in. "Thank you, Connor. You always seem to know just what to say."

He lifted his wrist computer. "Hang on, I'd like to get a recording of this. Would you say that last part again?"

She shook her head. "Say what?"

He lowered his hand with mock betrayal. "Fine."

Lenora pursed her full lips for a moment. "It hasn't been all bad being way out in the middle of nowhere, light years away from home, but I'd hoped we'd find some semblance of a civilization."

Connor nodded. "They can't all be like New Earth."

"For all its challenges, it was a dream come true. Until New Earth, we'd never encountered an alien civilization."

"There will be others," Connor said evenly.

"Hopefully, they'll be friendlier."

"It would be a nice change." He paused for a moment, considering. "I'm glad we got to do this—come on this mission. It'll help with structuring future missions, but I wanted this time with Ethan."

Lenora gave him a knowing look. Connor had made his peace with the past and the son he'd been forced to leave behind. It was an old wound that had scarred over.

Lenora squeezed his hand. "It's time. When this mission is over, we'll return home, but Ethan will more than likely stay out here." Connor nodded slowly. She gestured around the lounge. "Look at all this—everything that went into building this ship and all the other ships, the cities, and everything else. We all had a part in it, but none of us had the impact you did."

Once again, Connor found himself at a crossroads in his career. He was part of the old guard who'd fought wars and explored more than most people alive, but he knew it wasn't something he could keep up. At some point, he'd have to allow the future generations to take up the torch for humanity's future.

"Our survival is in the hands of many now, thanks to you. I know you hate being reminded of it, but it's true, Connor."

They regarded each other for a few moments. "It just feels like I'm leaving something unfinished."

Lenora nodded knowingly. "I think it might always feel like that."

His lips pursed a little as he thought about it. Maybe she was right. No matter when he stepped away from being on the edge, whether it be exploring other star systems or assessing future threats, he wondered if it would always feel like there was more to do and see.

# CHAPTER 3

Ethan Gates stood in Major Caleb Arvad's ready-room aboard the *Challenger*.

"The mission is yours," Arvad said.

"Thank you, Major," Ethan replied.

Arvad looked amused. "You knew it would be cleared."

"I had a hunch it would be. No way I could know for sure."

Arvad bobbed his head slowly and rubbed his chin. "Good hunch then."

"Maybe so. One of the challenges of this kind of long deployment is getting practical use of our training. We're supposed to be agile, but if we restrict exploits to include only star systems, we might miss something really interesting. Alternatively, if we take time to survey star systems, we don't cover as many sectors in our deployment window, but our teams get practical experience."

Arvad arched a dark eyebrow. "Why, Captain Gates, that sounded like something you prepared to say ahead of time."

Ethan tipped his head to the side a little, lips lifting. "Maybe a little. We need to be more self-sufficient, especially for the longer deployments. A year sounds like a long time, but it really isn't."

Arvad snorted a little. "A year is plenty long enough, at least for most people. Regarding self-sufficiency, our superiors agreed. I'm going to give you full autonomy for this mission. It'll be your operation from beginning to end."

Ethan stood a little taller. "I'll have a mission plan put together in a few hours."

"You mean you don't have one already?"

Ethan smiled. "I do, but I want to check with my team. They had some equipment maintenance concerns. I could give you the highlights of the mission right now if you wanted."

"A few hours is fine, and don't forget to consider the active scan data we'll get when we arrive at the target," Arvad said and paused for a moment. He exhaled a long breath. "This is our time to prove what we can do. A lot more could be riding on this than we think."

"I'm looking forward to proving what we can do, sir."

Arvad nodded in approval. "Dismissed," he said, lifting his chin toward the door.

Ethan left and bolted through the corridor, unable to keep the spring from his step. He served as the *Challenger*'s XO and was concerned that he wouldn't be allowed to execute as many field operations because of those duties. As it was, he rotated his XO duties with Captain Ester Talori, which freed Ethan up to command the direct action force on the *Challenger*.

Ethan stepped onto the elevator and sent out a meeting notification to his team leaders. Then he spared a glance toward a long list of unread messages, none of which were urgent—at least none of them had been marked urgent—so those messages could wait. Switching off his personal holoscreen right before the elevator doors opened, he walked down the corridor to a vacant assembly room where he found Tom and Flynn waiting for him.

"Captain Gates," they acknowledged.

"At ease, Lieutenants," Ethan said.

A notification appeared on his internal HUD. He skimmed it and it faded from view.

Tom Washburn was his second-in-command and was senior of the two because he had longer time in grade. "We happened to be close by, sir."

Flynn Rosen nodded. "I was collecting updates from the crew chiefs in the hangar."

Ethan had recruited them for this mission, and they'd proven to be just as good as their records indicated. He'd developed a keen eye for talent, a skill that could never be overutilized, especially when putting one's life in their hands. They were good men to have at his side.

The door to the assembly room opened, and Cynergy hastened in. She wore a black ship suit, form fitting, that hugged her athletic build. Her long, dark-blonde hair was tied back into a ponytail, and she looked as if she'd just come from an exercise session. He hadn't recalled her mentioning that in her schedule when they'd had breakfast together.

"I heard we've got mission clearance. All hands for this?" she asked with a hopeful glint in her honey-brown eyes.

Cynergy was not in the CDF. She led the civilian contractors and specialists who were mostly from Earth and were a mix of hybrid and human. Both Tom and Flynn's platoons had hybrid specialists attached to them.

In the past three years, there had been many changes and acceptance of Vemus-human hybrids like Ethan and his wife, which had become the norm. With time came trust as people acclimated to working with individuals rather than group labels.

The colonials were quick to adapt, due in large part to the Ovarrow serving among them. Hybrids had special capabilities that afforded them certain advantages, and that simply could not be ignored.

Ethan smiled. "That's right. All hands for this mission. We'll have two primary goals. First is to explore the planetary object with a focus on replenishing our stock of materials. There have been specific scans for ores, which also indicated significant ice deposits. Water is at a premium out here, so I'm aiming for us to replenish as much as we can in the window we've allotted for this mission. We'll receive better scan data when we arrive."

Each ship had water reclamation capabilities, but it was never a one-for-one equation. There was always a cost, no matter how much they tried to preserve.

They sat and Tom activated the holotank.

"I brought up the salvage and survey protocols. What's the approved timeframe for this operation?" Tom asked.

"At least forty-eight hours. I could push for more if we find something truly extraordinary, but there won't be much time to smell the roses," Ethan replied.

"That should give us enough time to collect samples for a decent survey," Cynergy said.

She would know. Most spacers knew the backwards and forwards of salvaging anything in space. She'd been raised as an outcast on old space stations in Earth's star system. Salvaging materials had been a way of life for the spacers, but that had all changed when the colonial expeditionary force arrived. Finally, having been given a choice, most spacers returned to the planet to begin life anew, but some had chosen to join the exploration initiative.

Flynn cleared his throat. "Can you define 'extraordinary'?"

Ethan nodded once. "We have the prioritized list of ores and minerals, so any significant deposits should be noted. Ice deposits, especially if the water is safe or requires minimal processing to make it usable, are of note. But they're no good to us if the ice deposits are mostly made up of ammonia or methane. And let's not forget evidence of an alien civilization."

Flynn glanced at Tom and frowned, as if he couldn't determine whether Ethan was joking.

"I'm serious. We could find an outpost there. That would be a shock," Ethan said and shrugged. "Perhaps a Vemus probe."

"Doubtful," Cynergy said. This wasn't the first time they'd had this kind of conversation. His wife was more of a realist when it came to "what if" scenarios.

"How do you know?" Ethan asked.

"Probes likely went to star systems, not rogue planets traveling through dark space, so yeah, doubtful. Or what's a more sensitive way to put it?" she asked, tapping her full lips with the tip of her finger. "Highly unlikely. I think I saw that in a CDF presentation sometime."

They grinned.

Ethan nodded, conceding the point. "Agreed, but until we actually find more evidence of the Vemus on other worlds, we're just shooting in the dark."

Cynergy crossed her arms and tilted her head to the side. "Would you care to make a wager on whether we'll find any evidence related to the Vemus?"

He regarded his wife with a playful glint in his eyes. "Oh, it's tempting," he said and frowned for a second. "You know, that's not a bad idea."

Cynergy's honey-brown eyes widened. "Really?"

He nodded. "Yes," he said and looked at the others. "We need to get our teams involved. Give them some kind of stake in this. Something to strive for. Why not this?"

Tom pressed his lips together in a thoughtful frown. "You want to start a contest as a way of motivating the team?"

"I just want them engaged," Ethan said. "Soldiers always perform better when they're engaged. We need to work on our pacing for the next deployment. Too much idle time isn't good for anyone, and we've had a couple of long stretches."

"That's because they're still trying to figure out how best to explore the galaxy," Cynergy said, drawing their eyes toward her. She raised her eyebrows. "What? That's what we're really doing. It's the end goal, and at this rate, it'll be a thousand years and we won't even cover half of it. Anyway, it's about time they called the initiative what it is."

Flynn chuckled and shook his head. "I like the current one—Explore the Stars. It conveys the right message without making the distances seem so extreme."

Cynergy shrugged and looked at Ethan.

Tom snorted. "If you really want to get lost in the woods, we can start talking about what they're going to call the alliance moving forward."

"Is it down to four names now?" Flynn asked.

Ethan knew he needed to get the meeting back on track but sometimes couldn't help himself. "It's down to two names. Confederation or the United Coalition of Planets."

Cynergy frowned. "What if we encounter an intelligent species that doesn't have a home world?"

Ethan stifled a grin. "You mean like space nomads? Well, they wouldn't qualify to join us because they don't have a planet."

Tom and Flynn's eyes widened for a moment, and Ethan continued. "Why so surprised? We must have standards. Not just anyone can join the alliance."

Cynergy shook her head, amused. "What if we combined the top two names?"

He shook his head. "Too wordy. Can you imagine the acronyms we'd have to remember?"

Tom and Flynn nodded.

"It does add complexity. Can't have that," Tom said.

Ethan made a "there you have it" gesture, and Cynergy sighed. "Right," he said. "Let's get back to business here. Tom, what's the status of our deployment vehicles?"

Tom became more serious, losing some of his amusement from a moment before. "Old. Worn out. They gave us castoffs to outfit the mission."

"It's not that bad. The vehicles and equipment provided were in working order," Ethan replied.

Tom brought up a report, and several windows appeared in the holotank. "Over forty percent have reached the end of their deployment life cycle and are due for a proper maintenance cycle. Combat shuttles and several older Talon V Lancer fighters are in good working order. Maintenance crews have had to remove thirteen percent of the EVA suits because of safety concerns and almost as many combat suits."

Ethan scanned the list. While the *Challenger* itself was a retrofitted Destroyer class ship with a completely revamped interior, which included a new I-Drive and computer systems, the CDF had had to scrounge to outfit the entire expeditionary force with the equipment they needed. This meant using vehicles and equipment that were still space worthy but probably wouldn't hold up indefinitely to sustained use. Some ships were using older NA Alliance vehicles that had been preserved in storage, which was Earth's contribution to the exploration initiative.

"There isn't anything new under the sun here," Ethan said. "We'd all like top-notch equipment, but sometimes we just need to work with what we've got." He paused for a moment, then continued. "So, safety issues aside, can we field a full team for the mission?"

Tom glanced at Flynn for a second. "It might be a tight squeeze for some, but to answer your question, yes. We can do it, Captain."

Ethan looked at Cynergy.

"My people will be fine. We're used to operating with old equipment." She frowned with a slight shake of her head. "That didn't sound right. Your old equipment is better than anything we've been using for decades, so you won't get any complaints here."

Ethan threw an accusing look at his officers. "There, you see? Stop complaining." He held up a hand before they could reply. "I understand the risks involved. In all seriousness, we only field a force that can perform the mission. It's not like the airlock is going to fail in one of these combat shuttles, right?"

Tom winced and glanced at Flynn. The two shrugged. "We can't make any guarantees about that, Captain," Tom said.

Over the next couple of hours, they went through the equipment and personnel they had available. It wasn't as dire as Tom had implied, but it was close. Ethan maintained a mental checklist he intended to push for to outfit the next exploratory mission. There would be more, of that he had no doubt. New Earth had the infrastructure to build ships and equipment. Old Earth's tech-base was increasing daily, but what they lacked in resources they more than made up for with sheer population numbers. Humanity had a bright future ahead of it, and that future would take them well beyond two planets separated by sixty light-years.

# CHAPTER 4

Ethan ended the meeting. Tom and Flynn left the assembly room, while Cynergy lingered behind.

"Do you need to report in?" Cynergy asked.

He shook his head. "Not yet. I'm going to wait on the active scan data once we come out of hyperspace."

They left and headed to their quarters. They had officers' quarters, so it was basically the size of a small apartment. The CDF had loosened certain regulations, and the *Challenger* was technically an exploratory ship that housed a mixed crew of military and civilians. Certain creature comforts were to be expected. They'd even made allotments for married couples. No one wanted to be away from their loved ones for a year at a time. There were no children aboard the ship, but Ethan supposed that would change in the future. The exploration initiative needed qualified people and couldn't limit their selection pool to only those who were single or married with no children. Given the current population growth, both on the colony and Old Earth, there were more married couples with children than without.

They stepped inside an elevator, and Cynergy eyed him for a long moment. "You're pretty quiet."

Ethan shrugged. "Just thinking about logistical stuff."

"You didn't get enough of that in the meeting?"

The elevator stopped, and the doors opened. "Not that. I was thinking about some of the things we talked about the other night. Bringing families on these deployments and all the challenges that would entail."

"Only for you military types. It doesn't take much to establish a learning curriculum, and there won't be a lack of experts in a variety of fields right here on the ship."

Ethan considered it—had been considering it for a few months now. By CDF warship standards, the *Challenger* had been positively gutted of its armament. They still had two missile tubes, point defense systems, and mid-range kinetic and energy weapons. It wasn't bad, but this ship would never stand against a purpose-built warship. There were proposals of even more minimalist ship designs for exploration and having those ships mixed in with more capable defensive ships.

They entered their apartment, which boasted a single bedroom, their own private bathroom with shower, and a work area that doubled as private living space. It was pure luxury when compared to some of the cramped living spaces he'd been in while serving in the CDF.

Cynergy removed her jacket and hung it in their closet. Her black ship suit was sleeveless, showing her long, slender arms.

"Did you come to the meeting straight from exercising?" he asked.

She regarded him for a moment and then came to stand in front of him. Their gazes locked. "Why? Are you saying I need a shower?"

Ethan smiled a little. "That depends."

She backed away from him purposefully and turned around, slipping her arms out of her shirt and pushing it down to the waist. He drank in the sight of her smooth, pale skin and her well-toned back, and her femininity was enough to increase his heart rate.

She went toward their bathroom with slow, purposeful grace and paused in the doorway, hand on her hip as she looked over her shoulder at him. "Coming?"

It was all the invitation he needed as he stalked toward her, removing his own ship suit as he went.

He loved married life.

---

Scan data populated the holotank, giving Ethan and the rest of the team leaders their first real glimpse of the planetary body sailing through dark space. Specific data feeds went right toward the workstations of the specialists waiting for them. More than a few scientists were excited at the opportunity of surveying a deep-space planetary mass. The theory was that the galaxy was full of them, but the opportunity to study one of these mysterious free-floating objects was rare. No one could say how a moon-sized object came to be traveling through space light-years away from the nearest star. Yet here it was.

"Scans show rich mineral deposits present on the surface," Luanne Atwater said. Her specialty was field biology and geology. "Rocky surface to the extreme. Indicates the mass has been subject to more than a few collisions during its travels."

"Probably has to do with how it came to be knocked out of orbit from whatever star system it came from," Cynergy agreed.

Luanne peered at her screen intently, and then her eyes widened. She looked at Ethan. "Captain, you're not going to believe this, but scans indicate a large metallic mass detection. Fifty-nine percent probability of it being artificially made."

"Put it on screen," Ethan said.

The image on the holotank updated to show a partial scan of just what Luanne described. It was a cluster of metallic structures partially exposed in a deep chasm.

"That's not very clear," Tom said.

Luanne nodded. "There are ice deposits all over that region, so it's as clear as we'll likely get until we get there." She looked at Ethan questioningly. "Are we going there?"

"That depends. Are there any other sites with better survey potential?" Ethan asked.

Luanne blinked in surprise and glanced at Cynergy.

"Captain," Tom said, "I've identified a few sites that are more than adequate for survey and salvage operations. I can have a prioritized list in a few minutes."

"Excellent, Lieutenant Washburn," Ethan said and studied the holotank. "I guess that just leaves the potential alien structure," he said, his gaze sliding toward Cynergy, considering.

"My team is ready in whatever capacity is required," Cynergy said. "We're more than able to handle the initial survey, and if we do confirm that this is of alien origin, we can coordinate with the CDF before proceeding any further."

"Excellent, then the potential find of the mission is yours," Ethan said.

"Thank you, Captain Gates," she replied.

Flynn cleared his throat. "Excuse me, Captain."

"Yes, Lieutenant Rosen."

"Scans also show deep fissures throughout the surface. I'm not sure how stable any of those regions are going to be. The ground could quite literally crumble beneath our landing gear if we're not careful."

Flynn made a passing motion toward the holotank, and a new sub-window appeared.

Ethan peered at the data and nodded. "We'll have to test potential landing zones before committing. Recon drones should help with the rest." He paused while considering the data on the holoscreen. "Let's identify at least five sites per group and pair up groups so no one is without any backup in case things are even more unstable than we can tell from here."

"Yes, Captain," Flynn replied.

Ethan glanced at the deep chasm where the metallic mass was located. There were many rocky protuberances jutting out of the walls. "Might be a tight squeeze in there."

Cynergy nodded. "Not beyond the specs of the *Mariner* shuttle. We should be fine."

The *Mariner* shuttle had been designed for salvage missions. It had a small flak cannon that could break up rocky material and not much else. Cynergy was right.

"All right, everyone," Ethan said, "we deploy in two hours. We've got forty-eight hours to make the most of this mission. Temporary base camps will be set up to maximize our time there. However, should circumstances change or we receive updated orders, we might need to return home quicker than we anticipated. So be prepared for that."

Ethan ended the meeting, and the attendees began to leave.

Cynergy looked up at him expectantly.

"I don't like that chasm. We'll send in recon drones first to map it out. If it's too risky, you'll need to abort," he said.

She nodded. "We'll know more when you get a closer look," she said and pressed her lips together.

He arched an eyebrow. "Regretting not making that wager?"

She gave him a dazzling smile. "I'd still make that wager. The likelihood of it having anything to do with the Vemus is beyond miniscule."

He shook his head. "You don't even hesitate to tempt fate, do you?"

Cynergy laughed. "Neither do you!"

# CHAPTER 5

"That's ugly," Lieutenant Kirk Bentley said to Ethan as they looked at the shuttle's main holoscreen.

"It does lack a certain symmetry that we normally expect from a lunar-sized object," Ethan replied.

Four shuttles departed from the *Challenger*, making their survey and salvage run to the rogue lunar body. S&S runs covered a wide range of missions, both large and small. The rest of the Expeditionary Force was far away, giving the *Challenger*'s crew exclusive access for this mission.

Bentley looked up at Ethan from the copilot's chair. "It looks like a smashed potato that's been gouged by a giant spoon." He looked at their pilot. "What do you think, Sergeant?"

Sergeant Chavez considered the oblong lunar object. "Reminds me of an Old Earth whale with a bunch of battle scars."

Ethan peered at the holoscreen. Giant canyons were easy to spot, even at their current distance. The lunar object fit the designation because of its size—371 kilometers wide and 609 kilometers long. There were flattened surfaces toward the edges, but scans didn't indicate any significant detections of things they were really interested in.

Ethan shook his head a little.

"What do you think, Captain?" Bentley asked.

"I can't decide between a smashed potato or an old, battle-weary sperm whale," Ethan said, giving Chavez a wink.

Several survey drones had flown in ahead of them and their data feeds updated on the shuttle's computer systems.

Ethan opened a comlink to the other shuttles in the group. "Okay, Challengers," he said, using the nickname he'd given his task force, "looks like we've got a beat-up beauty on our hands. Recon drone scans validate the long-range sensor data. Probe all landing zones before committing to them. All groups are cleared to proceed. *Mariner*, stay on the comms. Everyone else has a green light. Happy hunting." Ethan paused. The comlink session on his holoscreen indicated that the others had dropped off. "*Mariner*, looks like the canyons don't disappoint."

"Copy that, Captain," Cynergy replied. "There is definitely some kind of metallic structure in sector 92. Could be of alien origin."

Ethan studied the distant view of the sector. It was a deep canyon, and they couldn't see into the darkened depths. He blew out a breath. "Okay, you're cleared to proceed. Keep me updated as to your progress. As soon as you confirm whether that metallic mass is actually of alien origin, I want to know about it."

"Understood, Captain. *Mariner* out," Cynergy replied.

Ethan was quiet for a few moments, and Bentley cleared his throat. "Right. Sergeant Chavez, take us to our coordinates."

Ethan stepped out of the shuttle's cockpit, and Bentley followed him.

"Sir," Bentley said, "are you having doubts?"

Ethan shook his head. He'd scouted hundreds of moons and large asteroids during his time as a Talon V pilot, and he knew the ins and outs of the work that was going to be done. The Eagle class combat shuttles they were using were armored and could carry a lot of equipment, but they weren't the most agile spacecraft the CDF had produced.

"I hate dark spaces. We're relying entirely on scan data, which should be fine, but there could be anything in those canyons."

Bentley frowned. "We're way out in dark space a long way between star systems. Who knows what this smashed potato went through before we stumbled onto it."

"Looks like quite a bit. I really want an excuse to survey that sector."

"You are in command, sir. Make it so."

Ethan had come close to doing just that a few times. He shook his head. "Negative, the *Mariner* has got this."

Bentley glanced around. They were well out of earshot of the rest of the platoon. "Permission to speak freely, Captain?"

"Go ahead."

"Is this because Cynergy is commanding the *Mariner?* It's got to be a challenge among those of you who are married doing this job."

"It's not for everyone," Ethan replied. "There are risks in what we do. That's true for all of us. I could tell you some of the things Cyn had to do before we ever reached Earth's star system. Yeah, what we're doing here is risky, but it's right in line with what spacers were doing when we arrived. They went into those high-risk places to salvage for materials because if they didn't, they'd starve. People like Cyn, Hash, and all the other hybrids have been doing it for generations. So yeah, I'm not without concern for my wife. That goes without saying." He smiled. "At the same time, I want to go in there and see if we really did find some derelict alien spacecraft. Don't you?"

Bentley chuckled. "Heck yeah, when you put it like that. My father told me some of the things he'd encountered when his platoon was scouting worlds during the Krake War. High risk, high reward, but extremely deadly all the same."

His own father had had more than a few experiences he'd shared over the years, and those were just the events he chose to talk about. Ethan knew there were many things his father would never speak about—old wounds that were better left in the past.

Over the next six hours, the Challengers performed their mission, surveying large mineral deposits and collecting samples that were just too good to pass up. Flynn had also reported that the ice samples were within acceptable range to be used on ships.

The rocky terrain was extremely brittle and prone to collapse in many areas. Incidentally, the best places to land happened to be rich in ores and minerals, which reinforced the terrain.

Ethan walked up the loading ramp into the shuttle and went to the comms station. An analysis had just come in from the scientists aboard the ship.

Bentley joined him. "Is that the report?"

Ethan nodded, quickly skimming the data, and frowned. "Interesting theory."

Bentley read the report. "A sudden loss of atmosphere could explain the number of caverns being reported. Having all the water simply 'flash boil' also fits, but how could this little piece of rock have had an atmosphere?"

Ethan arched an eyebrow. "Didn't you read to the end?" Bentley's eyes flicked toward the screen and Ethan blocked his view.

"Fine, what did it say?"

"It only makes sense if this was actually part of a planet that suffered an incredible calamity."

Bentley blinked a few times and pursed his lips. "They're not lacking in imagination."

Ethan nodded and navigated toward the team status. "Doesn't look like the *Mariner* has found a derelict ship," he said, reading the latest status update. As he read, he felt himself leaning toward the holoscreen. "Damn it."

He'd always been a quick reader. It wasn't anything he practiced; it was just something he could do.

"They're flying into that cavern they found."

"At the bottom of the canyon."

"They sent recon drones in. It's not as if they're going in blind."

Ethan shook his head, looking at the timestamp of the message. "They're already inside." Cynergy had included that update at the end, probably buying herself some time before he could stop her.

"What do you want to do?" Bentley asked.

"We need eyes on top. Stay with the team here. I'm going to take Chavez and do a little reconnaissance over where the *Mariner* is."

Bentley nodded and then glanced toward the cockpit. "You do remember that Chavez is still a pilot trainee?"

Ethan gave him a lopsided smile. "That's why I'm going with him."

Bentley walked back down the loading ramp, and Ethan closed it.

He walked through the airlock into the shuttle's interior and removed his helmet, then went to the cockpit.

Sergeant Chavez looked up in surprise. "Captain," he said, beginning to stand.

"Stay there, Sergeant Chavez. We're going on a recon mission," Ethan said, claiming the copilot's seat.

Chavez sank back into his seat. "Do you want control, Captain?"

"Negative, you've got this," Ethan replied.

Ethan sent an update to the ship and Chavez engaged the shuttle's engines.

Ethan glanced down at the well-lit base camp amidst a dark surface as the shuttle rose up. "Here are the coordinates. We're doing a survey run over a network of canyons."

Chavez entered the coordinates and flew toward them.

The lunar surface wasn't in complete darkness. It had a peculiar rotation on multiple axes. It was in almost permanent twilight, forever on the verge but not quite getting there.

The shuttle's HUD marked where the other teams were located, showing tiny green icons along with their designations. They soon reached the sector where the *Mariner* was conducting its survey deep in the canyons.

Ethan activated the shuttle's scanners, which began mapping the surface. He opened a data comlink to the *Challenger*, borrowing computer cycles from the ship's systems. An analysis of the data from the shuttle's scans was compared with scans reported from the *Mariner*.

Chavez glanced toward him.

"Keep making a sweep of the area," Ethan told him and focused his attention on his holoscreen.

"Yes, sir," Chavez replied. "If you don't mind me asking, sir, what are you doing with that data?"

"I don't mind," Ethan said, navigating the interface and selecting certain terrain anomalies for the scanners to focus on. "Comparing the current scan data with what the *Mariner* reported when they made their own sweep."

Chavez glanced at the holoscreen. "And you're highlighting the changes," he said, nose wrinkling. "Why are there so many changes?"

It was just what he was afraid of. "This place is a brittle skeleton, undisturbed for God knows how long, and the stuff we're doing is having an impact."

"How can that be? We only just gotten here."

"One minute," Ethan said.

He sent a message to the other teams, ordering them to have their recon drones cover the base camp areas.

"Think of it like a stack of dominos. Once one of them falls, it starts cascading to anything within range of it."

Chavez considered it for a moment. "I get it. Like a house of cards," he said, and his eyes widened. "But that means our teams are in danger. Should we turn back?"

"Not yet," Ethan said. The young man looked unconvinced. "It's not an all-or-nothing equation. We weigh the risk, evaluate our surroundings, and then we—"

An alert appeared from his analysis, showing multiple seismic anomalies. Ethan frowned and shifted his gaze toward the video feed. The shuttle's bright lights pierced the gloom, and a ripple of swirling material made the lunar surface look like a shifting cloud, recently disturbed. The lunar object's weak gravity sent waves of material spraying across the surface, away from the rotational plain.

"Oh crap, that doesn't look good, Captain!"

"No, it doesn't. Get us higher. I need to see how widespread this is," Ethan said.

Chavez increased their altitude, and Ethan felt something cold settle into the pit of his stomach. A huge, expansive cloud covered the area for kilometers. He quickly updated the scan parameters, and it was worse than he thought.

He swore as he sent out a high priority alert to the other teams.

Chavez's eyes were wide. "Captain, we've got to go back for the others."

Ethan shook his head. "Not yet."

"But sir!"

"Sergeant, listen to me. The others are fine. The disturbance is moving away from them," Ethan said. He tried to open a comlink to the *Mariner* by increasing power to the subspace transceiver.

"Captain," Chavez said, "comlink from the ship."

A video comlink came to prominence. Major Arvad's face appeared.

"Ops just alerted me to your update," Arvad said.

Ethan made several decisions in the span of a second. "I'm pulling the plug on this, Major. I'm ordering the teams to make an orderly withdrawal."

Arvad nodded in approval. "Understood. I'm ordering the ship to move closer to you to be able to render assistance if necessary."

"Thank you, Major," Ethan replied.

"*Challenger* actual, out."

The video comlink severed.

Ethan never would've guessed that the potato-shaped moon would break apart under their feet, but that was exactly what was happening. And Cynergy and her team were caught underneath it all.

# CHAPTER 6

Ethan had received check-ins from the other teams, except for the *Mariner*. While subspace communications were extremely reliable over vast distances, there were some things that interfered with it. The *Mariner* could be having issues with its comms systems, and he wouldn't even consider that the shuttle had been destroyed.

Ethan quickly brought up the *Mariner's* last known location. Then he highlighted the cavern locale.

"The cavern could go off in any direction," Chavez said, studying the holoscreen.

"It's a shot in the dark. We need to fly low. Hopefully, we can detect the ship," Ethan said.

Chavez altered course and headed to the new coordinates.

Ethan knew their time was limited. The collapse was spreading, and there was no way for anyone to know whether it would impact the entire moon. They'd have to return to retrieve Bentley and the others.

"Decrease velocity," Ethan said.

"Copy that, sir."

The shuttle slowed and Ethan raised the power of all comms signals, increasing the sensitivity of their small array.

The comlink request to the *Mariner* flickered from amber to green, and Ethan felt a surge of hope pump through his chest.

"Ethan, is that you?" Cynergy said, her voice sounding slightly modulated from signal degradation.

"Yes, it is. What's your status?"

"Caverns are collapsing, and we're trying to outrun it," she replied and gave him their coordinates.

They couldn't retreat the way they'd come because the collapse had made it impassable. Ethan locked onto the *Mariner's* signal and gestured for Chavez to follow it.

Ethan's mind raced as he tried to figure out a way to help them escape. They needed to get out of those caverns before they were crushed.

"Can you give us a data link to the *Mariner's* systems?" Ethan asked.

A few moments went by.

"Can't get it to establish," Cynergy said. "We'll have to do this another way."

She began telling him the layout of the caverns as she flew the shuttle. The caverns were narrowing, and the shuttle had taken some damage that knocked out the subspace transceiver.

Ethan scanned ahead of their location and saw that there was significant disruption along the surface about a kilometer from their position. He relayed the coordinates to her.

"Got it," Cynergy said. Her voice tensed. She grunted and sounded like she was clenching her teeth. "Major impact. Lost two engine pods."

Chavez looked toward him, but Ethan ignored him.

"Understood," he replied. "We're moving ahead. Going to try to open the way for you."

Chavez's eyes widened. "Sir?"

"Give me the shuttle," Ethan commanded. Chavez passed the flight control of the shuttle to him.

Ethan kicked the thrusters in the posterior, and the shuttle lurched forward. "Bring the weapons systems online, Sergeant."

"Yes, Captain, weapons systems are online."

The shuttle was equipped with a mag cannon stored in the belly.

Ethan painted a target area. The surface was a swirling mass of rocky debris, making it almost impossible for them to see the actual lunar surface, but the scans showed a significant breaking up of the area.

Ethan banked hard on the flight controls, stressing the inertia dampeners, and the shuttle swung around.

"Fire!" Ethan said.

Chavez fired the cannon, blanketing the target area.

"Stay on it. We need to break it apart as much as we can if they're to have a chance at punching through."

Ethan tracked the *Mariner's* signal.

"Cavern is deteriorating fast," Cynergy said, her voice sounding high with strain.

"I know. You're going to have to punch through it. We're softening the area for you."

Cynergy muttered a curse and told the others to brace for impact.

Ethan waited until the *Mariner's* signal was almost to them. "Cease fire!"

The shuttle's weapons stopped their barrage of the lunar surface.

Ethan held his breath, eyes fixed on the dark lunar surface. A burst of lunar debris shot forth and there were several bright flashes as the *Mariner* ricocheted out of it. It tumbled through space, barely clearing the lunar surface. Ethan spotted small bursts from the maneuvering thrusters to slow the roll the shuttle was in.

Ethan sucked in a breath and flew the shuttle toward them.

"Ready the tether cables," he said.

The *Mariner* had sustained heavy damage, but it was still holding together. Several of the rear engine pods were gone, and large parts of the rear sections had been heavily impacted. Atmosphere was leaking out of the damaged sections in bursts that settled into a wispy nothing.

"Cynergy, are you all right?" Ethan asked, hoping and praying that they'd had their EVA suits on.

He watched as the shuttle continued its slow tumble in a long arc over the lunar surface.

"Captain, we need to get a tether on it before it falls back to the surface," Chavez said.

Ethan stared at the comms systems, but there was no response. Chavez shifted in his seat.

"Ready the tether," Ethan said.

He watched as the maneuvering thrusters stabilized the shuttle. The flight systems could handle that on their own. If they deployed their tether cables too soon, they'd run the risk of jerking the shuttle and causing injuries to the people inside.

"Steady," Ethan said, watching the shuttle. "Okay, now."

The tethers locked onto the shuttle's hull and Ethan gently sent power to their engines to stabilize the derelict shuttle.

A personal comlink from Cynergy's EVA suit appeared, and Ethan acknowledged it.

"Comms systems are shot. We've got injured, but all crew are alive and accounted for," Cynergy said.

Ethan blew out the breath he hadn't realized he'd been holding.

"Main engines are offline. Maneuvering thrusters are down to thirty percent," Cynergy said and paused for a moment. "We could use a ride back to the ship."

Ethan grinned. "I think we can arrange that."

"Thank you, Captain," Cynergy said. "Oh, and no alien ship. Luanne believes it was a convergence of various metals, but she's at a loss as to how they could've come together like that."

"Understood. We'll review the data when we get back. We're going to tow you to a safe distance and then go back to retrieve the team still on the surface."

They'd set up the base camp on a hardened surface that functioned like a large metallic island. Bentley and the others quickly disassembled the camp, and all were on the shuttle within fifteen minutes.

Ethan was glad the team was safe and that the others had made an orderly withdrawal with minimal loss of equipment.

"We've been monitoring communications," Bentley said to Ethan. "Scans are showing large regions being impacted, while others not so much."

He nodded. "We got lucky, and at the same time our protocols are what saved us." Ethan regarded Bentley for a moment, and he shook his head. "We got lucky. Should've had a rescue team on standby."

Bentley looked at the main holoscreen where a live video feed showed the *Mariner*. "There are no perfect operations. If you'd waited for us to break camp before going after them, they would've died. We were the lesser risk. I will go on the record because it's the truth."

Ethan felt an urge to thank him but knew it would've been inappropriate. Bentley was right, but it was still a tough call to make. This operation could've gone a lot worse. Now they just needed to do the post-op eval to determine what they could've prevented.

# CHAPTER 7

The *Mariner* was in worse shape than they thought. The deck officer assured Ethan that it wasn't beyond repair, but it was going to take a while. His first instinct was to scrap the shuttle altogether, but he wasn't the only one who wanted to prove what they could do. He found that engineers viewed the world a bit differently than people in other professions. Ethan was willing to give them a chance but advised them to manage that priority along with all their other duties.

Major Arvad met him in the hangar as the injured crew were brought to sickbay. Ethan stood at attention and saluted.

He gave Ethan a once-over and then looked at the *Mariner*. He exhaled a breath and shook his head. "They're lucky no one died."

"It wasn't luck, sir," Ethan said, and Arvad raised his eyebrows. "Cynergy's team is mostly made up of spacers—hybrids, at that. They practically lived in their light-duty EVA suits, and she ordered them to go to their own life support as they tried to escape the collapse."

Arvad nodded slowly. "What else?"

Ethan frowned. "I'm not sure what you mean, sir?"

Arvad began walking and gestured for Ethan to accompany him. They passed the other shuttles as they were going through their post-flight checks.

Arvad gave him a sidelong glance. "What else?"

"I'm trying to figure out if there was a way we could've anticipated this. I'll need time to review the data."

Arvad bobbed his head once. "Oh, I know you will. Not a doubt in my mind. We'll also go over it together before we push the reports up the chain."

Ethan knew there were other officers who would distance themselves from a disaster, although this might not qualify as that.

"Still feels like a loss. I'm not trying to be negative, but we had only just begun to achieve the mission objectives."

Arvad shrugged. "You got your people out. Unforeseen situations occur. It's how we improve, but I know you already know this."

Ethan sighed and glanced back down the flight deck at the shuttles, gritting his teeth for a second. "Sir, I almost lost two teams. I left Lieutenant Bentley and his platoon to investigate the whereabouts of the *Mariner*. If things had been different, they would've been in real trouble. They could've died."

Those thoughts had been creeping along the edges of his mind the whole way back.

"You're right. If things had gone down differently than what they did, Bentley's team might have paid the price, or," he said, holding up his finger, "you would've returned and gotten them out of there."

Ethan frowned, considering it. He would've tried.

"Ethan, the longer you do this job and rise up the chain of

command, you're going to find that there is no way anyone can account for every situation. We make decisions based on the data we have available. You had a hunch that the crew of the *Mariner* was in trouble. There was nothing unstable about the lunar surface in the base camp's area; hence, minimal risk of leaving at that time. And you also noted the direction of the collapse and made another judgement call before committing to continue after the *Mariner*." Arvad paused. "I reviewed the communications logs from the shuttles."

Ethan couldn't find anything wrong with what Arvad had said. "I understand, sir. I just don't like it. I feel like there was more I could've done, maybe at the planning stages. We needed an additional rescue force to cover our six, and we didn't have it." He paused for a moment as ideas kept coming to mind. "Better yet, I could've reassigned one of the teams to function as recon and emergency response so they wouldn't have boots on the ground."

"Perhaps," Arvad agreed. "And I could've had the *Challenger* closer so we could've sent support. As it was, things happened quickly. It all goes back to the fact that we'll need time to consider it and do a proper evaluation before we can improve our protocols. I've sent a preliminary report to COMCENT, so they're in the loop." He regarded Ethan for a long moment. "This site has been deemed too hazardous to exploit for resource, but ideas supporting these efforts are good and will be included in future exploration missions."

"Thank you, sir."

"Go get cleaned up. See to your people, and we'll meet up later this afternoon."

Ethan left Major Arvad and checked in with his team. Then he went to sickbay where Cynergy and the crew of the *Mariner* were getting cleared by the doctors.

He walked into the med bay and saw Hash sitting in the waiting area. He was a brilliant technical expert whose hybrid capabilities made him sensitive toward detecting people's emotions.

"Ethan, hello," Hash said. "Cyn is speaking with the doctors."

"Are you all right?" Ethan asked.

"Just a few scratches. Already healed," Hash said, waving away the comment.

Most hybrids could heal fast, with regenerative capabilities that sometimes exceeded what doctors could accomplish. They weren't impervious to injury or bleeding out from serious wounds, but they could recover quicker and with minimal intervention.

Ethan walked toward the back of the med bay and saw Cynergy leave one of the rooms. Their gazes locked, and Ethan felt a wave of relief sweep over him. He knew she was fine, and he could sense that she was free of injury, but seeing her set his mind at ease.

She strode toward him, and he wrapped his arms around her. For a few moments, he ignored the fact that they were standing in the med bay. They both knew how close they had been to losing each other.

They stayed in the med bay until each member of her team was discharged. Broken bones would heal in a day or two at the most. There were a few head injuries, and their biochips would be monitored by the ship's computer system until they were cleared by the doctor.

They went to their quarters, and Cynergy walked in ahead of him. She stopped and spun around.

"We explored the cavern because we were still hoping that there was an alien ship," Cynergy said. She'd crossed her arms and wasn't looking at him. He decided to wait her out. Cynergy lifted her gaze to his. "I have the scan data. I've never seen a mineral deposit like this. I can understand why the analysis AI thought it could be artificial. But I wanted to be sure. I knew going into the caverns could be risky," she said and shook her head. "I know better than that."

"You couldn't have known what was going to happen. No one anticipated this. Not you. Not me. Not anyone on the ship. We were all surprised."

She pursed her lips thoughtfully and looked away from him. "I do have a couple of ideas about that."

"What do you mean?"

"Mitigating the risk. I should've sent a recon drone into the caverns instead of risking the team. We're so used to doing things a certain way that we forget we have more resources available to us."

"Who's we?"

"Spacers," she replied, letting her hands come to her side. "I know it's been three years, but old habits…" She bit her lower lip for a second. "I also want to push forward with that prototype drone I've told you about."

"You mean the one for exploration?"

She nodded. "It can really help. It would be more capable than what we're currently using and would be able to perform near-planet exploration."

"But the drone might have to be sacrificed if we can't retrieve it."

She leveled her gaze at him. "Better than losing a team."

"True, and we can't visit every single planet, moon, asteroid, and anomaly ourselves. I agree with you there." He stepped closer to her, but she backed away.

Cynergy went to take a shower, and the closed bathroom door meant she wanted to be alone. He'd give her the space.

He sat down at his workstation and closed his eyes, trying to imagine what it had been like flying through underground caverns, searching for a way out. It was enough to rattle anyone's cage. Even seasoned pilots weren't immune to it.

He brought up a holoscreen and began reviewing his messages. It was a quiet, busy sort of work that didn't require a lot of mental cycles, and he accomplished little things while taking some downtime. He knew the value of taking a step back and simply being in the moment to get his bearings. Other people threw themselves into their work or other types of escapism, but, inevitably, they'd have to face it. Ethan had decided long ago that he wouldn't avoid those contemplative moments. Eventually, he'd learned to draw peace from them.

He scrolled through unread messages and saw one that was flagged. It was a video message from Lauren. He opened the file and her smiling face appeared. She looked happy. Then he watched the message and sat back in the chair, dumbfounded.

The door to the bathroom opened and Cynergy came out with a towel wrapped around her body that came to the middle of her well-toned thighs.

"What's the matter?" she asked.

Ethan started to speak and had to clear his throat. "Lauren is pregnant."

Cynergy smiled. "That's wonderful," she said, coming toward him, giving him a hug. "You're going to be an uncle."

He grinned. "Yeah," he said, his voice sounding a little wistful, and he wasn't sure why.

"Do they know the sex?"

Ethan frowned and then shook his head. "She didn't say."

"Oh, well, when is the baby due?"

Ethan felt his mouth go a little dry. "Three months."

Cynergy blinked. "Three months? Why'd she wait so long to tell us?"

Ethan raked his teeth over his lip. "I don't know."

She eyed him for a long moment, looking slightly amused. "Why are you so surprised?"

He shrugged. "I don't know. I just wasn't expecting it, is all. I just…wasn't expecting it."

"Well, I was," she said, walking toward the closet.

"You were? Since when?"

"Since New Earth. When they moved back," she replied. She let the towel fall to the ground, and for once he didn't let it distract him, but it was a close thing. She reached in and grabbed a ship suit. "She and Isaac spent quite a bit of time talking about where they were going to live."

Ethan tried to remember but couldn't. "I guess."

Cyn finished getting dressed and gestured for him to join her on the couch. She waited for him to sit and then plopped right on his lap. They grinned.

"I don't know why I'm so surprised by this," he said. "They're older than us. I don't know."

She watched him with honey-brown eyes that seemed to draw him in. "Isaac comes from a big family, and Lauren loves children. She's going to make a wonderful mother."

Ethan tilted his head to the side, staring at his wife. "What about us? What about you?"

Cynergy smiled, looking almost giddy at the thought. His heart began to race as if he was flying a space fighter through a debris field. "Of course I want a family."

"I know that. We talked about that. But I guess what I'm asking is whether you want to start sooner rather than later."

She regarded him for a long moment, as if she were making some kind of assessment. "Start what?" she asked, eyes gleaming.

Ethan rolled his eyes and stood up, lifting her up with him. He spun her around, and she squealed in delight. "You know what I mean," he said, slowing down. She'd wrapped her legs around him and he stared up at her.

"Not yet, Ethan," she said and kissed him. "You?"

"I hadn't thought about it."

She didn't look surprised. "And now?"

He frowned, not sure.

"We could start right now." She leaned in and nibbled on his neck.

"I just don't think now is the best time. I mean, the *Challenger* isn't exactly family friendly."

He sat on the couch again, and somehow she'd shifted to remain on his lap. She was really quite agile.

"Is there a perfect time?" she asked.

"I'm not looking for a perfect time but maybe a better time."

Her expression became more serious, almost somber. "We always had to consider the population growth on the space stations and outposts. Limited resources. Even though you say the ship isn't family friendly, this place would've been a luxury once upon a time."

He stared at her while caressing her back. "We've got our whole lives together, Cyn. Prolonging treatments give us centuries to live. Plenty of time to fill up several shuttles' worth of kids. Don't you think?"

She smiled and nodded, then rested her head on his shoulder. "I look forward to it, you know. Starting a family. I never thought I would. It just wasn't on my mind for so long, but then everything changed." She lifted her head off his shoulder. "Seeing

New Earth where you grew up—I want that for our children. Maybe not today, but someday."

Ethan smiled and held her close. "Someday."

# CHAPTER 8

Connor finished reading the mission report from the *Challenger*. He could tell that most of it had been written by Ethan, but there were places Major Arvad had influenced—something in the language used or the tone he'd come to recognize from the people he worked with, and his son, who he knew better than Ethan knew himself.

He leaned back in his chair and looked at the wall screen to his left. Landscape images of the region surrounding Sanctuary on New Earth cycled through in random order. Each of them brought back memories of his time on New Earth, and recently, a slight longing to return to his home. His preferences of the randomized images were selective so as not to distract him while he was working.

Blowing out a breath, he stood, pressing his palms into his lower back and stretching. He rolled his shoulders, expecting a snap, crackle, and pop, but his muscles just loosened up. He'd spent too much time in the chair recently.

His office had neutral carpeting that softened the pale walls, fooling the mind into believing the space was larger than it really was. There was a couch along one of the walls, with a table that could double as a holotank. A couple of chairs with smart cushions that could mold themselves to support a wide variety of body types sat opposite the couch.

He inhaled a deep breath and closed his eyes. The air held hints of a spicy pine that was pleasant to his nose.

A chime came from the door, and Connor used his implants to activate the holoscreen next to it.

"General Gates," Lieutenant Haley Jordan said, "Director Grayson and Colonel Martinez are here for your two o'clock meeting."

Connor glanced at the clock on the upper right side of the holoscreen. Lieutenant Jordan waited patiently for his reply, her bright blue eyes earnest.

"Send them in," he said.

"Yes, General," she replied. "Will you require anything else?"

"No, thank you, Lieutenant."

Martinez gestured for Dennis to enter first. While Martinez was tall and trim, Dennis Grayson was short and stocky, with a mix of muscle and a bit of padding to go with it.

"Thanks, Oliver," Dennis said as he walked past Martinez.

Dennis glanced at the wallscreen, peering at the image. He smiled. "Is that the early days of Sanctuary?"

The image showed the early construction of what had started as a small, remote town. Mobile HAB units from the research base could be seen to the left.

"That's right," Connor replied.

Dennis walked toward the screen. "Where are the Ovarrow Archives?"

"About a kilometer east of the HAB units."

Dennis nodded and turned toward him. "I toured them once. Remarkable find, that was."

So much of their knowledge of the Ovarrow had been built from what Lenora discovered in those archives.

Connor gestured toward the couch, and the men sat down. He sat in one of the chairs.

"I've reviewed the mission report from the *Challenger*, and am I correct in assuming both of you did as well?" Connor asked.

"That's right," Dennis said.

Martinez nodded. "Yes. Not what you'd call a run-of-the-mill survey and salvage mission."

"No," Connor agreed.

"Was there any way to determine the..." Dennis paused for a moment, considering, then shrugged. "Could we have detected the fragility of that lunar object before sending the teams in?"

Martinez shook his head. "No, and subsequent analysis post mission doesn't indicate where the origin of the collapse was."

Dennis looked at Connor.

"Sometimes, when you kick over a few rocks, a situation can take on a life of its own," Connor replied.

"Sir," Martinez said, "I can find no fault with how the operation was conducted, given the data that was available. Captain Gates advised his team to test the landing zones before committing to them. There is no way anyone could've predicted it would start a chain reaction."

Dennis eyed Connor thoughtfully. "Could it have just been bad timing?"

"We can't rule it out," Connor said. "Nor can we rule out causality. Our survey must've had some kind of impact. The astrophysicist on the *Challenger* believes that the lunar object was once part of a larger body, probably a planet that had an atmosphere. Whatever catastrophe occurred that sent that chunk of rock out into space left it in its current state."

Dennis nodded. "Yes, the flash boiling of water, but the team reports significant ice deposits there as well."

Martinez nodded. "That's right. I had the scientists here try to put a few models together to recreate the lunar object. It's all just possibilities, and you know how noncommittal that bunch can be sometimes. However, in this case, I don't blame them."

They were quiet for a few moments, and Connor leaned forward a little.

"There are dangers operating in space. That's the risk we all assume by coming out here."

Dennis rubbed his broad nose and stifled a sneeze. "I got the impression that Ethan was more than a little frustrated with the outcome of the mission."

Connor smiled. "Not the outcome but the fact that something that should've been routine with a managed set of risks became unpredictable. It's a tough lesson for anyone to learn."

Dennis glanced at Martinez. Something passed between the two of them, and Dennis shook his head, looking amused. "I don't know how you compact so many things into such a small sentence. Unpredictable, indeed!"

Connor chuckled a little. "I've lost count of how many times I've been in a similar situation. We try to account for all the risks as best we can, and then something unforeseen occurs."

"But how do we prevent it from happening again? They almost lost an entire shuttle and crew," Dennis replied.

Martinez cleared his throat, and Connor gave him a nod. "It's better to think of our protocols as not being edged in stone, but rather sliders that we adjust. The improvement suggested by Captain Gates is to have an emergency force kept in reserve that can be called upon."

Dennis considered it for a few moments and nodded. "That sounds like a good idea," he said and looked at Connor. "You don't agree?"

Connor tipped his head to the side a little. "It's not a bad idea. Something that is difficult for young officers to accept is that no matter how much they prepare or how many precautions they take, they will never be able to guarantee with one-hundred-percent certainty the safety of every team that goes on a mission."

Dennis shifted in his seat, looking uncomfortable. Martinez lowered his chin once. He understood, but Dennis did not.

"This isn't being pessimistic; it's practicality born of experience. Okay, so, in this one instance where everything occurred exactly as events unfolded, having an emergency response team in reserve would've covered the exposure of the platoon left on the ground. Seems like a win and something we can do, and we probably have done. However, it also behaves like a security blanket, making people feel safer than they actually are. Take this scenario with the lunar object. Instead of Ethan following a hunch that one of his teams was in danger, the suddenness of the collapse could have accelerated, hitting all the teams at once. There wouldn't have been anything an emergency response team could have done to help. The *Challenger* could've launched a response team, but the timing of these things is always an issue. Sometimes," Connor said, holding up a hand, "events occur so quickly that it's all we can do to deal with it in the moment."

Dennis sighed, looking sober and a little uncomfortable. He considered it for a few moments and then nodded slowly. "Geez, Connor."

He shrugged. "I know. Sometimes I'm like a splash of cold water when you're first waking up. Most officers have had to struggle with this."

"How will this affect the proposal for sending out single exploration ships like the *Challenger*?" Dennis asked.

"That's the real question. On the one hand, I want multiple ships assigned to explore a sector so there is always help available, but that might not be practical," Connor replied.

"I'm aware of the issues you've raised in the past about this—the dangers of exploration and the possibility of an alien encounter," Dennis said.

"Hostile alien encounter."

Dennis arched an eyebrow. "Potentially."

Connor smiled a little. This had been an ongoing theoretical debate between them.

"Will anything come of this report?" Dennis asked.

"It'll be sent to COMCENT and archived. Both Major Arvad and Captain Gates are free to conduct missions as they see fit, provided that their actions fall within the best practices of the CDF," Connor said. Dennis frowned. "I thought after all this time out here among the CDF you would know senior officers are allowed to act with a certain amount of autonomy. That's going to increase with these expeditions, especially the farther they travel from home."

"I see your point. And for the record, I think Captain Gates' quick thinking and performance under pressure are to be commended. I don't know if I could've done anything like that," Dennis said and eyed Connor. "The apple doesn't fall far from the tree."

"Much to Lenora's chagrin sometimes."

Dennis smiled knowingly. "I bet."

"More than you know, especially with what's going to happen next," Connor said.

Dennis frowned and glanced at Martinez, who also looked curious.

"Colonel Martinez," Connor said, "you're being given command to conduct operations for this last sector of exploration."

Dennis's eyes widened. "Congratulations, Colonel."

Martinez's gaze narrowed a little. "Thank you, General Gates. If you don't mind me asking, where are you planning to be during this?"

Connor felt the edges of his lips lift. Martinez had a sharp mind. "I'm going to the *Challenger* to observe the crew."

"You're leaving?" Dennis asked. "Can you do that?"

Connor chuckled and raised his eyebrows.

Dennis rolled his eyes. "Sorry, dumb question. Why are you going there?"

Connor could tell that Martinez had the same question in his mind. "When we return home, we'll be asked to give recommendations for the future of these expeditions. I don't like the idea of a lone ship exploring without any backup, but I might have to accept the very real possibility that this is the way things will be in the future."

"Surely you have a strong grasp of things from here, especially based on your considerable experience," Dennis said.

Connor snorted. "You just don't like the fact that you're losing a player in your Thursday night poker game. Martinez can take my spot."

Martinez grinned.

Dennis gave him a nod. "That's fine. Oliver, you're welcome anytime, but I still don't understand why you'd leave the ship, particularly at this juncture," he said, looking at Connor.

"You know how we review the mission reports and there is good data there? Sometimes I like to get input from both the soldiers and civilians who were in the thick of it. Do the people serving on the *Challenger*—or even the *Endeavor* or the *Horizon*

—do they have a preference for how the expeditions are conducted?"

Dennis pursed his lips and nodded. "I have to say that this past year of working with both of you has been quite illuminating. While I'll be happy to get back home, I will miss the company."

"Likewise, but we have a lot to do before then," Connor said.

The meeting ended, and Connor left his office. He walked to the deck where the offices of the scientists were located and found Lenora standing with a couple of holoscreens suspended around her.

She turned toward him and smiled. "I didn't know you were coming."

"What can I say? I missed you."

She grinned and kissed him.

Connor glanced at the holoscreens. "What are you working on?"

"Just some proposals sent for my review from the Colonial Research Institute."

"Clamoring for your return, are they?" Connor said.

"They miss me, and I miss them. I like teaching and fieldwork. It's not the same doing it remotely," she said, and then her eyes brightened. "Oh, I just learned that Noah is back on New Earth. He and Kara just had their second child."

Noah Barker was an old friend. Connor remembered first meeting him when they arrived at New Earth. He was young, brilliant, and among the most honorable men Connor had ever met. Lenora loved him like a brother.

"Now that's just put the nail in the coffin. We have to return to New Earth and start having kids as soon as possible. We can't have Noah overtaking us."

Lenora gave him a playful slap on the arm. "Not everything is a competition."

Connor chuckled. "Oh, yes, it is."

She rolled her eyes and minimized her holoscreens.

"Have you sent a message back to Lauren?" he asked.

She shook her head. "Not yet. You?"

Connor nodded. "Yes. It wasn't long. Mostly contained the things we'd already spoken about and probably nothing Lauren doesn't expect."

"I've recorded three messages so far, and I don't like any of them."

Connor smiled. Lenora could be particular about how she responded to personal matters. She wasn't one to fly off the handle, but she'd let you know if you'd misstepped in her eyes.

"Just remember, love," Connor said, and Lenora looked at him, "you can always say it later, but you can't take it back."

She pressed her lips together for a moment and nodded. "It hurts, Connor. I wish it didn't, but it does."

"Then tell her that. Better that you tell her you're disappointed than let it fester unspoken. Actions like that cause rifts, and there shouldn't be any with our daughter."

Lenora looked away from him and sighed.

He reached toward her and lifted her chin so she looked at him. "If you're coming from a place of love, you'll do fine."

She stared at him for a long moment and then hugged him tightly. They stood like that for a minute, soaking in the moment. Then, she pulled away.

"Thanks, I needed that."

He hadn't told Lenora about his decision to go to the *Challenger*. She must've sensed his unease because she peered intently at him.

"What?"

"I'm going to the *Challenger* for a few weeks. I want to observe the crew and a whole list of things."

She gave him an amused look. "Also to check on Ethan and Cynergy."

Connor blinked.

"Oh, come on, you know it's true."

Had he been so transparent, or was it that Lenora knew him like no one else did? "It's part of it. He seems fine, and he says Cyn is fine, too, but there is a difference in the things people tell you and how they actually are."

Lenora nodded. "I'm glad you're going."

"I have official reasons for going as well," Connor said. "Care to join me?"

Lenora snorted. "Didn't I just tell you the other day that I find ships confining, and now you want me to go to a smaller ship that has even less space?"

He smiled. "I thought it would be cozy."

She shook her head. "I'll pass."

"I'll tell Ethan not to take it personally."

She shot him a playful glare. "You better not."

He'd known it was a long shot at best, but he'd had to ask.

"Shocking, as it might seem, I do have a lot of work to get done while preparing for the trip home. Things are lining up."

Connor nodded. "I understand. I'll see you at dinner then."

# CHAPTER 9

Connor walked into the hangar bay with Colonel Martinez at his side, giving him a sidelong glance. "Any last-minute questions?"

Martinez shook his head. "Not at the moment, General."

Connor arched an eyebrow but didn't say anything.

Martinez frowned. "Is there something I should know, sir?"

Connor shook his head.

He nodded. "Good. I'd start thinking the past four years serving with you had been wasted if you didn't think I was up to the task."

Connor chuckled. "Well said. I have absolute confidence in your abilities to command this last leg of the expedition."

Martinez shook his head. "You make it sound like you'll be unreachable."

"I won't be, but this is yours. The next expeditionary force to be sent out, you'll be the most senior officer in command."

Martinez smiled. "I look forward to that day, General Gates."

Connor smiled. Martinez hadn't disappointed him once in

the last four years. Sean Quinn couldn't have picked a better officer to replace him. Thoughts of his old friend…old protégé…pricked his thoughts for a few moments.

They walked across the hangar to the shuttle that would fly him to the *Challenger*. The loading ramp had been lowered.

Martinez came to a stop and snapped a salute at Connor. "Safe travels, sir."

Connor returned the salute. "Happy hunting, Colonel."

They shook hands, and Connor walked up the loading ramp. Once inside, three tall soldiers stood at attention. All of them were equal to his six-foot-four-inch height. He knew them all.

Connor frowned thoughtfully. "Captain Carver, was there a minimal height requirement for this protective detail?"

"Of course, General," Carver replied.

Connor smiled and looked at the others. "Lieutenant Deacon. Sergeant Cole. Drew the short straw, I see."

Cole shook his head. "Negative, General. This is where the action will take place."

Sergeant Cole had dark skin and eyes full of the confidence that came from years in the CDF.

"Never know what can get stirred up," Connor replied.

Cole smiled and stood to the side, making a path for them.

"General Gates," Carver said, "I've sent your itinerary to the *Challenger*, and your gear has been secured in the cargo hold. We can be underway as soon as you give the word."

"Thanks. Let's get moving," Connor replied.

Transitions between ships could only occur when not traveling through hyperspace. Traveling through uncharted space required that they emerge into N-space to update their navigation charts. They also dropped transit buoys that could feed updated information to other ships traveling in range so those ships wouldn't need to make a stop. They were trailblazers in a region of space that only the most powerful telescopes had peeked into.

Connor settled down in the passenger area and the shuttle left the *Reliant's* hangar bay. He brought up the technical specs for the *Challenger* and began reviewing the finer details of the ship's current configuration. He planned on comparing them with the proposed updated designs for future exploration ships. He was presiding over the dawn of a new class of ship that was decidedly not a military vessel but still needed some kind of defense measures in place. There were compelling arguments to demilitarize ships designed for long deployment expeditions, and Connor hoped he wasn't witnessing a tragedy in the making. Exploring space was dangerous, but he was practical enough to know that not every dangerous encounter could be met by carrying the most weapons.

The shuttle began its final approach to the *Challenger*'s main hangar bay, and Connor felt the transition in the ship's artificial gravity field. It was akin to taking a long step over a large gap.

The shuttle landed, and the loading ramp lowered to the deck.

Captain Carver waited by the door.

Connor stood and walked through the door. The crew of the *Challenger* waited in parade rest on the deck as Connor descended.

Major Caleb Arvad waited at the bottom of the ramp. "Welcome aboard the *Challenger*, General Gates."

"Thank you, Major Arvad."

"General, I believe you know my XO, Captain Gates."

Connor smiled as he locked eyes with his son. "Indeed, I do."

Ethan stood at attention, looking every bit the fine officer that he'd grown to be.

Major Arvad guided Connor through the hangar and

proceeded to lead him on a tour of the ship. He met department heads, both military and civilian. It was always interesting for him to observe the distinction between the two groups. CDF soldiers would answer questions and not volunteer anything unless asked directly, which had to do with military protocol. Civilian response to his presence was more cautious, almost dividing into a couple of camps—either an inquiry as to why he was there or wondering if they'd done something wrong. Connor left assurances where he could, along with a promise that he would make time to get to know all of them.

The tour ended at the bridge, and Connor sat in Major Arvad's ready-room. He'd meet with his son later that day, so it was just the two of them. Captain Carver waited outside while the rest of his protective detail saw that his belongings were brought to his cabin.

Arvad relaxed as he gave Connor a briefing of the previous mission. He was more or less in line with what Connor had thought the takeaways would be.

"This might be a surprise, but I didn't come here because of what happened on that mission," Connor said.

Arvad nodded. "I read the memo. You want to evaluate ship operations and how they would serve as a model for future solo expeditions."

He quoted the memo almost perfectly. "What do you think? Speak as candidly as you want."

Arvad sipped his bourbon before answering. "We're capable of performing the mission. I believe you'll hear things about getting better equipment to do the job, which is probably nothing you haven't heard before. I think we need the ability to be more self-sufficient."

"How?"

"It's part of why I pushed for the survey and salvage mission.

Demonstrate our ability to acquire raw materials that could be processed into things we can use."

"Are the current fabricators and printers up to the task?"

Arvad considered that for a moment, pressing his lips together. "Not an easy question to answer." Connor chuckled, dipping his head in acknowledgement. "It depends on the length of the mission. If we did another twelve-month rotation, accounting for travel to and from New Earth—or Old Earth for that matter—would eventually limit our range and ability to resupply. If I take into consideration the wear and tear we've observed, I think we'd fall short with the current generation of fabricators. They're designed to bridge the gap for shorter deployments but under the purview that home isn't as far away."

Connor nodded. "You've hit the target right in the center. It's always tradeoffs."

"There are options for expanding engineering workspaces to increase as the need occurs. We'd leverage gray spaces that could accommodate temporary workspaces for various groups."

Connor pursed his lips, intrigued. "Interesting. This would allow you to reconfigure at will, based on priority."

"I thought you'd like that, sir. However, I have to confess that it wasn't my idea."

"Whose was it?"

"Ethan's. He's given this a lot of thought and has very good ideas. I'll be sorry to lose him after this mission."

Connor sipped his bourbon, enjoying the taste as it warmed his chest. "Did Ethan put in for a transfer?"

Arvad shook his head. "Negative, but he's reached the ceiling in terms of rank and responsibility. He'd be wasted if he remained in his current role."

Connor regarded Arvad for a moment. He'd studied his military record and knew that Caleb Arvad wasn't free with his praise. He was consistent and fair.

"What are your thoughts on him commanding a ship like the *Challenger*?"

"He's performed his duties as an executive officer without fail. He's got all the right instincts for command. There are times he can be a bit brash, but that lines up with his age and experience. He not only gets the job done but will push himself and those under his command to improve. The people who work with him are very engaged. This isn't just limited to CDF soldiers but to the civilians as well."

"What are your criticisms of him?"

Arvad considered his response for a few moments. "The things I've highlighted in his record. Those strengths he has can sometimes work against him. At times there aren't good solutions, and when we re-evaluate post-mission performance, he's more likely to put himself in morally gray areas because he works so closely with his wife. I'm of two minds when it comes to that. It's a blessing, but it does open a great deal of risk, which is true for anyone in similar situations. It hasn't held Ethan back, nor has it interfered with his performance, but the potential for conflict of interest is there."

"What about the fact that he's a hybrid? Any concerns about that?"

"Not anymore, General. I didn't know what to expect at the onset of this mission, but I've come around to the fact that Ethan's hybrid nature is something he should lean into. It's another layer I just don't have, and I need to make more of an effort to account for that when considering personnel capabilities and rosters."

Connor chuckled. "You and me both."

Arvad sighed, looking relieved. "I'm glad to hear you say that, sir."

"For all the advantages that being a hybrid affords them, it does leave them vulnerable sometimes," Connor said and paused for a moment. "Thank you for your candor. I recognize that the personal relationship I have with Ethan can make some people hold back in their evaluations."

"Ethan makes it easy. You know, there are some people who are just born for the job. He's one. And he's never leveraged the fact that he's your son to gain anything, and not just under my command. It's all over his record."

"He used to be sensitive about it, but he's settled into his role and what he needs to do to advance. Which is why I was surprised to learn that he hadn't sought a promotion to major."

Arvad frowned. "I put my recommendation in for him six months ago."

Connor nodded. "We'll sideline that for now."

"General, if you don't mind, I have a question for you."

"Go ahead."

"It's my understanding that your involvement with this assignment was temporary. What will your involvement be moving forward, sir?"

"You want to know if I'll be going out on another twelve-month deployment?"

"If you were, I'd request to join it, sir."

Connor was sure Arvad wouldn't be alone in that. "As it stands now, I have no plans for another deployment. There's a need to help guide the effort back on New Earth, and I'll probably be doing that."

"Thank you for indulging me, sir."

Connor grinned a little. "You're not the only one to wonder

what I'll be doing next. It's become the topic of the day with my wife."

"Per your instructions, I've assigned a daily escort to accompany you and your protective services designate."

Connor nodded. "They can coordinate with Captain Carver. Wouldn't do for me to get lost on the ship."

Arvad chuckled. "I seriously doubt that, sir."

They spent the next hour going over the ship's performance, confirming what Connor had already suspected of Major Caleb Arvad. He was every bit as good an officer as Connor had suspected.

When the meeting was over, Connor was brought to his quarters. He was only there for a few minutes when Ethan came to see him.

"Your mother misses you," Connor said as they sat on the couch.

Ethan snorted. "Didn't want to brave the smaller ship, I see. I just spoke to her before coming here. She told you to take it easy on me."

Connor laughed. "Why would I suddenly change things now?" Ethan shrugged. "She's the one you have to worry about."

Ethan eyed him for a moment. "So, how does it feel becoming a grandfather?"

"It feels great. We're happy for Lauren and Isaac."

"So, it's all right if we call you grandpa in private then?"

"Only if you'd like to talk about when you and Cynergy will start having children."

Ethan blinked, and Connor could've sworn that his son's complexion paled just a little bit. He grinned. "All right, truce, no grandpa jokes then."

Connor smiled. "It's good to know you can surrender with

dignity." He regarded his son for a long moment and then asked, "Is there anything you want to talk about?"

An almost nervous laugh escaped Ethan's lips and he shook his head. "You see, statements like that make me feel like I should be confessing something."

Connor raised his eyebrows. "Is there?"

He shook his head. "No."

Connor nodded. "Tell me about the mission."

Ethan frowned. "You read the report. It's got everything in there."

He leveled his gaze at his son and tilted his head to the side.

Ethan sighed. "Things happened fast. I almost lost Cynergy."

"Does it change anything? For you or for her? Will she be joining us?"

"We talked about it, and no, it's not going to change anything. We are what we are. This works for us. As to your third question, I didn't think you wanted to stay in your quarters. Cynergy is meeting us at one of the engineering workspaces. She's got something she wants to show you."

Connor nodded and regarded his son. "Just promise me one thing."

"Okay, what do you want me to promise?"

"If it becomes too much, that you'll change this working relationship you have with Cynergy. I'm serious. I don't want to see either of you suffer because…well, you know what can happen out here. Worrying about loved ones will wear on anyone's nerves. I'd rather see you stop before something irreversible happens. Do you understand?"

Ethan looked away for a second. "I understand, Dad. Cyn was a little upset. She didn't like being trapped like that. It's one of the reasons she's pushing for this prototype probe she's come up with."

It was interesting to see how they'd both come up with different solutions in the aftermath of the mission to the lunar object. Ethan attacked the problem from a resources standpoint to be better able to address the risk, while Cynergy chose a more technological solution. Connor had to acknowledge their resilience. He'd seen others who'd had an extremely close call completely back away and change their lives because of it, be it a different career focus or leaving the CDF altogether.

"All right, let's go see what she's come up with."

Ethan blinked. "Oh, I thought you had other meetings set up."

Connor smiled. "I do. You're it." Ethan sniffed. "You should know by now that I make my own schedule. It's one of the benefits of being a general."

# CHAPTER 10

As the week went by, the *Challenger's* crew had gotten used to having Connor aboard. Gone were some of the long stares as he entered the room, along with the deafening silences. But there was still the show of respect due a CDF General, and Connor knew that his reputation preceded him wherever he went. However, after meeting with various department heads and their teams, the crew and passengers had come to know the man behind the legend—as Ethan liked to put it.

Captain Jack Kershaw, the *Challenger's* lead engineer, came to Connor's side. "Apologies for that, General Gates. The I-Drive requires her share of attention when she wants it."

They stood outside the vast containment center of the I-Drive.

Connor nodded. "I don't want to get stranded out in the middle of nowhere. We don't know what kind of neighborhood we're in."

Kershaw was a man in his thirties whose hair had gone white

in his late teen years. He used to have red hair, but for some reason, his hair color had changed. He'd told Connor that the doctors could've "fixed" the problem, but after the shock had worn off, Kershaw had found that he liked the color. Not only that, but the women whose attention he'd sought liked it as well.

Kershaw grinned, giving Connor an approving nod. "Very good, General Gates. As I was saying," he said and began gesturing toward the wallscreen that showed the stunning brilliance of the I-Drive's core, "the ship builders did an outstanding job with this core. She'll continue to perform within specs as long as we follow the maintenance protocols. In fact, it's a toss-up as to what will fail first—the core or the superstructure of the ship." His expression became serious. "It's all the other systems we cram into a ship that the potential cascade of failures can stem from."

Connor nodded. "A ship is more than the core. What are your recommendations?"

Kershaw smiled and his gaze flicked toward the ship's clock. "How much time do you have, sir?" he asked, pausing for a moment. "A good team can keep a ship running for the duration of the proposed deployments, but it also depends, and I want to give you an accurate answer to your question. We don't know the kinds of stresses the ship will be called upon to endure. If we encountered a hostile alien race and needed to run, we might have to push things beyond specs to save our own lives. These ships are becoming less like warships and more like civilian exploration ships. However, the expectation from the outside world is that we'll still be able to push the limits on them like we would a CDF warship, and that's unrealistic when pushed to the extreme."

Years in the CDF had contributed to Kershaw's opinion, which was likely shared by many military personnel.

"What about longer deployments?"

Kershaw frowned in thought for a moment. "How much longer?"

Connor chuckled. "Engineers refuse to allow themselves to be trapped by generalities. Well played, Captain. Anywhere from two to perhaps five years."

Kershaw's sky-blue eyes widened for a moment and his brow furrowed in thought. "Assume resupply missions?" he asked and then shook his head. "We'd have to assume that; otherwise, we'd run out of supplies." He scratched the back of his head while he considered. "It's possible… highly probable that the ship could function for two years without a major overhaul. The range of the mission, as well as preparedness for exploration missions, might be limited at the end of such a long deployment."

Connor nodded. "So, your opinion is that two years is the upper limit."

Kershaw gave him a lopsided smile. "Assuming the ship is in good working order before deployment, then yes, that's my opinion. The problems arise when I add the crew into the equation."

Connor suspected where the engineer was going. "What do you mean?"

"We're not machines. All work and no play wears the best of us down. And we're limited in recreational downtime. At the end of the day, it's obvious we're still on a ship. I suppose if there comes a time when those lines are blurred, perhaps longer deployments are possible."

"Interesting."

Kershaw frowned. "Why is that, sir?"

Connor shrugged. "You just hit on something my wife and I discussed not too long ago. She'd rather the ship was more like being planet-side than being on a ship to help make being on them more enjoyable."

Kershaw snorted. "She's not wrong."

"No, she's not, as she is fond of reminding me from time to time."

"Are those lengthy deployments really being proposed?"

"It's definitely a consideration," Connor replied.

Kershaw blinked a few times as his gaze sank toward the floor.

"Is something wrong?"

Kershaw looked at him and shook his head. "No, it's just that for being out here that length of time we'd have to account for families being aboard and have additional capacity available for children being born."

"That's right, Captain. A population that's not growing isn't a good sign for any civilization."

"Would you do it, sir? Would you start a family out here far away from everything?" Kershaw asked, all the lightheartedness leaving him.

Connor considered it for a few moments. "I honestly don't know. Maybe I'm a little old-fashioned. Interstellar travel is new, and the younger generations will grow up with it as commonplace."

Kershaw bobbed his head slowly a few times and then his gaze flicked toward Connor. "Sorry, sir, it's just a lot to consider. I can see why you came to the ship to do this evaluation." He glanced around the large area. Members of his team were working at terminals across the way. Then he turned to Connor. "We're going to need a bigger ship that's going to need to perform a variety of functions. This design isn't meant for that. I suggest an entirely new design instead of trying to shoehorn requirements into an older ship design that's not meant for the use it's being put to."

It was always gratifying when Connor observed someone else

who finally understood the momentous task they were taking on. "Now you're getting it. Care to come up with a few proof-of-concepts for COMCENT and the new Confederation to consider?"

Kershaw blinked. "Sir, that's outside my wheelhouse. I don't design ships."

Connor arched an eyebrow. "Once upon a time I was never going to be a general or create a military force from the ground up."

"Yeah, but you're...well, you're you, sir." Connor stared at him. Kershaw nodded. "All right, I'll see what I can come up with, basing it off our discussion. I'll even run it by my team. Make it a collaborative effort."

Connor smiled. "Excellent. I look forward to seeing it whenever you have a few designs to share."

Kershaw blanched as if he'd been given additional work to do, but he quickly recovered.

Connor grinned. "Can you have those designs in by the end of the week?" he asked with a deadpanned expression.

Kershaw's eyes widened and then he laughed. Connor smiled. "How about by the end of the deployment before we return to New Earth? These would probably still be considered high-level designs that would need further proofing, but I'm sure I could get a few analysis cycles out of the ship's computer before then."

"Excellent, and make sure you note who contributed."

Kershaw swallowed. "General, I have to ask, but is there an opportunity in the works here?"

"Sometimes opportunities come knocking. It's up to us to open the door and let them in."

Kershaw looked as if his well-ordered world had suddenly got turned upside down, but there was an excited glint in his eyes.

Connor left main engineering. Sergeant Cole waited for him in the corridor.

"Next up on the list?" Connor asked.

"Dinner, sir. I'm to escort you to the officers' mess."

"Doesn't quite have the same ring as the dining lounge, does it?"

Sergeant Cole shook his head and grinned.

Later on, Connor sat in the officers' mess where off-duty officers took their meals. Across from him were Ethan and Cynergy. Major Arvad sat to his left, and there were other officers and civilian senior operators in attendance.

Cynergy smiled warmly at Connor. She had long, golden-blonde hair and large, attractive brown eyes. They'd lost some of the edge they'd had when Connor had first met her. Ethan and Cynergy weren't the only couple at the table, but there was a closeness he'd observed between his son and his wife. It was as if the space between them wasn't really there. It was almost like an unconscious deference they gave each other. He approved. It had taken him and Lenora years to reach that kind of intimacy.

They ate, and when the meal finished, several people took their leave until it was just Connor, Ethan, and Cynergy.

She stood and gestured toward the door. "I've reserved some time in port observation. A better view than here."

Waiting for them outside was Lieutenant Joe Deacon.

Cynergy looked up at him. "Can I help you, Lieutenant?"

"He's with me," Connor said.

"Protective services," Ethan said, and Cynergy nodded.

They made their way through the ship to one of the observatories. Cynergy looked at Connor. "You have protective services with you everywhere you go?"

"Depends on whether I'm on deployment or not, but yes, more or less."

She glanced at Ethan. "They've always been around as long as I can remember."

"All of you had some kind of protection?"

Connor shook his head. "Ethan and Lauren didn't require it so much, but for me and Lenora, yes."

"For good reason," Deacon said from behind them.

Cynergy looked at Connor expectantly.

"There have been a few incidents over the years."

Ethan nodded. "The department was conceived by Sean."

"General Quinn?"

"The one and only," Ethan replied.

"In the early days of the CDF, Sean took it upon himself to stay as close to me as possible."

Cynergy frowned. "I just hadn't expected it, but I guess it makes sense."

They entered the observatory and went to a closed-off section. It was dimly lit, and the room had dark walls. A huge wallscreen displayed a video of the vast expanse of a breathtaking starscape. In the distance was a nebula the color of yellow sand, and on the far side was a cluster of red that reminded Connor of an eye.

"Is this what I have to look forward to?" she asked Ethan.

"Only if I rise to the rank of general."

Lieutenant Deacon took a position near the entrance of the room and became still.

Connor looked at Cynergy. "It's not as invasive as you might think. You'd be surprised at how often someone like Lieutenant Deacon has watched out for me and my family."

"But New Earth is so peaceful. I expected it back on Earth, but it doesn't line up with what I remember of New Earth."

"It is peaceful, but that wasn't always the case. When push comes to shove, there are things you need to do to ensure the protection of your family. Things weren't so different for hybrids or other spacers, were they?" Connor said.

"I guess not. I was always on the move."

A few moments of silence passed between them.

"I had something I thought you might be interested in," Ethan said.

"Shoot," Connor replied.

"This is going back to the subject of expanding the exploration initiative and it being hampered by the fact that ships and crews must return to either New Earth or Old Earth to change crews and resupply. I think we need to build fast transport ships to facilitate crew changes and resupply runs. Definitely crew changes, and we can establish supply depots in certain sectors. We can even reduce the supplies required for those ships by utilizing stasis pods."

"So purely a transport vessel that doesn't have all the accoutrements of a full-on ship," Connor said and Ethan nodded. "Not a bad idea."

"Good enough to present to the Confed Exploration Initiative Council?"

There hadn't been a decision made on what the future alliance between New Earth and Old Earth was going to be called, but in certain circles people had adopted referring to it as Confederation.

Connor shook his head, and Ethan frowned. "Why not?"

"Why don't you push for it? It's your idea, after all."

Ethan glanced at Cynergy for a moment. "Yeah, but I'm..."

"Just a captain in the CDF. They're a dime a dozen and don't have the weight to influence or shape future policies. Is that it?"

Ethan blew out a breath. "Something like that."

Connor speared a look at his son. "Well then, you know how to fix that. What are you waiting for? Caleb submitted his recommendation for your promotion almost six months ago. All that's left is for you to submit your own record of intent."

"It's not that simple."

"It is from where I'm standing," Connor said, regarding his son for a moment. "You've got solid ideas, Ethan, and it's up to you to push them forward. You'd have an easier time or increase the likelihood of seeing those ideas bear fruit if you rise up the chain of command."

"Yeah, but there is a cost."

"What cost?"

"Rising so far in rank that you aren't allowed to be on the fringe. Conduct missions. Always sending others in your place. I've heard you talk about this over the years. How you missed the times when you could just go out in the field."

Connor had said and thought about those things over the years, and yet he'd still found a way to be in the heart of the worst battles fought by the CDF.

"It's true. When you're leading missions, you must delegate. The burden is too much for anyone to carry by themselves. But there are tradeoffs. There are always tradeoffs. There is a balance that can be maintained, and," he said, looking at both of them, "working below your ability will take its toll on you. It comes in the form of having an unsatisfying life. It'll eat away at you, the people closest to you, and everyone around you if you let it."

Connor watched as both Ethan and Cynergy exchanged looks. "I'm trying to help you. Both of you," he said. The edges of Cynergy's lips lifted. "Both of you are forces to be reckoned with. Why do you think you're snatched up by people who know what to look for, but it's only a temporary setup. You're meant to blaze your own path, and that's not going to work if you don't have the clout to achieve what you really want."

Ethan frowned in thought for a few seconds. "So, putting in my request for promotion to major is the answer?"

Connor shook his head. "It's not *the* answer. It's a step, one of many you'll take. You've got it in you to command a mission like this. With both of your backgrounds, I know you want to keep pushing the boundaries. You look at that starscape," he said, gesturing toward the view of the heavens on display, "and you want to know what's out there. When I look at it, I understand some of that, but mostly I just want to go back home to New Earth." He paused for a few moments, gathering his thoughts. "Your mother is right. Maybe it's time to let the younger generation take the helm and stand the watch for a while."

Ethan stared at him thoughtfully.

Cynergy put her hand on Ethan's shoulder. "Your mother doesn't like extended space travel. She can't wait to go back, especially now with Lauren starting a family."

"Is that what's going to happen to us? When we start a family, we'll go back home?"

They stared at each other for a long moment, and Connor cleared his throat. "This is a conversation you should have when I'm not here."

"No, it's fine," Cynergy began, and Connor shook his head.

"No, it's not. You're husband and wife. You guys need to strike your own balance," Connor said and frowned. "Unless you're pregnant, too?"

Ethan paled, and Cynergy quickly shook her head.

Connor laughed. "You guys," he said and blew out a breath. He couldn't stop laughing but knew he had to. He gave Cynergy a hug. "Did you see how scared he looked?"

Cynergy looked at Ethan, who rolled his eyes.

"Okay, I'll stop now. If your mother was here, she probably would've elbowed me in the ribs by now."

Ethan relaxed and put his arm around Cynergy's shoulders.

Connor regarded both of them. "It's not enough to have good ideas. You need to have people in authority willing to listen and support you. Your sphere of influence will increase as you rise in rank."

"What about Uncle Noah?" Ethan said.

Connor chuckled, knowing his son sought to regain some perceived lost ground. "What about him?"

"He's been able to do lots of things without climbing the rank ladder."

"That he has, by partnering with both the CDF and Research and Development leaders in the colony. He also invented the technology that allowed us to explore like we can today. He's a great man and a good friend. Do you see yourself going in that direction?"

His son was a soldier. They both knew it.

Ethan shook his head. "No, that's not for me. But if you're right, these expeditionary initiatives will come under the joint purview of both planets, separate from the CDF."

"Probably not for another twenty years. These things take time. Look how long it took the Ovarrow to integrate into the colony. It's still an ongoing process, but you were raised in a world where Ovarrow were around; whereas, I still remember when they first came out of stasis."

Ethan considered it for a few moments, and Connor could almost see his mind at work.

"Thanks for bringing it up. I meant to talk to you about it—promotion and other things—but I've been working on coming up with ways to allow us to explore farther from home."

"I'm glad we got to talk about it," Connor said and looked at Cynergy. "How are the prototype probes coming along?"

Cynergy smiled at the mention of her new pet project. "We'll be able to use some on the next star system we explore."

# CHAPTER 11

At nine o'clock in the morning, ship time, which was incidentally set to New Earth time, a meeting began.

Connor sat at the pale conference table next to Major Caleb Arvad. Ethan and Cynergy sat next to them. A holotank was active in front of them and showed the *Reliant's* meeting room.

He spotted Lenora among the attendees and sent her a quick message in text.

::*I see you.*::

She peered at her personal holoscreen for a moment and then lifted her gaze to the video feed, smiling a little.

::*I see you, too.*::

A second went by and another message appeared on Connor's holoscreen.

::*I miss you. How's the eval going?*::

::*I miss you, too. Eval is going well. It's not as cramped here as you thought it was going to be.*::

She shook her head a little. ::*I'll take your word for it. I sent my message to Lauren.*::

Connor wanted to ask about the message, but Colonel Martinez started the meeting.

"Hello everyone. I'll be running the meeting and commanding the exploration of our final assignment of this deployment," Martinez said and looked at Connor. "Unless General Gates has had a change of heart on this matter?"

Connor shook his head. "Negative, Colonel Martinez, you've got the ball. Take it all the way."

Martinez smiled. "Excellent," he replied and gave a nod toward someone off-screen. "Data is coming your way about the systems we'll be exploring. We've detected a small star cluster of a few dozen stars. At least thirty percent of those stars are G-type main-sequence stars. Preliminary analysis shows systems commensurate with that of New Earth and Old Earth. Rocky planets are closer to the star, with gas giants acting as a shield to the inner planets. The data is there, but the size of the inner planets is well within range of Earth norms. In layman's terms, some are a little smaller while others are larger. No super-earths like we've been encountering in other parts of the sector. I'd like to highlight our science team led by Dr. Aksu, who identified this cluster as having the greatest potential for what I hope to be a momentous find."

Major Arvad glanced at Connor. "They must've worked all night to put this together."

All comms channels were muted when a speaker was active, so there was no chance of their conversation being overheard.

Connor nodded. "It's what they live for. Keenan rotates the schedule of his team, so they've worked at all hours."

"How does his team enjoy that?"

"They're the ones who pushed for it."

"This brings me to the deployment details for the mission," Martinez continued. "Given the uniqueness of the find, we will be splitting up. Each ship will be performing a survey of multiple star systems. Priority should be given to the star systems that have the greatest chance of supporting life. Caution is the order of the day if any of the teams hit the jackpot. Based on the discovery of the Vemus probe on Earth, the current theory is that there were other probes sent out to discover other worlds like ours. If significant Vemus presence is detected, the planet should be avoided until backup units can arrive."

Connor pressed the button for speaker request and his session became active. "I just wanted to add to that. The secondary priority of our search is for Phantoms. While not an official name, it's the reference that's been adopted for the advanced alien species that ferried the colonial probes to Old Earth."

Martinez nodded. "Follow standard scanning protocols and focus on anomalous activity in the star system. Since we haven't detected them, the recommendation is to focus on gravitational anomalies. The Phantoms seem to be able to travel through space using technology that we're not familiar with. However, they must also come into N-space, and when they do, the working theory is that they generate gravitational anomalies. The chances are small, but we've got to look. In the event that you encounter these beings, First Contact Protocols should be followed." He paused for a few moments and then continued. "I know there are various opinions on how the exploration initiative should be conducted. Splitting up our forces does give us a chance to test out firsthand singular exploration initiatives. Even if the future holds other task forces, there is a strong likelihood that single ships will be designated to explore entire sectors. Part of your planning should account for the delay in backup being provided by other ships. I've accounted for this in your assignments. Also, I expect that this last leg of our mission will be performed with the same level of excellence shown throughout this past year. Let's finish this race strong."

The meeting ended and Arvad brought up the data pack from the *Reliant*.

"Colonel Martinez has positioned the *Reliant* in the centermost location of the cluster," Ethan said.

Connor nodded in approval. "Excellent. I would've done the same."

The star cluster spanned across five light-years, with most systems within a fraction of that distance.

There was a three-dimensional model of the star system, and several stars were highlighted. The cluster loosely formed a spiral, with the head pointing toward the outer edge of the galaxy. Their assigned stars were near the bottom of the spiral that angled toward the center of the galaxy. Connor wondered if Martinez had given their assignments using a randomized association, using the *Reliant* as the anchor in the center of the cluster. It was an option for general assignments. If he were planning this, he might've taken into consideration the capabilities of the ships and their crew. Not all teams were built the same, and over the last year there had been ships that proved better suited to certain types of exploration.

"Looks like we've got the farthest to travel," Arvad said. "We'll need to plot a course to a better location that will give us the best insight into those target systems."

Before the meeting, Arvad had been assured that Connor's function was strictly as an observer.

"Major Arvad," Cynergy said, "we have a prototype of the probe ready to deploy. I request that we use it for one of these systems."

Arvad considered it for a few moments. "Is this the probe that can perform precision surveys by way of entering a planet's atmosphere?"

"Yes. Its more robust engines allow for faster travel and the ability to enter and exit the atmosphere. The onboard sensors will be able to sample and survey as needed," Cynergy replied.

"I won't make a decision on this now. I want the results of our own scans before committing to anything," Arvad said.

"Understood," Cynergy replied.

Connor noticed Ethan staring thoughtfully at the star cluster. He rubbed his chin.

"What's on your mind?" Connor asked.

Ethan blinked. "I was just wondering how the cluster came to be here."

Cynergy nodded. "It's rather small for a cluster. They can contain hundreds or, in other cases, thousands of stars spreading across massive distances."

"That's what I was thinking. Could this little cluster have broken away from a larger cluster, or did these stars form here?" Ethan shrugged. "The thought just popped into my brain. Doesn't have any bearing on conducting the mission."

Arvad looked at Ethan. "I'll need to know the status of our away teams and equipment."

"Yes, Major, I'll get right on that," Ethan said and stood.

Cynergy left as well, leaving Connor and Arvad alone.

Arvad looked at Connor. "A year sounds like a long time, but it really goes by fast."

Over the past year, the expeditionary force had explored many star systems and space anomalies. Scientific discoveries had been made and confirmed, and there would be plenty of work to be done when they returned home.

"This cluster is quite the find. It's an excellent candidate," Connor said.

"Have you seen the technical specs of Cynergy's new probe?"

"Yes, she showed them to me last night."

"A lot of systems aboard that probe. It goes against the established design doctrines that treat probes as expendable objects."

Connor nodded. "If the discovery is worth sending in this specialized probe, the loss of it could be justified, or a retrieval mission could be done if appropriate."

Arvad stood. "Care to accompany me to the bridge, General?"

Connor nodded. "Absolutely."

# CHAPTER 12

A lot had changed in the last two days. The crew of the *Challenger* focused on their assigned tasks with an excited diligence that Connor approved. Over his many years of military service, he'd found that the most effective crews were the ones who were most engaged with the mission. This came in part from having good people in the appropriate positions. He remembered the early days of the CDF, when he'd had to make do with the candidates that were available. There had been many slots to fill, and he'd ensured that the rigorous training methods would weed out the worst of the bunch. That had been nearly forty years ago, and the population of New Earth had soared. The CDF was no longer lacking in recruits with a wide range of capabilities and ideas. They weren't without faults and tensions, but their two wars had brought them together. Then, traveling to Old Earth, learning the fate of humanity, and reestablishing contact had forged humanity anew. There were still disagreements, and even though the population of both planets numbered well into the millions, it was nowhere near the almost countless billions that had inhabited the Sol System. Humanity had been given a second chance, and he knew all too well the value of that. Most people understood the basic fact that humanity as a whole had almost been snuffed out of existence. The Vemus might've been the catalyst, but severe tensions between old alliances couldn't be discounted—all of which were gone. Certain traditions still existed in the current population, but there was quite a bit of time between those old alliances and the world that existed today. Connor still remembered that old world, as did most of the adult first-generation colonists who'd arrived at New Earth. He knew what a civilization could accomplish when dedicated to specific goals. He'd seen it in both humanity and among the Ovarrow.

Connor looked around the *Challenger*'s bridge. The crew consisted of both human and Ovarrow. Among them were trainees from Old Earth who would one day serve in the Confederation. He wouldn't bring himself to consider that they might be called the United Coalition of Planets. Noah had seen to that with his offhand comment about what they would do if they encountered a species that didn't have a home planet and wanted to form an alliance with them. If they were to expand this Confederation in the future, wouldn't it be prudent to account for possibilities they hadn't encountered yet? That had been over a year ago, and he wondered if Noah understood how some of his more innocuous comments sometimes spawned lives of their own.

On the main holoscreen was a star system that had a planet roughly eighty-seven percent of the mass of Old Earth. They spent the better part of the day scanning the three star systems assigned to them, but there was only one real candidate for exploration. They'd deployed Cynergy's probe to that star system with its thirteen planets. The core system of planets was similar to that of both Old Earth and New Earth star systems. It was a model that was conducive to life, but it didn't occur everywhere.

Major Arvad came to stand beside Connor. "Should be any time now."

Connor nodded and turned toward Cynergy. She sat at the auxiliary workstation on the bridge, staring intently at the holoscreen.

One of the sub-windows on the main holoscreen for the data comlink sessions flashed, indicating an update was being received.

Connor gave a nod to Arvad, and they both walked toward Cynergy.

"Probe data has been received. I'll put the updated data about the star system on the main holoscreen. There is a planet in the habitable zone. It does have an atmosphere. Five major land masses, with three of the largest around the polar regions. Average surface temperature is just above freezing," Cynergy said and paused with a frown. "Analysis suggests that the climate wasn't always like this."

"The planet could've suffered from some kind of catastrophe. Are there any indicators of a civilization?" Arvad asked.

"Possibly," Cynergy said, and a group of a dozen smaller images appeared on the main holoscreen.

Connor peered at the images from the probe, which progressed from inside the lower atmosphere as it made several orbits around the planet, then flew along the equatorial line. The landscape was mud-colored and frozen, looking almost barren, but there were large shapes, as if they were covered by some kind of structure. They could be naturally occurring phenomena, or they could be covering cities.

"Do you have control of the probe?" Connor asked.

"Yes, I have a subspace comlink established."

"Good, can you have it fly lower over one of these regions to give us a closer look?" he asked, gesturing toward one of the images.

Arvad nodded. "They could be buildings, but I'm not sure. Reminds me of ice building up during a bad storm, but this looks extreme…and dirty."

"Could be an artificial ice age," Ethan said. "Something triggered it, like what happened on New Earth. Rapidly forming ice."

Connor considered it and shook his head. "There isn't any glaciation. This has to be something else."

The rapid ice age experienced on New Earth had been triggered by the Ovarrow in their war with the Krake. They were losing the war and had adopted a strategy to make the planet—already ravaged by war on a planetary scale—unlivable, while a portion of the Ovarrow population weathered the small ice age in stasis pods. It had been a strategy born of the most desperate of circumstances.

"Could be a massive storm," Ethan said thoughtfully. "We'll see what the science team makes of the data."

The probe flew over one of the continents, heading north along the coastline. Connor glanced at the planetary data, which indicated that oceans covered about sixty-eight percent of the planet. He considered what Ethan had said, wondering if he was right. Could a massive storm dislodge a significant amount of water and debris covering the continents, almost like a massive flood, but on a planetary scale that indicated a massive shift of the tectonic plates?

The video feed from the probe showed that it had come to a hover position over a landmass. It slowly sank toward the ground. The ground looked like a rock formation worn smooth by wind and rain. Gray and brown patches streaked through similar-colored ice.

The probe scanned the ground and then landed. Cynergy deployed the scientific caching kit, and the probe began taking soil samples and running analysis on them. A preliminary report appeared, showing the composition of the atmosphere based on the ice and soil samples.

Suddenly, the video feed shifted to the side, and then something dark blurred by as the probe fell into a roll. The *Challenger*'s bridge immediately became quiet. Connor expected the video feed to cut off at any moment, but it kept working.

The probe eventually slowed, but some kind of muddy water had covered the optics. While most people stared in shock at the main holoscreen, Connor noticed Cynergy navigating the control system for the probe. She looked at him and lifted her chin toward the main holoscreen.

There was a flash of red light, and the camera optics became clear of the mud and water. The probe looked as if it was teetering on the edge of a dirty pond, and it began to inch toward the water in slow motion.

Cynergy growled in frustration, and Ethan went to her side. "I can't get the engines to come online. They won't respond."

The probe dropped into the water and rolled over. The video feed went to cloud depths and displayed gray sky far above the walls of a chasm. The probe sank from view, and the telemetry data indicated it had sunk to a depth of fifteen meters. The probe's systems began to shut down, and it broadcasted a distress beacon.

Connor looked at Cynergy. "I can't get it back online."

Something about that last image before the probe sank tugged at his mind. "Can you bring up the last few seconds of video before the probe sank?"

Cynergy did as he requested.

"Play it back at half speed," Connor said. "Hold it there."

Just before the probe sank under the water, its camera showed the walls of the chasm. But they weren't walls. They looked to be some kind of artificial structure buried in the mud and ice.

"That's not naturally occurring," Arvad said.

Connor nodded. "No, it's not."

Arvad looked at Connor. "What do you want to do, General?"

Connor considered it for a few moments, but he really didn't need that much time. He looked at Arvad, and then at Ethan and Cynergy. "Let's go get our probe."

## CHAPTER 13

After twenty-four hours, the *Challenger* was still orbiting the dismal planet. Connor had studied the images from the probe. He'd seen so many different planets, but they'd mostly been variants of New Earth in alternate universes. There was a commonality among them, despite the sometimes deadly differences in climate. During those expeditions into alternate universes, they eventually had an idea of what to expect, or had a better search protocol. On this planet, there was none of that. It was an entirely different star system.

The planet itself had three small moons, with the largest orbiting closer to the planet than the farther two. The scans indicated that the gravitational influence of the smaller lunar objects stabilized the larger, which put the planetary wobble a few degrees beyond that of New Earth. Some of the planetary scientists put forth the theory that it was the greater wobble that caused the planet to have colder temperatures. The entire planet could be going through a colder season, but the season could last for decades. They were working on analysis models to predict the orbital patterns of the moons to determine when the season would end.

Connor walked onto the bridge where a video feed of the planet was on the main holoscreen. He walked toward the command center, where Captain Ester Talori, alternate XO of the ship, sat. She was a bit taller than the average woman, with thin, dark-brown hair, a pronounced nose, and brown eyes that were almost black. She stood and saluted Connor.

"General Gates, sir," Captain Talori said. She looked surprised to see him, but her expression changed in an instant. "Apologies, General Gates," she said, gesturing toward her holoscreen. "I was working on some analysis."

Connor's experience with Ester Talori was that she didn't startle easily. "That's fine, Captain. What were you working on?"

"Sir, I was conducting some alternative analysis models on the lunar object dataset."

A flicker of annoyance caused his face to tighten. "Captain," he said, putting a little edge to his voice, "your focus should be on the mission at hand. The away teams will be heading to the planet soon."

Captain Talori stiffened at the rebuke, shoulders going back, her eyes forward and not looking at him. "Yes, General."

Connor looked at her for a moment and then glanced at the main holoscreen.

"General Gates," Talori said, and Connor turned toward her, "I wasn't being negligent in my duties, sir. This *was* for the mission."

The skin above his eyes pinched together. "Okay, Captain, enlighten me."

Talori made a swiping gesture, and the holoscreen near the command chair shifted toward her, becoming larger. "Sir, Captain Gates and I have been working on analysis of all the data collected from the lunar object mission. We were trying to determine when the disturbances occurred that caused the collapse."

"The reports indicated it was from the survey teams and the brittleness of the object itself."

She nodded. "Yes, but we decided to dig a little deeper. I started looking for patterns of sensor data that didn't make any sense. The protocols used in operations would highlight patterns that appeared above a certain threshold. I created a filter based on smaller data points that ordinarily would've been considered garbage data."

Connor nodded a little, following her logic. "But they would give rise to a bunch of false positives."

"That's why I accounted for that in my filter," she said and gestured toward the holoscreen. "What I found were small gravitational anomalies that really don't make any sense, but they're small, so it's easily overlooked." She brought up a lunar object scan and had it zoom in to a particular area, far from where the survey teams had been operating. "This is tracking the collapse and the subsequent debris that was projected above the lunar surface. It doesn't look like anything is wrong."

Connor watched it and then nodded.

"I've added a filter that diminishes the view of everything that looks normal," Talori said.

The model of the screen changed, most of it becoming moderately transparent. There were indicators of the direction that the collapse traveled, but it appeared that there were several origin points. Not all of them were located where the survey team had been operating.

"The most interesting part is this," Talori said, zooming into the image.

It reminded Connor of a river or stream going around a rock, except here the rock appeared and disappeared in milliseconds.

"Are they errors in the scan data?" Connor asked.

Scan data was gathered by an array of sensors that were then pieced together by the ship's computing core.

Talori shook her head, looking pleased at the question. "Negative, General. I've had the ship's analysis AI scour the data, and it's authentic. These tiny micro gravitational disturbances *did* occur. This is what I was looking at when you arrived. I'd tasked a subroutine on the secondary computing core, giving it a lower priority so as not to take away from higher-priority tasks. It's taken days to run and create this model. What I'm not sure is how or whether this had any significant effect on that lunar object."

Connor nodded in appreciation. "This is impressive, Captain Talori." He paused for a moment in thought. "You said both you and Ethan worked on this?"

She nodded. "Ethan was frustrated by how events seemed to get away from him. It's a frustration we shared because I was supposed to be watching his back from here."

"Would active scans have detected this?"

"Possibly, sir. Depending on whether we're just taking a snapshot of the area or were maintaining the scans over a period of time," she said and gestured toward the holoscreen. "With the lunar object, we didn't maintain the scan until the away teams left the ship. It was snapshots until then. The anomalies don't appear during that time, but you see it for yourself. They come quickly and are gone. It's possible we just missed it."

Connor nodded, understanding. "How resource intensive would it be to add a filter like this to our active scan data?"

She considered his question for a moment. "I could assign it a high priority and see what the analysis AI says."

"Do that," Connor said. He regarded her for a moment. "Excellent catch, Captain Talori. I have to admit that now I'm curious. Are these events naturally occurring or is something else happening?"

She smiled. "Me too, sir," she said and paused for a second, but then seemed to have arrived at some kind of conclusion. "Sir, one of the reasons I've been so keen on this, aside from the lunar object, has to do with the Phantoms."

Connor was familiar with the unofficial name of the mysterious aliens that assisted the colonial probes to reach Old Earth a little over forty years ahead of schedule. "What makes you think this has anything to do with them?"

"I can't draw anything more than conjecture. It's just an anomaly that challenges our understanding of the galaxy. However, I can't help but wonder what else we could be missing." She shrugged. "It's like an itch in the middle of your back, sir."

Connor smiled a little and nodded. "I understand. Carry on with that filter. I'm curious to learn if anything is detected here."

"Thank you, General," she replied and returned to her workstation.

Connor walked toward the main holoscreen, peering at the area the shuttles were flying to. He thought about his conversation with Ethan the other night. There was a part of him that missed going on missions. It wasn't just the going but the team. The longer you were part of a platoon or even a company of platoons, the more you developed a camaraderie with the people you served with. He'd been fortunate to work with so many good people throughout his career, many who were no longer alive. He thought of his old friend Kasey Douglass, his second in the Ghost Platoon. He'd been a well-grounded man who looked out for Connor over their years serving in the NA

Alliance military and helped him immensely with the formation of the CDF. Sometimes he even found himself missing friends who were still alive, but both career and life choices prevented them from interacting on a daily basis—people like Noah, Diaz, and to a certain extent, Sean Quinn. He recalled Diaz at his side during the Krake wars. Diaz had almost died, and while Diaz wanted to fight at Connor's side, he'd made the difficult choice to serve in the CDF away from combat teams. He had a large family, and his close brush with death on that world in an alternate universe had shaken him to his core. Connor had never resented Diaz's choice to step away from active duty. And here he was many years later, light-years from home, wondering if now was finally the time for him to take a step back and allow others to forge ahead and stand watch to protect humanity. He snorted to himself. He'd never thought about it like that in the beginning. The colonists had needed someone to protect them, but at some point during that time he'd begun to count himself among the colonists, especially when they'd believed they were the last of humanity. What else could he have done? He'd had the skills, knowledge, and more military experience than anyone else in the colony. But those times had long passed, and as he stood on the bridge of a converted warship, he began to accept that perhaps it was time for him to return home. Others could go on the dangerous missions. But he knew there would always be a part of him that wanted to be with them—the same part that wanted to be at Ethan's side while he forged his own path in the CDF and what came next, and also be with Lauren as she continued her medical career and began a family. It was an impossible task, but that didn't stop the father in him from wanting those things. He'd enjoyed these past months, watching Ethan grow into an even better officer than he'd been before. His son had a bright future ahead of him, and it was time Connor took a step back, allowing him to seize it on his own.

# CHAPTER 14

The shuttle wobbled a little as it went through the atmosphere. Most people didn't notice it, but Ethan had always tried to spot the moment when they truly entered the lower atmosphere of a planet.

The planet's size was ninety-six percent the size of Earth but had a much slower, fifty-seven-hour rotation for a single day. Seventy-four percent of the planet was covered with water and had average temperatures slightly above freezing for less than half the day.

He glanced at the icons that showed the other shuttles. His shuttle flew point, while the *Mariner* was on their six. The other two shuttles flew toward another continent to begin their survey of the area.

Sergeant Chavez peered at the video feed and sighed. "This place looks depressing. It's like the beach in the middle of winter, all grey and dreary. Even the ground looks like it's dying. Toxic atmosphere to boot. Wonderful."

They'd just penetrated a thick cloud cover that was a mix of ice and water layers. For a few moments, it had sounded like they were flying through a hailstorm, but they were actually just flying through ice clouds.

"Makes you wonder what kind of civilization could've evolved here," Bentley said.

The land mass looked like dark, wet sand dredged up from the bottom of the ocean, the kind that was full of dead things. Ethan glanced at the levels of sulfur in the atmosphere and was glad not to have to breathe it. He imagined it was the kind of stench that took up residence in the back of your throat and was all but impossible to get rid of without significant decontamination.

"We're only seeing the land masses," Ethan said.

Bentley glanced at him. "It looks like someone either dumped wet sand on the continents or these land masses are new."

Chavez twisted in his seat toward him. "New? How could that be?"

"Tectonic shift or upheaval forced the continents to push upward," Ethan replied. Chavez began to ask another question, but Ethan kept going. "Alternatively, or possibly a cause for the upheaval, is the draining of the oceans across the planet, exposing areas that were once underwater."

Lieutenant Bentley gave him a confused frown, and it was shared by Sergeant Chavez.

"Where did the water go?" Bentley asked.

Ethan looked amused. "It's still there," he began and chuckled. "It's under the planet's crust. Didn't you guys ever study basic planetary science?"

Bentley blinked and shook his head. "Must have missed the class that taught how water somehow went under the crust."

This wasn't the first time Ethan had discovered that his

education was somewhat unique in the colony. Given who his parents were, it shouldn't have come as a surprise, but it wasn't just him. It was common in Sanctuary where the schools had strong ties to the Colonial Research Institute.

"It's actually not that complicated," Ethan said. "Fissures in the crust allow seawater to get sucked underneath the planet's crust, but that isn't always the case. It's not an all-or-nothing kind of process because of the mantel. You could just refer to them as deep-water wells. So, pressure pulls seawater in and eventually there is an expansion of the crust because of the displaced seawater."

Bentley frowned for a few moments in thought. "Wouldn't that create tidal waves?"

Ethan nodded. "Probably. We'd have to ask Luanne Atwater about that. She'd probably know, but let's assume it does. On this scale, it must've been an extremely turbulent time. That might explain some things we're seeing here."

"Not the structure where the probe was lost," Chavez said.

He was referring to the split-second image sent by the probe's camera. "*Possible* structure. I don't want to jump the gun here."

"Captain's right," Bentley said. "We'll need to confirm it as we retrieve the probe."

Chavez made an uh-huh sound and then became quiet.

They flew toward the waypoint where the drone's distress beacon was detected. Ethan gazed at the dismal landscape and tried to imagine the upheaval he'd so flippantly described to the others. If anyone did live here, he didn't think it would have been possible to survive that kind of catastrophe. Even if they were technologically advanced, there were only so many safety measures to be taken. They hadn't encountered any signs of technology in the upper atmosphere and nothing on any of the moons. If there *was* a species here, it wasn't space faring. Which meant that if Ethan's theory was correct, it was highly unlikely they'd survived, but that didn't mean there wouldn't be evidence of them.

He looked at the large expanse of the continent. It was desolate and almost devoid of plant life, but not completely so. They were darker colors, some a deep purple like that of an eggplant on fields of vines with broad leaves. There were no forests or even shrubbery. Chavez was right. This planet was depressing to look at. But regardless of their personal tastes, they had a job to do, and he was determined to find out if that structure glimpsed by the probe's camera was really what it seemed to be.

Lieutenant Bentley peered at the landscape and then looked at Ethan. "We're heading toward an epicenter of sorts. See how things seem to converge on that area ahead?"

Ethan studied the flowing landscape, and Bentley was right.

"How can we know for sure, sirs?" Chavez asked.

"We can't. Not without scans and running detailed analysis using the *Challenger*'s computing core. Too many variables to consider," Ethan said and then added, "Still, the observation is compelling."

He sent a message to the other shuttles, alerting them to what they were seeing and confirming whether there were other occurrences on the other continents.

As they flew toward the gray epicenter, they saw large cracks on the surface. They were approaching the chasms that the probe had flown over.

An area ahead of them was highlighted on the HUD, showing where the probe had landed and subsequently fallen.

"Take us around to where the gap opens wider and we'll begin our descent there," Ethan said.

Chavez did as he was ordered, and the *Mariner* followed them.

Ethan had told Cynergy that he was taking point on this descent and that the *Mariner* was their backup. She hadn't been pleased, but she also knew there was no point in arguing with him.

Contrary to what he expected when they'd flown down, the walls of the gap receded inward, and the area opened wider than what the surface indicated. It began to rain in a steady fall, and there was a body of water at the bottom. Ethan glanced at the video feed above them, not liking the precariousness of their location. If there was a major collapse, they'd be in real trouble.

He initiated a scan of the area, searching for any structural weaknesses, and it came back negative. It looked like natural-forming shelves had produced a wavy pattern that stretched out for hundreds of meters.

"Take us into that open area away from the water," Ethan said, gesturing toward an area where the ground leveled off.

Chavez flew them toward the area and sent several engine bursts downward to test the stability of the landing zone before setting the shuttle down. They'd have to walk to where the probe had last been located, which would take them past the alleged structure that had been spotted.

"Time to gear up," Ethan said. "Not you, Sergeant. Stay on the ship. Be ready for an emergency evac. Monitor comlink activity."

"Yes, Captain," Sergeant Chavez said as he settled back into the chair.

Ethan went to the back of the shuttle with Bentley, and they put on their combat suits. They were a lighter-class NexStar series nine combat suit that was equipped more for exploration than fighting a battle. They had protection, and the combat suit jets would help them navigate the terrain.

The loading ramp lowered to the ground, and the platoon

exited the shuttle. Ethan walked down the ramp and spotted where the *Mariner* had landed. Its team was also exiting their shuttle.

The charcoal-colored wet ground was solid enough to stand on, if a little slushy, and each of their steps gave way a little before it firmed. The temperature was near freezing and ice deposits were almost everywhere, which was probably one of the main reasons the area hadn't collapsed.

Ethan peered into one of the shelves and saw that it went deeper than he'd initially thought.

"They look like caves," Bentley said.

Ethan heard some of the other soldiers groan, and considering their recent experience with caves, he couldn't blame them.

Corporal Brand Lasky reported that scans showed the probe was nearby, and they set off to find it.

The paths around the shelves gave them plenty of footing, but the ground was a mix of ice and slush. The tread on their combat suits produced small spikes that reduced slipping.

Recon drones were deployed and began tracking ahead, and they soon came to the area where the probe had tumbled down. Ethan picked out the impacts on the walls as it had approached the ground.

Cynergy met him near where the probe had rolled into the icy water, and they found themselves in close proximity to one of the shelves. Layers of ice had built up along the walls, but it resembled the structure of an arch. There was a base structure, and then the curve at the top disappeared into the frozen, coarse substance that passed for sand.

Ethan looked at Lieutenant Bentley. "Have Lasky go get a core sample from over there. He needs to confirm whether there is a structure hidden under all that ice."

"Yes, Captain," Bentley said.

Ethan turned to Cynergy. She was staring at the water. One of her arms was lifted, and she had her personal holoscreen active.

He walked over to her. "Any luck reaching the probe?"

She shook her head. "No, it's offline. Just the beacon is active. I can get a general area. Hash and Luanne are offloading our submersible drone. We'll connect a cable to it and raise the probe."

Ethan nodded. "All right. We're going to have a look around."

She eyed him for a moment. "Don't go too far. I don't like this place. I feel like we're standing in a giant graveyard. Reminds me of some of the old derelict space stations."

Those old space stations had been filled with the bodies of people who'd lived there. There was no decomposition in space, so those bodies would stay in their frozen state forever unless someone properly disposed of them.

"We won't stay longer than necessary," Ethan said. An alert appeared on his internal HUD. "I've gotta go."

He left Cynergy and the other hybrids to retrieve the probe. They'd settled into a quiet survey of the area, and he noticed that the CDF soldiers were behaving the same way. They were on task and focused.

Ethan crossed the area to the team of soldiers that was extracting a core sample from the ice.

Lieutenant Bentley saw him approach. "There is a structure under the ice. Some kind of alloy, but the analysis can't match it to anything we've encountered before."

Ethan's eyes widened and he peered up at the beginnings of the arch. There were dark streaks through the ice, making it all but impossible to see the structure underneath.

"Have them take other samples to confirm these results,"

Ethan finally replied. He wanted them to triple check it before he broke the news that they'd found the ruins of an intelligent alien society. Primitive species couldn't build structures like this. That had required sophistication and technological progress.

Ethan remembered the massive shelves they'd flown past and wondered if each of them had some kind of arch. Usually, arches were used as a boundary. His gaze slid down the interior structure. It was curved on the edges, almost oval in shape. The interior was dark.

A short time later, three more ice core samples confirmed the same result as the first. Recon drones flew in a few hundred meters along a long corridor and came to a stop. The video feed showed some kind of wall with wave patterns that varied in color from a deep metallic purple to pinks and greens.

Ethan ordered the platoon inside for a closer look. The walls of the corridor were made from a very coarse black sand that had been compressed and frozen. There were swirly ribbons of compacted debris that they couldn't really identify. They finally reached the wall and saw there was a jagged opening at the bottom. Several of the soldiers were able to push the wall down. It wasn't attached to anything but looked to have been wedged in place.

The recon probe flew inside, its bright lights revealing a wide expanse. Ethan and the others followed the probe. The ground began to slope downward. A huge metallic wall of angular planes emerged from the edges of their lights. It was made from the same material as the wall that had blocked the entrance.

Ethan blinked in surprise, and Bentley gave him a questioning look. Something in the design tugged at his memory. The structure looked as if it were grown instead of shaped.

"What is it, sir?"

"It reminds me of exoskeletal material, but this is metallic," Ethan replied.

The structure rested at an angle, slanting away from them. More than two hundred meters were exposed before it disappeared into the far wall.

Ethan looked to the right where the metallic structure showed a more severe curve to the ground, but he suspected it went on beneath it.

"Exoskeletal, but that would make this of Vemus origin!" Bentley said and then shook his head. "Maybe it's just similar and there is no link between the two. It looks like some kind of building maybe?" Bentley asked.

There were twisted ribbons of a lighter shade of material swirling across it. "Maybe," Ethan said finally. "Let's search for a way inside."

## CHAPTER 15

They divided up into teams of four and began exploring the alien structure. One team used their combat suit jets to descend lower into the cavern.

Ethan went toward the far wall. The dark cavern narrowed. As they walked, the ground crunched beneath their feet. Broken ice crumbled under their weight.

"Captain," Corporal Lasky said, "I think you're going to want to see this."

Lasky squatted down to the ground and gestured to an area in front of him. In the ice was a long tentacle the color of sandstone. Ethan angled the light of his helmet toward it. Several other tentacles twisted, disappearing beneath the ground. Circular suckers lined most of the tentacle, and it looked to have serrated edges. The tentacle was ten centimeters thick and extended from a thick membrane that might have been the back of its head. The ice distorted the view.

Corporal Lasky gestured toward it with his rifle. "Looks like a tentacle from an octopus or a giant squid. Ever seen one of them in the historical vids?"

Ethan panned around the area and saw something like an arm and perhaps a shoulder. The body was broken apart, but it appeared as if it fit together. "Not like any octopus I've ever seen."

There was a bulbous mass that might have been a head, but he couldn't tell. The body must've suffered some kind of mass trauma, but the ice kept it close together.

They found more of the strange bodies frozen over in the ground and part of the wall. He couldn't see any wounds, but it was clear that whoever they were, they'd been dead for a long time.

The recon drone flew to a wall across the way and gave an audible chime. Ethan shined a light at a far wall, and the sight made him suck in a breath. The wall extended upward about forty meters before curving overhead. Buried within the wall were more of the tentacled creatures. A tangle of tentacles surrounded a large head, with large, black, lifeless eyes frozen in place. He supposed there was a mouth of some sort buried amid the tentacles. Beneath them were shoulders and arms, almost humanoid, but covered with some kind of pale-colored, bulbous mass.

"My God," Bentley gasped. "There are thousands of them in just this area alone. They're holding weapons."

Clutched in the hands of the dead were long dark shafts that could've been staves or long rifles.

Several of the soldiers lifted their weapons, pointing them at the wall. A few muttered curses sounded over the comlink.

"They can't be alive. Can they, sir?" Corporal Lasky asked.

"Doubtful," Ethan replied. "They're frozen solid."

The sight of it was unsettling. They looked as if they'd all been frozen while charging toward them. Ethan frowned and glanced back at the metallic wall. Bentley followed his gaze.

Sergeant Wilson let out a hearty grin. "Lasky, go stand by the wall over there. See if one of them moves."

Lasky shook his head. "No way am I going over there."

"It'll be fine. We need a picture of you with the aliens."

"We need a sample, Corporal," Ethan said.

Lasky simply stared at him for a moment. "Yes, sir," he said.

"Go with him, Sergeant," Ethan said to Wilson.

The two made their way toward the wall, and a comlink chimed on Ethan's suit computer. He tore his eyes away from the dead and shuddered.

Cynergy's face appeared on his internal HUD. "The probe is wedged in place. We're not going to be able to retrieve it intact. I was able to access a control panel and have initiated a data dump. The probe will come apart if we force it out of there." She peered at him. "What's wrong?"

Ethan told her what they'd found.

"What do you think they were doing?" she asked.

Ethan wasn't accustomed to seeing so many dead bodies. He made himself turn around and take in his surroundings. "It looks like they were trying to reach this building we found." He frowned. "At least, I think it's a building. We're scouting the area."

His gaze sank to the ground, and he tried to make sense of what he was seeing given what they suspected had happened in this area. It made him wonder if there had been some kind of battle being fought here and these were the remnants frozen in the ice and sand. But why were they here in the first place? Who were they fighting? The aliens wore what looked like a dark green uniform, but it could also have been the color of their skin. He couldn't tell.

"There's something strange in the probe's data storage," Cynergy said.

"What did you find?"

"Telemetry data seems to be cut off for a moment. The probe reports entering the atmosphere and then skips ahead. It's like there is lost time, but it wasn't recorded. It's strange."

"Does the flight path match the trajectory it was on?" Ethan asked.

Cynergy's eyes focused on something else for a few moments, and she shook her head. "No, it doesn't. It's off by over three hundred kilometers."

Ethan frowned. "Are you able to run a diagnostic on the probe?"

"I can try. I'll make sure the data dump includes the system logs," she said and paused for a moment. "I've got to go. I have Hash scouting the area, and it looks like they've found something."

"All right, stay alert," Ethan said.

She gave him a warm, knowing look and the comlink severed.

Corporal Sansky and Sergeant Wilson returned to them.

"I got the sample, Captain. Unknown organic life-form, probably aquatic in nature, is the preliminary analysis," Sansky said.

Wilson shook his head. "You think?"

"It's what the computer told me."

Ethan nodded. "Okay, secure the sample. We'll let the biologists take a look at it when we get back."

They continued to scout the area. More than a few of them kept glancing back at the ice tomb of alien warriors. Ethan found himself doing it as well, as if trying to glean some kind of message from them.

Lieutenant Bentley sent him a comlink. "Captain, we're scouting the lower level and, well, you've got to see it. This is a massive structure."

A video feed from Bentley's combat suit was added to the comlink. It showed a superstructure that extended far beyond what they could detect. It was dark, with a dull metallic sheen marred by the ice and dark sand.

"We'll make our way to you," Ethan said and ordered the others to Bentley's location.

They returned to the back of the massive wall where it ended, going to the depths below. Ethan could see the combat suit lights of the soldiers sent to meet them. The drop was just over seventy-six meters. The CDF soldiers leaped off the ledge and used their suit jets to control their descent, increasing the output as they neared the bottom.

Ethan landed, his combat suit absorbing the impact, and he strode forward, clearing the way for the others nearby. Soon, the rest of the platoon had joined him.

The exposed areas of the deep purple metallic wall were smooth, and parts reflected the light. They followed the wall and skirted around the edges. More than a hundred meters in the distance, the wall opened, exposing the vast framework of the interior superstructure. The inside was even more cavernous than what they'd already seen. Massive support beams were connected by circular couplings forming an unfinished barrel. There were several levels of them, and they ended at differing intervals, narrowing, and something about the design seemed to tease a thought from his mind.

Ethan caught up to Bentley, who gestured up.

The structure was remarkably intact, considering the acidic atmosphere.

"This is more than a building, sir," Bentley said.

Ethan blew out a hard breath. He walked a short distance ahead, studying the layout, thoughts stacking in his mind, pointing toward something he was at a loss to admit. "If I had to guess, I'd say it's a ship, or part of one."

"A ship!" Bentley replied. "That can't be right. This thing is massive in scope, and we're only seeing a small part of it. No way this thing could fly."

"It doesn't look like they finished building it."

"There's nothing to indicate they could produce enough power to clear the atmosphere," Bentley said and stopped.

Ethan gestured above them, where the long circular framework narrowed. "Those look like some kind of engine pod could be mounted there. As far as power output, we'd need to find a power station," he said and frowned, taking in the sheer size of it. "Or stations. If their tech is anything like ours, they'd need more than one power core."

Bentley stared up at the ship, cocking his head to the side, considering.

"We need to send an update to the ship," Ethan said.

"There is no indication this species had this kind of technology."

"I don't know," Ethan admitted. "It looks like it was under construction. For all we know, we're looking at things upside down. Nothing could be where it was intended before whatever happened here…occurred."

Bentley stared at him for a long moment. "Or someone triggered. Those were soldiers back there frozen in the ice. But who or what were they fighting?"

They received a comlink from Sergeant Wilson. Another alien body was frozen in the ice.

"We're coming to you," Ethan replied.

Because of the terrain, the alien ship angled on a slant,

creating a large gap underneath it. They reached the area where Sergeant Wilson and his squad were located.

"Captain, it's down there on the ground like the others," Sergeant Wilson said, leading them toward the area.

The ice glistened under the lights from their combat suits, giving the area an almost ethereal glow. Ethan saw the same aliens they'd spotted earlier.

Wilson came to a stop and gestured in front of him.

Ethan peered at the area and saw the same octo-aliens they'd seen earlier. They were frozen over a dark depth that the light couldn't penetrate.

Sergeant Wilson increased the strength of the lights from his combat suit. Bright light penetrated the dark, frozen gloom, and beneath the octo-aliens was another creature in the black depths. A large, clawed hand appeared as if it was frozen in mid-attack by the other creature. Several large, black tentacles fanned out behind it. Its body twisted away, so Ethan couldn't get a good look at it.

The soldiers in the area all became quiet as they watched the frozen scene beneath their feet.

Ethan increased the output of his combat suit lights and ordered the others to do the same. Luminous depths were suddenly exposed to the lights, and more of the aliens appeared.

"Gah!" Corporal Lasky exclaimed as he jumped back a few steps. "Look at its mouth. Look at the mouth!"

Beneath the ice was a black alien with its mouth wide open. Sinister-looking, pointy teeth, each the size of a finger, could be seen. Dark lips peeled back as if the alien had been roaring before it was about to attack. Dark slits were above the mouth, looking more like nostrils than anything else, but it was difficult to see.

Ethan could pick out the ropy musculature of its long arms.

The skin looked solid, as if it were armored and sinewy at the same time. If there was an alien designed for killing, this was it.

He took a step back and surveyed the area. The frozen battle scene made it look as if the octo-aliens were either running away or regrouping.

"Sir," Lieutenant Bentley said, coming to his side and speaking quietly through their private comlink, "I don't want to sound like an alarmist here, but what if these things are simply hibernating in the ice?"

Ethan knew what he meant. Vemus could hibernate in the vacuum of space, which was a much harsher environment than this ice. If the creatures frozen in the ice were somehow related to the Vemus, they needed to confirm it.

"You're not being an alarmist. We need to confirm it," Ethan said, and looked at Corporal Lasky. "We need another sample, Corporal."

"I'm sorry, Captain, my sample kit is full, and my backup unit is malfunctioning," Lasky said.

Bentley shook his head. "Brooks," he called out to their platoon's medic, "give Lasky your bio-kit for sample collection."

Brooks came forward as he reached inside a storage compartment. He pulled out a kit and handed it to Lasky.

Corporal Lasky looked as if someone had stolen his favorite dessert.

"Sergeant," Ethan said to Wilson, "you and your squad cover him. Keep those weapons ready. If that thing so much as twitches, pull Lasky out of there and light that area up."

"Yes, sir," Wilson said, and ordered his squad mates to cover the area.

Ethan and the others moved away, coming out of the gap.

A deep sound echoed throughout the expanse, resonating from frozen walls, amplifying and distorting the source. Ethan spun around, looking for the source, and faced the squad of soldiers in the gap.

Something large and metallic groaned, as if it were suddenly straining under a colossal weight. Ethan's gaze sank toward the squad of soldiers.

"Get out of there!" Ethan shouted.

He watched as Wilson gestured toward the others and the CDF soldiers began running.

Lasky looked as if he was struggling to move, and Wilson spun around. He raised his weapon and fired. Lasky tried to jerk backward, but something dark clutched at his arm.

Ethan darted toward them, weapon raised.

A burst of ice chunks went straight up, and Ethan watched Lasky get yanked toward it. Wilson bellowed as he fired his weapon, and Ethan was at his side.

A clawed hand clutched Lasky's arm as he tried to scramble away. Ethan aimed his rifle at the arm and fired at full auto. High-density darts chewed through the alien's arm, freeing Lasky. Ethan reached down and helped the CDF soldier get away from the alien.

Together, they backed away from it.

"It's alive! That freaking thing grabbed me," Lasky cried.

"Keep it together," Ethan said to him. "We're not out of this yet."

A few moments later, they were out from underneath the alien ship.

Sergeant Wilson gestured with his rifle back the way they'd come.

Ethan saw more of the ice chunks get pushed to the side. "Explosive rounds!"

They changed the configuration of the nanorobotic ammunition and fired a burst of explosive rounds right at the alien as it tried to pull itself from the ice. There was a bright flash and the sound of grisly meat slapping the ice.

"Let's get out of here," Ethan said.

They hastened back the way they'd come. More deep sounds echoed around the ice cavern.

They reached the wall, and the soldiers leaped up, using their suit jets to ascend to the top. Clearing the top of the wall, Ethan got an emergency message from Cynergy's team.

They were being attacked and requested an evac.

# CHAPTER 16

Captain Jack Kershaw eyed Connor over his coffee cup. They sat in Kershaw's office near main engineering. "It's only been a few days, General Gates."

Connor looked at the holoscreen that showed a couple of the ship designs Kershaw had been working on. "I realize these are a work-in-progress."

Kershaw seemed to relax a little. Sometimes, engineers didn't like to be pinned down before they'd absolutely made up their minds about a solution. Then they hardly ever relented. It was dedication to a decision already made that Connor could relate to. He was never one to constantly second-guess a decision after the fact.

"Just a couple of concepts. High-level-type stuff trying to push different kinds of ship designs," Kershaw said and flipped through a couple of concept images on the holoscreen. "If I remove some of the constraints that come from building a warship, then it really frees things up."

Connor nodded. "I imagine it would."

Kershaw narrowed his gaze just a little. "I wouldn't compromise safety for the sake of a design, but these are a few ideas I've been playing with in my off time."

"They're impressive," Connor said.

Captain Hank Carver stepped inside the office. "General, Captain Talori is requesting to speak with you."

Carver was part of his protective detail, and Connor had routed the comlink request to him while he met with Kershaw.

Captain Kershaw stood. "Please, General Gates, use my office. The XO wouldn't contact you if it wasn't important."

"Thanks. Stick around," Connor said.

Carver made a passing motion toward the active holoscreen and the video comlink became active.

Captain Ester Talori looked at Connor. "General Gates, I've been working on that filter we spoke about, the one for tracking anomalies. I'm in CIC and we ran an analysis on the sensor data we've received. I got a hit, sir."

Connor's eyes widened a little. When he'd given Talori the go-ahead to create the data filter, he wasn't sure if it would yield any results. "What did you find?"

"An occurrence with the space probe as it entered the atmosphere. We received a data dump from the team on the planet, and it appears that an anomaly occurred just as the probe entered the atmosphere. It suddenly moved position approximately three hundred and eleven kilometers. On top of that, its course was altered, changing the trajectory toward a specific continent."

"You've compared the scan results with the data dump from the probe?" Connor asked.

"Just the preliminary data provided by the team below. They were attempting to get more information from the probe itself but were having issues reaching it," Talori replied.

Connor frowned. Years of combat instincts began triggering his suspicions. A one-off anomaly in dark space was one thing, but to have a similar occurrence at a planet they were visiting was beyond impossible for a random event.

"Connect us to the bridge," Connor said.

The others in the room noted the command in his tone and stiffened.

"At once, General Gates," Captain Talori said.

A few seconds later, Major Caleb Arvad joined their comlink, and she quickly brought him up to speed.

Arvad looked at Connor. "No way this can be a random occurrence. We haven't detected anything on active sensors."

"That's because whoever is doing this doesn't appear on sensors. Set Condition One. I'm coming to the bridge," Connor said.

Major Arvad relayed Connor's orders and a ship-wide broadcast sounded.

"Action stations. Action stations, set condition one throughout the ship," said the comms officer on the bridge.

Captain Kershaw shot to his feet and quickly left the office.

Connor and his protective detail left the office also, but he kept the comlink to CIC and the bridge active for a few moments and was about to sever the connection when Arvad forestalled him.

"General, two teams on the planet are under attack. An evac is underway," Arvad said.

It felt like the final teetering domino was about to fall, giving way to a cascade of events that were about to surge with blazing speed, setting things into motion.

Connor stared at Arvad. "Is it the same continent the probe went to?"

Arvad looked away for a few seconds and then nodded. "It is, sir. It's Ethan's teams."

Connor quickened his pace down the corridor. "Understood. I'll be at the bridge as quick as I can."

"I'll have an update for you when you get here. Emergency response teams are being activated and heading to the hangars as we speak," Arvad said.

The comlink severed and Connor hastened down the corridor, with Carver sprinting to catch up.

His thoughts raced as he processed all the new information. Nothing had been detected with active scans, but someone had to be there. Someone had to be making these things happen. Attack could be imminent. The question remained as to what form the attack would take.

All their assets began listing in his mind, but first and foremost was that they were alone. There would be no backup coming to help them. He gritted his teeth in frustration as he ran but then banished the irritation. They could have an entire battle group here with the CDF's most powerful warships and it might not make a bit of difference. Safety in numbers didn't necessarily translate when dealing with a foe who had achieved this level of stealth and demonstrated the ability to manipulate the actual space they traveled in. If they could manipulate space and time to target a space probe, guiding it to their intended target, what would stop them from doing the same thing to their ship or the shuttles as they tried to escape?

Main engineering was as far away from the bridge as you could get. He had to travel the length of the ship to reach the bridge, and despite focusing most of his attention on what was ahead, his mind kept wandering, as if trying to anticipate an attack from an unseen assailant.

He gritted his teeth as he ran. The ideas in his mind were all possibilities but lacked proof that any of those horrible things were about to occur.

He and Carver rounded a corner, with Carver shouting for the soldiers in the corridor to make a way for them to get through.

Then the lights in the corridor suddenly went out. It took a few seconds for Connor's implants to enhance his vision for darkness. Emergency lighting became active along the floor.

Several people shouted in alarm, and he heard someone cry out in pain. Too many damn civilians and not enough safety drills. They were scared, and he couldn't just barrel through them. He had to help. When people were scared, they tended to develop tunnel vision to the exclusion of everything around them. It was up to the preparedness and training of the CDF to help protect the other spacers. With that in mind, he took charge of the soldiers around him.

## CHAPTER 17

The CDF soldiers moved swiftly through the ice tunnels. Gray light came from hundreds of meters away. Ethan watched as the scout team moved ahead and a fire team covered the area with weapons ready.

He'd sent a comlink to the shuttle, and Chavez was heading to their location. Ethan checked the location of Cynergy and her team through the specialized EVA suits they wore. They could be considered light-armor suits but without the full complement of protection and abilities of a NexStar combat suit.

They exited the tunnels, passing by the wall of the octo-aliens frozen in place, casting accusatory looks by the trick of the light as if convincing them to take some kind of action. Ethan ignored them as they went by. He searched for Cynergy and her team, expecting them to be near the entrance, but they weren't there.

He checked their EVA suit status, which maintained a connection to the shuttle. Slush gave way to dark water where their probe had fallen in, but Cynergy's locator showed that they were farther away from their location.

They made their way past other shelves along a long lake. Soldiers kept watching the dark interior of the shelves, anticipating some kind of attack.

The combat shuttle flew overhead, and Chavez opened a comlink.

"Looks like there is something two shelves farther from your location, Captain."

Ethan ordered the soldiers to move on. "What's there?"

Chavez was silent for a few moments, and Ethan watched the shuttle hover in the distance. "My God," he said, repeating it.

"Focus, and tell me what you see, Sergeant."

"There are bodies at the edge of the water. They're torn apart. There's something in the water, sir."

Ethan yelled out to the others. "Double time."

The CDF soldiers quickened their pace, but a steady downpour of rain made the ice and sand even more slippery, causing them to go slower than Ethan wanted.

Ethan spotted the bodies, and his breath caught in his throat as he searched for Cynergy. Blood had spattered the dark sand, mixing with the ice and slush. Something had gouged through their EVA suits, exposing them to the atmosphere. They'd been members of Cynergy's team, people he'd known and spent time with. EVA suit computers had protocols to help protect the wearer in the event of trauma, but three of them were dead. Internal organs had been torn out of them, and their faces were frozen in pain and horror as their lifeless eyes stared through him.

Ethan spotted movement off to the side, and he raced toward it, his heart thundering.

Luanne Atwater reached toward Ethan. Her skin darkened, shifting to hybrid nature, which was her best chance for survival. She had a deep gouge across her middle. The edges of the EVA suit were ragged, as if the gouge had been caused more by blunt force than sharpness.

Corporal Brooks, the team medic, began sealing the wound with an emergency medical gel infused with healing nanites. They were encoded to follow different protocols if the subject was a human or a hybrid. Some hybrids had excellent healing capabilities, and healing nanites encoded for humans could interfere with hybrid regenerative capabilities.

Ethan knelt down and took Luanne's hand. She looked as if she was struggling to speak.

"We're here. You're safe," Ethan said. "What happened to the others? Do you know where they are?"

He heard Bentley telling the soldiers to cover the tunnels nearby, while Wilson called out that there were tracks leading into the tunnel.

Luanne stiffened, gasping in pain. "They came out of the water," she said, her voice sounding harsh. "They took them."

Ethan glanced at the murky water, unable to see more than a short distance. "Did you see where they took them?"

Luanne swallowed hard. Dark blood was inside her mouth. She coughed a little, and some dribbled down her chin.

"She's bleeding internally," Brooks said, pulling a syringe from her med kit and pushing it into the medical port at the neck. "She won't be conscious for much longer."

Luanne's eyes fluttered closed as she became increasingly groggy.

Ethan glanced at the water and then at the tunnels. Sometimes injuries were so severe that it left a person confused. He had to be sure.

Luanne's eyes opened, and he leaned toward her. "Are they in those tunnels? Is that where they took them, or did they take them into the water?"

Luanne's body relaxed as she lost consciousness because she was fighting to survive her injuries.

Ethan checked the EVA suit locators. There were several located in the water far beneath the murky depths, while a vast majority gave a general location of the immediate vicinity.

He clenched his teeth in frustration. "Lasky, can you isolate the missing team's suit signals?"

"On it, Captain," Lasky replied.

Lieutenant Bentley hastened over to him.

Ethan opened a comlink to Chavez in the shuttle. "Cover the tunnels."

"Copy that, Captain," Chavez replied.

Ethan walked toward the tunnels, peering inside.

"Those creatures could be inside, sir," Bentley said.

Ethan glanced at Lasky, who was staring intently at his holoscreen. He shook his head and looked at Bentley. "The longer we stand here, the longer those things are getting away with our people."

A howl sounded from the depths of the darkened tunnels, startling some of them. Ethan tried to see what was inside, but the tunnel twisted out of view. He had to make a decision.

"Lasky, what's your status?" Ethan asked.

"Can't get a lock on their signal, sir."

Ethan looked at Bentley. "We go in."

The CDF soldiers moved into the tunnels. They left a few soldiers behind to help load Luanne onto the shuttle and to send a submersible drone to investigate whether there were any bodies in the water.

Cynergy had twenty people on her team, specialists from across varying disciplines. Some were human, while the majority were hybrids.

The tunnels didn't have alien bodies frozen in their walls.

Human tracks were easily seen among much larger claw marks, and Ethan couldn't be sure which tracks had come first.

Cynergy's last message indicated that her team had found something worth investigating. Could she have gone into the tunnels, leaving a small team behind? Perhaps something attacked and was now following the team that had gone into the tunnels.

As they made their way through the tunnels, Ethan hoped the signal to Cynergy and her team would become stronger, but it hadn't. Something must be interfering with it. Locator beacons didn't use subspace communications, and neither were they available in combat suit comms. Long-range communications were established through the shuttle.

The locator signals began to weaken and then went offline. Ethan stared at the list of names as their EVA suit statuses suddenly displayed red. That could only happen if the suit was severely damaged or the wearer had shut it down.

"They're offline," Bentley said.

Ethan's mind raced. If they charged blindly ahead, they could run right into a trap. The lighting at the end of the tunnel became brighter, as if it led back outside. They raced toward it and came to a stop.

The tunnel opened into some kind of small valley. Layers of frozen sand shelves surrounded them, the tops of which went on for several hundred meters. The scouts searched, looking for some trace of the other team but couldn't find anything. Strange sounds came from the tunnel entrances above, similar to the sounds they'd heard from the alien spaceship.

Once again, Ethan had to make several decisions in the span of a few moments. His wife was in serious trouble, and they were about to be attacked. The only way he was going to find his wife and the others was to use his hybrid nature to track them.

"Bentley, I need to do something here that's unorthodox," Ethan said.

The CDF lieutenant frowned. "What do you mean, sir?"

"I'm going to try tracking them, but I have to remove parts of my suit."

Bentley's eyes widened. "Captain, you don't know what this atmosphere will do to you. It's toxic for us."

"Maybe not for me," Ethan said.

He embraced his hybrid nature, and his skin darkened to almost black with a purplish hue. The most appropriate application he could think of that would protect him was preparing to go underwater. He'd done it many times, even to depths that required specialized equipment. He was a Vemus hybrid and had the ability to rapidly adapt his body, enhancing his strength, the way his body moved and protected itself, and even manipulating the way his mind worked. There was always a balance that needed to be maintained; otherwise, it would affect his ability to command.

"Captain, are you all right?" Lieutenant Bentley asked.

Ethan nodded. "Just adjusting," he said, his voice sounding somewhat strained with effort. He didn't know why, but embracing his hybrid nature made his voice sound husky because his body went through changes that affected almost everything. It wasn't just outward appearances. Scientists still marveled at their capabilities.

His abilities were a subset of what a full Vemus was capable of, but while a Vemus adhered to a rigid hierarchy of control with an Alpha that dominated and commanded the others, Ethan and the other hybrids were immune from those influences.

Hybrids could sense Vemus and other hybrids like themselves, which came from subsonic sounds they made. Ethan focused his mind and began to search for Cynergy. Her unique hybrid signal would be clearest to him because she'd changed him into a hybrid to save his life. The bond was intimate and extremely powerful, and it was his best chance of finding her.

Ethan retracted his helmet. Cold rain spattered his face, and his eyes stung because of the toxic elements in the atmosphere. Soon, his adaptations accommodated the higher acid count and his vision cleared.

This was an alien world. There were new sounds, an atmosphere he'd never experienced, and other things that he couldn't pay attention to at the moment. He focused on what he knew to be Cynergy, forcing all the other noise out of his mind so he could locate her.

He had it!

Cynergy's unique signature became apparent to him. It was audible only to other hybrids and the most sensitive equipment, well beyond the capabilities of his combat suit.

Ethan looked at Bentley and gestured toward their left.

"The missing team is this way," Bentley said to the others.

Ethan took point, keeping his weapon ready. Several scouts went ahead of him, taking their directions from him.

Sergeant Saul Wilson came to Bentley's side. "What's going on with Captain Gates, sir?"

"He can't speak right now."

Wilson frowned and shook his head. "I've seen him like this before. He could speak then."

"Focus, Sergeant. He can't talk right now because he's holding his breath."

Wilson blinked and then stared at Ethan.

"How long can he hold his breath?"

"I have no idea," Bentley said, glancing up at some of the nearby tunnels. "Keep that explosive ordnance ready."

"Understood, Lieutenant," Wilson said.

Ethan slowed down, listening, and then spun toward a tunnel entrance. A muffled sound was coming from inside. He gestured with his rifle and lifted his chin toward the tunnel.

The soldiers understood and moved forward.

They entered the tunnels and had only gone a short distance when they entered an underground cavern. It looked as if this was some kind of convergence point for the tunnels. Ethan looked overhead. Water cascaded from above, splattering on various levels, making its way to the bottom.

They heard the sound of weapons fire, and Ethan charged forward. The CDF soldiers had to leap to catch up to him.

On a lower level, several hundred meters away, he spotted the other team surrounded by the nightmarish figures in black. The creatures were large, with black tentacles coming out of their backs. They moved lethally fast as they propelled themselves like a highly agile alien spider. They had four thick legs beneath powerful tentacles, some of which had a vicious-looking claw at the end. Powerful arms with clawed hands gripped the ice, and the creature roared with a gaping maw full of long, pointy teeth.

Only some of them fired their weapons, while the others brandished theirs. They must be low on ammunition.

Ethan protracted his helmet and inhaled a breath. "Give them covering fire," he said and ordered his soldiers toward strategic positions.

The CDF soldiers fired explosive rounds down to the area below, careful not to shoot too near the survivors. Explosive rounds were a slower-velocity round but packed a powerful yield. Legs and other body parts were blasted off the creatures, sending them in temporary disarray.

Ethan updated his ammunition configuration for high-heat yield and ordered several of the others to do the same. They pushed forward, taking full advantage of their surprise attack.

The soldiers used suit jets to jump down to the lower level where the attack was occurring.

As soon as Ethan landed, Bentley shoved him to the side. Ethan spun around. A creature had landed right where he'd been a moment before. Ethan fired his weapon, center mass, careful not to hit any of the other soldiers around them. The creature folded on its side and scampered away.

Another one landed just to his right. It slashed out at him with a clawed hand while lunging forward.

Ethan twisted to the side, barely avoiding the attack, and then slammed the stock of his rifle down on the arm. Then he swiped upward in a powerful arc, catching the creature in its jaw. The force of the blow spun even the large creature off-balance.

He brought his weapon up, about to squeeze the trigger, but the creature hesitated. Its large head cocked to the side as if it weren't sure what to make of him.

A tentative subsonic beat emanated from its chest and was taken up by the others. Soon, the sound of it was overwhelming, as if expanding beyond the area.

The creature lunged toward him as Ethan fired his rifle in full auto. The creature hit him and the force of it knocked him backward off his feet. Alarms came to prominence on his HUD as it flashed red.

Ethan rolled away, trying to put some distance between himself and the creature, and he felt something wet across his chest. Stinging, biting pain spread outward, but he had to ignore it as the creature stood, rearing up to its full height. It was head- and shoulders taller than him.

Ethan brought up his rifle, and the creature spun, its thick, long tentacles swiping around, catching him in the chest. He flew through the air from the force of the blow. He tried to engage his combat suit thrusters, but they wouldn't respond, and he spotted the critical failure message just as he crashed into the wall. Then he landed on the ground, hard.

He pushed himself to his feet and shook his head, trying to clear it. A loud roar sounded off to the side, and he jumped. He pulled out his combat knife, attaching it to the end of his rifle as he embraced his hybrid nature. This seemed to draw the attention of even more creatures as they came barreling toward him.

He spotted Cynergy over a hundred meters away. Her helmet was gone, and her blonde hair looked unkempt. Her skin darkened as she embraced her hybrid nature. She turned toward him as if drawn by some unseen force. They locked gazes for a few moments amid a battle that was becoming more chaotic by the minute. Something powerful pushed through his body, as if all his muscles had suddenly come to life, followed by a protective instinct that overruled reason.

Three creatures bounded toward him, cutting off his view of Cynergy. Ethan moved forward, darting quickly to the side and narrowly avoiding the creature's tentacles and a vicious claw that plunged into the ice and sand beneath them.

Ethan fired his weapon at the creature as he tried to get past it, but something grabbed his ankle and yanked him off his feet. He swung through the air and was slammed onto the ground. Ethan twisted to the side, thrusting up with his weapon. The creature lunged toward him, its wide mouth opening for the kill. Ethan fired his weapon at the creature's face, high-density darts breaking through its teeth. He surged to his feet and brought his weapon down on the creature's head. He must have struck some part of its brain because the tentacles all became rigid as the creature stiffened and then collapsed to the ground.

He spun around, looking for the other CDF soldiers. He could hear weapons fire from behind him, but there were more creatures dropping in from the ceiling. They looked like a bug infestation, but these creatures were monsters.

He heard Bentley call out to him and then bellow orders.

Ethan tried to locate Cynergy but couldn't find her. And although he tried to detect her again, he was too distracted. More of the alien creatures were closing in on him.

Then the creature he thought he'd killed stood up. The damage he'd inflicted to its skull was almost completely regenerated. A shocking recognition exploded in his mind, and various facts seemed to assert themselves.

The creatures they were fighting weren't just some kind of dangerous aliens. They were alien Vemus!

# CHAPTER 18

The *Challenger* was experiencing abnormal power issues, and it was at the point where Connor barely noticed the occasional flickering lights. Life support systems hadn't been affected, despite the ship's computer systems alerting them to critical system failures. Engineering teams had been deployed to assess those systems, and all were performing optimally with the exception that either sensors reported malfunctions or some the of computing cores were incorrectly reporting issues.

He watched as medical teams treated people with injuries.

Captain Carver stayed at his side, and it wasn't long before the rest of his protective services team came to his location.

"Elevators are experiencing power issues," Lieutenant Deacon said. "Real ones. A group of pilots are trapped in one of them."

Connor nodded. "I need to get to the bridge."

Carver nodded and checked his personal holoscreen. "Looks like the service elevators are still active, or we can always climb the emergency tubes."

Connor sighed. He'd rather avoid being trapped in an elevator. They started to head down the corridor away from Main Engineering, and Sergeant Cole grabbed his arm. He had his hand pressed to his ear, listening.

"Sorry, General," Cole said. "CIC is reporting loss of contact with the away teams on the planet."

Connor's gaze narrowed. He started to respond and then opened a comlink to the bridge. At least communications were still working.

"General Gates," Major Arvad replied.

"I just heard that we lost contact with the away teams on the planet."

"Not all of them. Just Captain Gates's teams. The others are on the far side of the planet. I've ordered the rescue team to depart immediately."

Connor frowned in thought for a moment. "Have they left yet?"

There was a few seconds' pause before Arvad replied. "Negative, pilots are en route to the hangar."

He shook his head and looked at Deacon. "Pilots trapped in the elevator?"

Lieutenant Deacon nodded.

Connor heard Arvad confirm the location of the rescue team.

"They're cut off," Arvad said, sounding frustrated.

Connor understood. "They're the backup pilots, aren't they?"

"From the CDF. The others are deployed. There are spacers qualified to pilot the shuttle, but they wouldn't be my first choice to send on a rescue mission."

"Agreed. Get our pilots out of the elevators and to the hangar bay. I'm making my way to you."

"Yes, General," Arvad said, and the comlink severed.

Connor took a few steps down the corridor, his protective detail walking with him, and he stopped.

"Sir, what's wrong?" Captain Carver asked, brows furrowed in concern.

Connor ground his teeth for a second, then brought up his personal holoscreen. "Everything. This whole thing feels wrong. Coordinated."

He brought up the data feeds to the ship's operations subsystem and filtered out all but the critical systems errors. He then brought up a high-level model or schematic of the ship. Damage reports were concentrated amidships that seemed to isolate the bridge and officers' crew centers.

"Is this some kind of attack, sir?" Carver asked.

Connor nodded. "Either that, or our computing system needs a major overhaul." He stared at the screen and frowned.

"Sir, we can get you to the bridge," Carver said.

Connor shook his head. "No, we're going to the main hangar. It's between us and the bridge."

Carver blinked and then nodded in understanding.

Connor had maintained his flight status ever since he'd authored the first qualifications for the CDF. They'd changed and been updated, but he could still fly a combat shuttle.

They quickened their pace to a run, with Sergeant Cole taking point, shouting for the way to be cleared. By the time they reached the hangar, the pilots were still trapped in the elevator, but teams were there working on the problem. Connor wasn't about to wait around.

He strode across the hangar deck, drawing more than a few surprised looks from the crew.

A combat shuttle was located across the hangar, and deck crews raced around it.

The deck lieutenant hastened over to him. "General Gates,"

she said, "I had no idea you were coming. Is there something I can help you with, sir?"

Connor looked at her, and her name appeared on his internal HUD. "Is that shuttle ready to fly, Lieutenant Bowden?"

Her eyes darted across the deck at the shuttle, and she nodded. "Yes, General. The shuttle is prepped and ready to depart. I was told that the rescue team has been delayed."

Connor nodded and quickened his pace. Lieutenant Bowden nearly ran to keep up with him, eyeing him questioningly.

"We're the rescue team, Lieutenant," Connor said.

Bowden's large brown eyes widened.

"Are the weapons systems on it ready?" Connor asked.

Her expression became serious. "Absolutely, General. The Panther VII Combat Shuttle has got teeth and then some, sir."

The edges of Connor's lips lifted. "Good job, Lieutenant Bowden. Now make sure your crew is clear because we'll be leaving as soon as I can get through pre-flight checks."

"Yes, General," she said and began shouting orders at the deck crew.

As they closed in on the shuttle, Carver leaned toward Connor.

"How long has it been since you've flown a shuttle, sir?"

Connor glanced at him. "Thinking of staying behind, Hank?"

Carver shook his head. "I'll never leave your side, sir. We just want to know if maybe one of us should pilot the shuttle."

They hastened up the loading ramp, and Connor walked straight toward the cockpit. Before heading inside, he turned toward his protective detail, who eyed him expectantly.

"I assure you I've had more time in the cockpit than any one of you," Connor said.

Carver, looking amused, bobbed his blond head once.

"Deacon and Cole, why don't you get into those combat suits. I have a feeling this is going to be danger close," Connor said.

Deacon and Cole went back to the armory.

Carver gestured to the side compartment. "EVA suits, sir?"

It was more of a suggestion than a question.

Connor nodded.

The EVA suits were modeled after the multipurpose protection suits (MPS), which had saved his life more than a handful of times. He sent his credentials to the EVA suit cradle, and his user preferences were downloaded to the suit. The golden material wavered as the suit went through its integrity checks. Then it split down the middle as the smart material pulled away, allowing him to put it on like a jumpsuit. The EVA suit adjusted to his six-foot-four-inch frame and soon fit like an extra layer of clothing. The suit could assist his movements and would give him some light combat protection if it came to it. A metallic rectangle lay across his shoulders, which was where the helmet was stored.

Carver did a quick check of his own suit, stomping his feet a little to check the fit. "Feels a little snug. I'm going to need to cut back on desserts for a while."

Connor chuckled. If Carver was gaining weight, it was because he exercised like a fiend.

"What did you expect with all those extra protein allotments at meals?" Connor said, stepping into the cockpit.

He sat in the pilot's seat and sent his authentication to the shuttle's computer systems. Pre-flight checks all indicated the shuttle was green across the board.

Connor opened a comlink to the bridge and requested permission to depart. After receiving clearance, he engaged the engines.

Once they were through the hangar bay doors, the operations officer passed his comlink to Major Arvad.

"General, we're sending you updated coordinates for the away team's last check-in," Arvad said and quickly brought Connor up to speed.

"Received the coordinates."

"Ordinarily, I'd recommend patching the shuttle's computer systems to the *Challenger*'s systems, but given what's been happening, I don't think it's a good idea," Arvad said.

"Agreed. What's the recommendation for fixing the problem?"

Arvad frowned. "Full computing core reset. That's the recommendation I'm getting from my department heads."

Connor cursed inwardly. Full computing core resets would take hours, leaving the ship even more vulnerable than it already was. "That's not going to work."

Arvad nodded. "Not without backup, but the nearest ship—the *Reliant*—is just over twenty hours away, best speed. That estimate doesn't account for their own away teams returning to the ship."

"Are the ship's weapons systems affected by the malfunctions?"

"We've checked them, and diagnostics don't indicate any issues."

"What about the nav system?"

"I wouldn't want to engage the I-Drive with our computing core having the issues it's been having, so we've got limited maneuvering capability."

Connor nodded and looked at the tactical plot on the shuttle's main holoscreen. He noted the *Challenger*'s location. "I want you to move the ship to support the rescue mission."

"We can do that. What kind of support do you have in mind?" Arvad asked.

"Precision strikes for marked targets only. No heavy weapons."

Arvad's eyebrows pinched forward. "We'll have your back, General Gates."

"I know you will. I'll be in contact when we reach the target," Connor said.

They flew toward the planet.

"Sir, I've been reviewing the last mission update from the away team," Carver said.

"What did you find?"

"Quite a lot, actually. Looks like Ethan found some kind of underground structure that appears to be an alien spaceship under construction. They've found bodies of what he's calling octo-aliens frozen in the walls. He's sent images of them."

Carver put the report on the holoscreen and peered at the aliens, taking in the sight of them.

Carver shook his head. "They look like soldiers."

Connor nodded in agreement.

"Oh, and there is another kind. These are...well, here, look for yourself."

Another image came to prominence on the holoscreen. It showed the octo-alien, and behind it, dark, frozen eyes looked like something emerging from the depths of a nightmare. It was black and savage. A clawed hand reached toward the octo-alien.

"That's a new one," Connor said.

He'd seen many creature variants over his military career—savage monsters grown in laboratories—and what he saw on the holoscreen was every bit as disturbing as the creatures from the Krake War and the Vemus.

"Ethan's last update was that they lost contact with the other team, and he was going to investigate what happened," Carver said. "And the data shows records of biological samples they'd gathered. Nothing to indicate they were in any danger, outside the obvious, that is," he said, lifting his chin toward the holoscreen.

Connor nodded. "They could be in some kind of hibernation. Does the data indicate anything to do with the Vemus?"

Carver shook his head. "Negative, sir."

Ethan wouldn't put that in the report unless he had conclusive evidence.

Connor studied the images of the aliens on the holoscreen. They could be related to the Vemus, but he might be grasping at something he wanted to be true because it was a convenient explanation.

"What First Contact Protocols should we follow, sir?" Carver asked.

"With the loss of contact from the away team, I'd say we shoot first and ask questions later," Connor replied.

Carver blinked in surprise.

"We assess and assume hostilities unless whoever they are prove otherwise," Connor said in a measured tone.

"Understood, sir."

He flew the shuttle toward the planet and soon they were through the atmosphere, following the course to Ethan's last known coordinates.

They flew over a dreary landscape that made the continent look like it had suffered some kind of major calamity.

"Does the report indicate what they thought happened here?" Connor asked.

"The samples collected indicate the land is covered with a soil and sand mixture that's sourced from the planet's oceans. Massive tidal forces," Carver said and looked at the video feed on the holoscreen. "This isn't the nicest planet we've explored on this mission. Ice and frozen sand cover the coastal areas for hundreds of kilometers, maybe more. I'll be happy once we retrieve the other team and head back to the ship."

The planet had a dreary look to it. Vast clouds covered the continent, and as Connor peered at the vista, it showed the appearance of a raw upheaval he'd never witnessed. He'd seen planets decimated after an attack or having suffered an extinction-level event by a super volcano, as well as planets frozen over by a terrible ice age. Life on those worlds had been either wiped out or struggling to survive on the wrong side of the apocalypse, with little hope. This planet had certainly been through something momentous, but he didn't let his mind dwell on the mysteries. He was here to rescue the missing teams.

Ethan could take care of himself. A lifetime in the military ensured that Ethan was an excellent soldier, but Connor also knew that sometimes, despite all the training and ability of the individual, when your number was up, it was up, and there was nothing anyone could do about it. He'd watched too many soldiers die, their deaths occurring so suddenly that the survivors were haunted by the loss for years. He knew because he'd suffered the same. He carried the lost with him every day, and he prayed that his son wouldn't be added to that list.

Connor pushed the shuttle's engines, increasing their velocity and coming up against the limits of atmospheric flight. They flew over the vast coastal areas, and the waypoint flashed on the main holoscreen.

"Receiving a distress beacon, sir," Carver said. "It's automated. It's a shuttle from the away team."

Automated distress beacons provided the location of the problem but lacked more details than that. The fact that a message wasn't attached to the distress beacon meant that the shuttle was down, possibly crashed, and the survivors hadn't been able to include more information.

The landscape became more elevated in the region where Ethan had last reported from. There were ravines and gaps between huge mounds of dark, frozen sand. They looked as if they covered buildings.

Connor saw multiple levels down between the gaps and what looked like tunnel entrances, perhaps the odd-shaped windows of an abandoned building. The gaps narrowed and opened in various places. He glanced ahead and saw black smoke billowing up in the distance.

"There's our target," Connor said.

Carver nodded and opened a comlink to the others. "Approaching the target."

Deacon acknowledged and advised that they were ready.

Carver watched the holoscreen for a few moments. "It looks recent. Scanning for comlink chatter."

He became silent, and Connor looked at him.

"They're fighting some kind of hostile alien force. Large predators," Carver said, his brow furrowed in concentration.

Connor nodded. "Send out a broadcast. Let's let them know help has arrived."

Connor flew the shuttle toward the billowing smoke and reached the crash site of a combat shuttle. Flames engulfed the interior, and there was a long skid from where the shuttle had crashed. A mix of CDF soldiers and civilian specialists had gathered away from the shuttle and were firing their weapons at a horde of large, vicious-looking creatures that galloped toward them.

Connor banked the shuttle hard to line up his approach and cross over the creatures. "Weapons free!"

Carver engaged the shuttle's mag cannons and peppered the

creatures from overhead. The output of ultra-high-density slugs broke the creatures apart, stopping them in a long gristly line.

Connor swung the shuttle around, making another pass.

A comlink registered with the shuttle's comms system.

"CDF shuttle, this is Lieutenant Kirk Bentley. We've got wounded here in need of immediate medical attention, and we're running low on ammunition."

"Copy that, Lieutenant Bentley. This is General Gates," Connor said, holding the shuttle steady while Carver used the mag cannons to hold the enemy at bay. "We'll create a window for you. Is there anyone unaccounted for?"

"Yes, General. Almost the entire crew of the *Mariner* has been taken by the creatures. We were effecting a rescue when we were overwhelmed and had to retreat. It was then we discovered that our shuttle had been attacked and brought down."

Carver glanced at him, eyes wide, the question evident on his face.

"They took down a combat shuttle?" Connor asked.

"We think they overwhelmed it somehow and surprised the pilot. The creatures are tough and can penetrate our armor."

Connor looked at Carver. "Get ready to put some heavy explosives right inside that tunnel."

"Copy that, sir."

"General Gates," Lieutenant Bentley said, "their falling back is a ruse. The enemy is smart, sir."

"Where is Captain Gates?"

Bentley sighed. "He's been restrained, sir."

Connor blinked a few times, not sure that he heard correctly. "Say again?"

"I'm sorry, General Gates. We've had to restrain some of the hybrids. We think the creatures are some kind of alien Vemus. We've all been exposed."

Connor felt the pit of his stomach drop, anchoring him in the seat. By rescuing them, they'd all be exposed, making him wonder if Lieutenant Bentley had delayed informing them because he feared they'd get left behind.

"Understood, Lieutenant. No one will get left behind," Connor said. He looked at Carver and gestured toward the tunnel. "Light them up."

Carver fired several high-yield explosives right into the tunnel. Bright flashes of light came from within as the explosives caused ice and dark, frozen sand to break free and collapse.

Connor flew the shuttle toward the survivors and then ordered Deacon and Cole to lower the ramp for an emergency evac. He watched the rear camera feed as the survivors ran up the loading ramp while some of the wounded were carried onboard.

"General," Carver said and lifted his chin toward the main holoscreen.

Fire and debris could be seen through the smoke inside the tunnel, but it didn't reach the top. Connor peered into the gloom, looking for movement, and then something caught his eye from above.

On the upper levels, he spotted the alien Vemus gathering. At first it was just a few of them, but then more came.

"How many of them are there?" Carver asked but then shook his head. "We've got to get out of here."

Connor glanced at the shuttle's rear camera feed. Survivors were still coming aboard. It wasn't that they were moving slowly; it was that there were so many of them. He'd lost count of how many wounded there were.

Connor brought up the shuttle's scanner interface. Then he contacted the ship.

"*Challenger*, actual," Major Arvad said.

"Rescue operations are underway. I'm painting a targeting

area no more than fifty meters wide. Are you receiving?" Connor asked.

"Confirmed targeting data. Aligning weapons," Arvad said. A few moments passed, and the number of alien Vemus looked to have become thousands with no sign of slowing down. "Target acquired, General."

"Fire!"

Two seconds of silence, and then a loud boom came from overhead. Heavy mag cannons fired a volley of medium payload with forty percent yield. One moment, the alien Vemus were gathered at the tunnel entrances of the open areas above, and the next, a hail of destruction caused an implosion and a deep fissure appeared in the area ahead of them.

Connor heard screaming from the back of the shuttle. He spotted Deacon and Cole at the end of the loading ramp, firing their weapons. There was shouting, and Connor thought he saw an alien Vemus blur past the camera. Both Deacon and Cole backed up the loading ramp.

"We're aboard, sir!" Deacon said over comlink.

Connor shoved the thruster controls, using the output of the shuttle's engines as weapons, burning anything that approached. More alien Vemus scrambled out from the newly formed crater, and hordes of them rushed toward the shuttle.

He flew the shuttle out of the gap with alien Vemus throwing themselves toward them in a vain attempt to capture the fleeing shuttle.

"Look at them," Carver said, awe in his voice. "Have you ever seen anything like this?"

Connor glanced at the shuttle's rear camera feeds. Even though they were kilometers in the air, he could still spot a darkened mass right in the area they'd been in.

"Sir?" Carver asked.

Connor tore his eyes away from the video feed. "Yeah," he replied. Memories from the two wars he'd fought pushed their way to the forefront of his mind. "I have. The Vemus we fought to protect New Earth. They attacked like a swarm, attempting to overwhelm us. And the other," he said and paused. "During the Krake Wars."

"Reminds me of the vids I've seen of ryklars," Carver said.

Connor glanced at his copilot for a moment. Carver was thirty years old and hadn't even been born when millions of ryklars were on the verge of attacking colonial cities in response to a latent purge protocol.

"Similar. The same reckless abandon in their attack. They don't have reason; they just follow instinct," Connor said.

Carver blew a breath through his teeth. "At least we were able to rescue the survivors."

Connor glanced at the cockpit door.

"I can take over if you want to go back there and check things out, sir," Carver offered.

He considered it for a few moments. Ethan was back there, restrained. He needed to see it for himself. "Passing flight control to you."

"I've got flight control," Carver replied.

Connor stood and left the cockpit. The back of the shuttle was crowded with survivors, and many of them were wounded. All of them looked shocked to even be alive. Sounds of a struggle came from the back of the shuttle. Several CDF soldiers in combat suits looked as if they were pouncing on something or someone.

A deep growling sound came from beyond them.

"I need to give them more to sedate them," a woman said.

"Do it, or they will tear through the shuttle," Deacon shouted, his voice sounding strained.

"But more could kill them," a man said.

Connor didn't recognize the voice. Sounds of an unearthly deep growl caused a shudder from the onlookers. Several flinched, and he pushed his way forward. On the ground were several hybrids fully embraced in their hybrid form, with skin almost black as night, exposed through combat suits that barely covered them. Connor locked gazes with piercing green eyes. He expected recognition, but all he saw was the animalistic intensity of something feral.

There were two more hybrids in the same state. All were held down by soldiers in heavy combat suits. It took Connor a few seconds to recognize that there were other hybrids, unaffected, who were also holding the afflicted down.

Ethan's muscled body became rigid, and Connor's eyes widened as his son began to push the heavily armored soldiers off him. He knew his son was strong, especially when he fully embraced his hybrid nature, but this display of strength astonished even him.

"Can't let him break free," Deacon cried.

A medic stood nearby, actuator in hand, but she didn't move.

"Sedate them," Connor said, his tone hard. "Now, Corporal."

The medic crawled between the struggling soldiers and pressed the actuator into Ethan's thigh. A sedation cocktail plunged through as Ethan continued to struggle against the others. The medic quickly did the same to the others, but it still took a few minutes for the medicine to work.

Corporal Brooks looked at Connor. "General Gates, I don't know what this will do to them. They're in a heightened state of agitation. I've never seen it before."

"No one has," said a man, a hybrid who had been holding Ethan down. He stood taller than Connor. "General Gates, I'm Wade Walsh. I'm one of the specialists with Cynergy's team."

Connor glanced around, looking for Cynergy. She'd have answers about this, but he couldn't find her. "Where is she?"

Walsh shook his head. "We don't know. We think she and most of the other team were taken by those…things."

Lieutenant Bentley stood and retracted his helmet. "General Gates, Ethan led a rescue mission to go after the other team. We caught up to them. They were engaging the…enemy. He tried to reach them, but that's when all hell broke loose. They came at us from everywhere."

"What happened to them?" Connor said, gesturing toward his son.

"They're the reason we're all still alive. They fought like I've never seen. Our weapons are effective, but they are just so damn agile and powerful. Something changed during the fighting. It's like Ethan and the others weren't themselves."

"What makes you think those creatures are some kind of Vemus?"

Bentley considered it for a second. "Because Ethan told me. He said he could sense it."

"He's right, General," Walsh said. "I could feel it, too. It's similar to the Vemus we encountered back home. Earth. But it's also different. Similar enough for us to recognize but not an exact match with the Vemus. Different species maybe."

Connor looked around at the survivors. Vemus transmission came from physical contact. Most of them were wounded. All of them had been exposed.

Connor looked at his son. His eyes were closed, but his breathing was rapid, almost labored. It matched the two others. They could be infected. They'd need to confirm that, and none of the medical equipment on the shuttle could do that.

He blew out a breath. "Okay, quarantine protocols. You've all been exposed," he said, and looked at Deacon and Cole. "That includes us. Observation protocols are to be followed. Report anything out of the ordinary. Like this." He gestured toward his son. He regarded the others and put steel in his tone. "I don't like it any more than you do, but it's what we have to do."

Lieutenant Bentley nodded. "Understood, General. We'll follow the protocol."

Connor moved away from them and gestured for Deacon and Cole to follow him.

"Sir, how can we be exposed? We're wearing our combat suits," Deacon said.

"You've got their blood on your suits. Once you come out of them, you'll be at risk like everyone else," Connor replied.

"Yeah, but we could just stay in our suits. Go through decontamination."

Connor nodded. "Yes, we all will. I need you to keep an eye on them back here. Alert me to anyone who looks like they're starting to turn into a Vemus. It's all we can do right now."

Deacon nodded. "Understood, sir."

Connor went back to the cockpit where Carver had them on a course for the ship.

He sat in the pilot's seat.

"I heard, sir," Carver said.

Connor nodded and then opened a comlink to the ship. It was routed to Major Arvad.

"Major, we've got a situation here. Contact with a Vemus contagion is highly likely. We need to follow alpha-quarantine protocols," Connor said.

Arvad's eyes widened.

Alpha-quarantine protocols required certain steps be taken to purge those who were infected or exposed to prevent the spread of the contagion to the rest of the ship. This was accomplished by fire and/or flushing out the hangar to the vacuum of space.

He was effectively handing Major Arvad a loaded weapon with orders to kill them if they started to become a Vemus.

Connor thought about Ethan, who could already be turning into a Vemus, and kept his features locked in stone.

"Understood, General," Arvad said and spoke to someone off-screen. The comlink was muted while he did it. Then he looked at Connor. "Hangar bay two is being prepped for your arrival. Portable life support equipment will be brought in and activated before you arrive."

"Thank you, Major."

Arvad's gaze softened. "I'm sorry, General."

Connor met his gaze. He didn't want to jump to conclusions, and they'd take every precaution necessary to avert the worst, but he knew he had to face the very real possibility that it might already be too late.

"I'm sorry, too," he replied.

## CHAPTER 19

The *Challenger*'s secondary hangar bay was sealed off from the rest of the ship, and quarantine measures were put in place to isolate the area. Armed CDF soldiers were stationed at the entrances to the hangar, which now functioned as a security checkpoint.

Connor stood on the hangar deck, surveying the room. In a relatively small amount of time, they'd cleared the hangar and set up the temporary spaces that were required for establishing a functional quarantine area. There were examination stations where assessments were made, along with waiting areas for those being kept for observation. Connor glanced at the temporary HAB unit where two CDF soldiers stood guard. Ethan and two others had been immediately taken into isolation there.

He, along with the others, was placed in a waiting area while the ship's doctors examined the people with the most severe injuries. Normally, Connor's rank would have moved him to the front of the line, but it wouldn't matter in this situation. He was still required to wait out the quarantine period to be sure that none of the survivors had contracted the alien Vemus contagion.

While he waited, he thought about the planet they'd just visited. He'd always expected that a Vemus-occupied world would be obvious to spot. Though it had been hundreds of years since Old Earth's Vemus Wars, there were telltale signs evident even today. A systematic collapse of a once thriving civilization left its evidence in the destruction of cities, and entire regions wouldn't be livable until they restored the ecosystem. Humanity had spread throughout the star system, but one only had to enter their space to witness the massive destruction of stations and colonies in order to grasp the devastation that had nearly annihilated them. But this planet didn't have those telltale signs at all. There was very little evidence of what Connor and many others would consider an advanced civilization built by a highly intelligent race. The entire planet had suffered some kind of calamity that had more than a few scientists at a loss for theories to explain what had happened. The theories that had been put forth —one of them by Ethan—were based on what they were able to observe. Connor never would've thought it was possible for entire oceans to move under the planetary crust, raising continents, but that's what Lieutenant Bentley had told him.

He shook his head, trying to imagine what destruction on this scale would look like. There were cities covered by ice and frozen sand. Were the inhabitants of this planet aquatic in nature, so they spent their entire lives underwater? Had they built their cities under the water, or were they a combination of surface and underwater dwellings? When the Vemus probe became active on Earth, it had originated from deep in Earth's oceans and spread among mammalian life there before moving to land-dwelling species.

Connor's musings were interrupted by a nurse calling his

name, and he was taken to an examination area. He'd already been through a decontamination station, and his EVA suit had been left there for further processing. Nothing had been detected during that process, so it was doubtful that he carried an alien contagion.

After waiting in the area for about a minute, the doctor walked in. She was tall and slender, and her long blond hair was tied back. She regarded him with pale blue eyes for a moment. She had the calming presence to her that he'd learned to recognize in the doctors he'd known, his daughter among them.

"Hello, General Gates, I'm Doctor Williams. You can call me Cassie if you prefer," she said and extended her hand toward him.

He shook it. "What's the prognosis?"

"Not as dire as we'd feared. Your biochip doesn't show any indicators of being infected with the Vemus contagion, and your nanites are routinely following a protocol to alert and report significant variances in your physiology," she said.

Connor arched an eyebrow, reading between the lines. "But this could be different."

She grimaced a little, her eyebrows squeezing together. "Yes. It's been reported that this could be an alien variant of the Vemus. We're analyzing the samples that were collected, and we'll update our protocols based on those findings, if it's applicable."

He frowned. "Why wouldn't it be applicable?"

"We're different. We're humans. The species that resides on that planet is not the same as us, to put it simply. The Vemus contagion we're familiar with adapted to Old Earth's environment and basically armed itself to spread across the planet. We don't have unaltered samples of the Vemus as it first arrived there. The probe was lost, and the likelihood of us finding a probe on this planet isn't very high. However, we might not be as vulnerable as one might believe."

Connor gave her a dubious look.

"I'm an optimist, General Gates. Traditionally, adaptation takes time."

"I'm a realist," Connor replied.

"Yes, I know. Let me assure you that we're being cautious, but I won't spread fear when there isn't a reason to be afraid. Everything I've said to you is fact."

"Then how do you explain what happened to the hybrids?"

"I can't explain it, yet. The hybrids are a smaller subset of our species."

Connor leveled his gaze at her. "You're going to have to do better than that, Doctor."

She took a few moments to consider her reply. "So far, we haven't found evidence that the hybrids have been infected with the contagion either." She held up her hand, forestalling his question. "You asked. Please allow me to answer. Hybrids are resistant to Vemus contagion, at least the contagion found on Old Earth. However, their exposure to the alien Vemus has had an effect on them, and we're not exactly sure what's happening. This could be their own adaptive capabilities going into overdrive because of their contact with the alien Vemus, but that doesn't necessarily mean they're infected. In fact, the blood samples drawn from your son and the others showing the same affliction don't indicate any foreign contagion markers."

Connor looked away from her, processing what she'd told him. "Ethan isn't infected, but he came into physical contact with them."

"It doesn't look that way," she replied, and shook her head. "No, at this moment, Ethan is not infected."

"Then what's happening to him? He's not himself. He's…"

Connor paused for a moment and heaved a sigh. "It's like he's feral. Not in control of himself."

Dr. Williams gave him a sympathetic smile. "We don't know what's happening to him. I've spoken to the other hybrids, and even they aren't sure."

That wasn't reassuring at all. Hybrids in general were the foremost experts on being a hybrid.

"Can I see him?" Connor asked.

"I have to caution you about that."

Connor exhaled through his teeth. "I'm not afraid, Doctor Williams."

Her gaze conveyed understanding and sympathy. "This is your son. If it didn't affect you to see him like this, I'd say you're more machine than man."

Connor snorted, but she wasn't wrong. "You'd be surprised. Is there a medical reason I can't see my son and the other hybrids in isolation?"

She regarded him for a long moment. "You can observe them, but we're limiting actual physical interaction for a time."

"If they're not infected, then why can't I be in the room with them?"

Her eyebrows peaked, and she wet her lips. "What if we're wrong?"

He couldn't argue with that simple logic. It was effective. He'd used simple logic himself countless times, so he understood it all too well. "I understand. Is there anything else I need to know?"

"I wish I had more to tell you, General Gates. The good news is that for the moment, aside from some of the more serious injuries, I'm hopeful that the survivors will make a full recovery. I just wish there were more survivors for me to treat."

There it was. That was the quality he would always respect.

Doctor Williams cared. There was a note in her voice that said she longed to do more, and he realized she might know some of the people who were missing. He almost asked her, but didn't.

"Just to confirm," Connor said, "we still have at least another seventy hours of quarantine. Is that right?"

She nodded. "That's correct. Unless we discover a reason for it to be extended."

It was doubtful that it would be shortened, so no need to bring that up. "Okay, one more question before I go. Who is monitoring Ethan and the other hybrids?"

"That would be..." she said, glancing at her personal holoscreen, "Charlie Harris. He's the closest thing we have to an expert with hybrids." She frowned. "That is, among those who aren't hybrid."

"Thanks, Doc," Connor said and left the examination area.

Once outside, he found Lieutenant Bentley waiting for him. He wore a dark blue ship suit and stood at attention, giving Connor a salute. There was a weariness around his eyes that came from post-mission downtime and a whole lot of worry.

"General, I'd like permission to go with you to isolation," Bentley said.

"Are the walls that thin around here?"

He smiled a little. "What walls, sir? I just figured you'd be heading there after the doctor cleared you."

Connor nodded. "All right. Walk with me, Lieutenant."

They began to cross the hangar.

"Any idea how the attack began? What set them off?" Connor asked.

"Sir, I've been thinking about that since before the shuttle got here, trying to put the timelines between the two teams together. There are only a handful of survivors from the spacer team," he said and grimaced. "I'm sorry, sir. That's how we refer to the civilian survey and salvage team."

Connor nodded. "It's fine. Go on."

Bentley looked away for a few moments before continuing. "The survivors from the other team are critically injured, with one exception. Wade Walsh. He helped me subdue Ethan and the others."

"How did he escape what happened?"

"He said he was flung away. Their tentacles are strong, and it knocked him away right toward us."

"Lucky for him."

Bentley nodded. "Yes, sir. The timeline for them is spotty. They were attempting to recover the probe, and one of the recon drones found something—I don't know what—and the data from the drone is gone. It wasn't uploaded to the shuttle."

Connor frowned. "Walsh doesn't know?"

Bentley dropped his chin toward his chest in frustration. "I can't remember. We just knew they were missing and not responding to comms."

"Okay, we'll get back to Walsh in a minute or ask him when we're finished in isolation."

Bentley swallowed hard, his eyes becoming distant for a second while he tried to recall what had happened. "We found that ship. At least we thought it was part of a massive ship. It still looked under construction, but there was no building equipment or anything like that. Ethan said it reminded him of the Vemus exoskeletal material, but it was different. It was some kind of metallic alloy. We only saw part of the ship. The rest of it went beyond where we explored. That's when we saw one of the alien Vemus trapped in the ice with the octo-aliens. Then we started to hear strange noises. I've got recordings of it from my suit cams."

"I'll review those later," Connor said and gave him a nod to keep going.

"As we were leaving, the alien Vemus broke through the ice, and we fired our weapons at it. Then we got out of there. Too many strange things were going on without enough information. Ethan ordered us back to the probe. That's when we found out the other team was missing, and we set off to find them with Chavez flying the shuttle," Bentley said and paused. His expression became pained.

Chavez hadn't survived the shuttle crash. Connor waited for Bentley to compose himself, choosing not to rush him. He understood the weight that the loss of a friend could bear on someone. He knew it too well.

"Sorry, sir. He was a good man."

"You don't have anything to be sorry about."

Bentley relaxed a little and sighed. "Chavez scouted the area ahead and found an ambush site that only had one survivor. We examined the bodies. Field Biologist Luanne Atwater was critically injured. Ethan tried to get her to answer his questions about what happened to the rest of the team, but the pain was too much, and she lost consciousness. So, we tracked the other team. Uh, wait. Ethan removed his helmet, using his hybrid capabilities to track the other team."

Connor frowned in thought for a moment. Ethan exposing himself to an alien atmosphere they couldn't even breathe was reckless. That was his first thought, but then he understood why his son had risked it. Would he do any less if Lenora was missing? Not a chance.

"Understood," Connor said.

Bentley stared at him for a moment. "I've seen him do it before. I've seen him hold his breath for over an hour like that. Both him and Cynergy. I think Hash could do it too. It was good that he did because those tunnels were like a maze. We wouldn't have found the other team if it weren't for him."

"Did he show any signs of something being wrong?"

Bentley shook his head. "Negative, sir. He was fine. He was fine until the fighting started. He went back to normal so he could resume command, but at some point during the fighting he changed again, back to hybrid. I've never seen anything like it. We've done combat drills with the hybrids, and they can do some amazing things, but the way they fought the alien Vemus… It was beyond the capabilities of the standard combat suit, or darn close to it."

Connor's gaze narrowed thoughtfully. "Were you concerned about him? That something was wrong with him and he wasn't himself?"

Bentley thought about it for a moment. "It all happened too fast. So many of the alien Vemus showed up. They just kept coming. Ethan was the one who said they were like the Vemus. He said he could sense it. Some of the other hybrids confirmed it. Then we lost the other team."

"What do you mean, lost?"

"They were just gone, sir. One moment, they were fighting across the cavern and we were trying to push toward them. Then they were gone."

"Were they killed?"

Bentley shook his head. "Not that I could tell, sir. I didn't see any bodies. I think the alien Vemus might've taken them somewhere," he said and shook his head. "I don't know, sir. It's all chaotic in my head. They're probably dead. I don't mean to sound so pessimistic, but they were trying to kill us. And they seemed drawn to Ethan and the hybrids."

They reached the isolation area, and the two soldiers eyed them.

"General Gates, we're not supposed to let anyone into the isolation area," one of the soldiers said.

"Tell Doctor Harris that I'm here to see him," Connor said.

One of the soldiers headed inside while Connor and Bentley waited. The remaining soldier waited patiently, then cocked his head to the side for a second before nodding a little and telling them they were clear to go inside.

Connor walked in first, passing the other soldier on guard duty.

A short man followed the soldier. He looked about twenty pounds overweight and had brown hair that was unkempt. His narrow eyes locked onto Connor, and he looked a little uncomfortable.

"General Gates, hello. I'm Charlie Harris. I just got the message that you were coming," he said and shook his head. "Sorry, no, that's not right. Cassie sent the message ten minutes ago. I just got the secondary alert that I hadn't read yet. We've been extremely busy, as you probably already know."

Charlie Harris spoke quickly, and Connor couldn't decide whether he'd had too much coffee, or he had an excitable personality.

"Doctor Harris," Connor said by way of greeting and acknowledgement.

His eyes crinkled a little around the edges, and he gestured behind him. "I'm sure you want to see…" he paused. "I'm sorry, but in what capacity are you here today? It'll help me understand how to frame my statements. Are you here as General Gates or as Connor Gates, father?"

Connor regarded him calmly. "Both."

Harris blinked a few times in a quick, rapid flutter while his brain processed the information. "Okay then," he said and started walking. "They're located just up ahead."

Harris led them down a narrow corridor toward the rear area and brought them in front of a window. The smart glass was opaque to the point that they couldn't see inside.

Harris turned toward them and regarded Connor for a moment. "I'm just going to show you," he said, keying in something on the control interface.

The smart glass became translucent, revealing a large room where three patient beds stood with their backs elevated. Ethan and the two other hybrids were strapped to each bed. The male and female on either side of Ethan displayed skin so dark that it verged on black, and their eyes were closed. Their muscles twitched, as if responding to some kind of unseen stimuli.

Bentley leaned toward the glass, peering inside. "Are they breathing in unison?"

Harris nodded. "Yes, it's amazing, isn't it? Some of their physiological responses seem to have linked up. Hybrids can do this. It's what helps them coordinate so well."

Connor stared at his son as Ethan sucked in a breath. It was sudden, and Connor expected him to wake at any moment. It was unsettling to watch it mirrored by the two people on either side of him. Ethan then exhaled forcefully, and his body seemed to relax for half a second. Then he moaned as if he was caught in a dream, and his arms tensed against the restraints that were keeping him in the bed.

Connor glanced at the restraints. They were made of heavy-duty smart-mesh that stress would strengthen.

Connor looked at Harris. "They're not asleep, are they?"

Harris shook his head. "Their brain patterns indicate a trancelike state."

"Why are you keeping them together?"

"Because when we tried to separate them, they became violent, and the level of sedation they'd already been given was not safe. If I'm to have any chance of figuring out what's wrong with them, I need to see what happens as they wake up. The restraints are a precautionary measure to protect them and us."

Connor remembered seeing three soldiers in combat suits holding Ethan down, and even then it looked as if they were barely able to do so.

"Have you tried to speak to them?" Connor asked.

"I have, but they won't respond to me. I was hoping you would try." Harris bit his lip, arching an eyebrow.

Connor nodded. "Okay, but not from out here. I need to go in there."

Harris's mouth opened a little. "I don't think that's a good idea."

Connor sighed. "Look, Doctor Williams said there's a good chance they're not infected with the Vemus contagion, so if *they're* not infected, *I* can't be infected."

"With respect, General Gates, only time will tell about that."

"Fine, then I'll accept the risk. If you want me to try to speak to him, I'm going in that room," Connor said.

Harris bobbed his head once. "Have it your way, General Gates. I'm only going to say that it goes against my recommendation."

"Noted," Connor replied.

Harris led him to the door and entered his credentials. Connor walked through and the door shut behind him.

The room was cooler than the hangar. He could hear atmospheric scrubbers cycling through the air. There was a sterile smell, as if it was completely sanitized.

Connor walked over to Ethan's bed and stopped two meters away from it for a moment. Then he stepped closer.

"Ethan," Connor said. "Can you hear me, son?"

Ethan didn't respond. Not even a twitch.

"Ethan," Connor said, forcefully. Then he added, "Captain Gates, report!"

Ethan's face twitched. It was slight, but it wasn't mirrored by the others.

Connor took a step, closing the distance. "Ethan, it's me. It's your father. I'm here."

Ethan's breathing rate increased, but the others remained the same. He turned toward Connor and slowly opened his eyes. They were a brilliant green. He seemed to be looking at Connor and past him at the same time. Then Ethan opened his mouth, exposing his teeth in a snarl. A hissy growl came from deep in his throat, and he lunged away from Connor.

The restraints held Ethan in place.

Connor grabbed Ethan's shoulders. "Ethan, listen to me. Listen to my voice. You're on the ship. You're safe." He repeated the last several times, hoping it would penetrate Ethan's mind. "You have to hear me, son."

Ethan squeezed his eyes shut and then shook his head from side to side as if he were in anguish. Then his whole body bucked in a violent burst, and the bed skidded forward. The others did the same.

Connor jerked backward in shock.

"Get out of there!" Harris said.

Connor backed away, but wouldn't take his eyes off his son, not sure if Ethan was in there.

The three hybrids gasped for breath as they exerted themselves. Connor glanced at the holoscreens above each of their beds. Vital signs spiked for all three of them, and then they just dropped—not to normal but out of the red zone.

He heard the door open, and Connor backed through it. As it shut, he released the breath he'd been holding.

Harris came over to him and smiled. "Thank you, General Gates."

Connor blinked, confused. "For what?"

"He responded to you. It might not have looked that way, but he did. Ethan is still in there. He broke the connection to the others somehow and responded to you."

Connor looked away from Harris and at his son. All three hybrids bucked against their restraints again, but it lacked the intensity that it had before, as if it was just an echo.

"It didn't look that way to me," Connor said, and glanced down at Harris.

"He's still in there. We just need to figure out a way to get him to stop what he's doing."

"How do you know he's doing anything?"

"He's the leader, the alpha in there. The others are following his lead. He responded to you, his father, which means there is still hope that he can be saved."

Connor let out a long sigh and watched his son. He'd never felt farther away from him or more useless than right at that moment.

# CHAPTER 20

"General Gates, are you okay?" Dr. Harris asked, staring at Connor intently.

Connor looked away from the isolation room and nodded. "I'm fine. We need to focus on next steps." He raised his chin toward the window. "What do you need to help them?"

"Time," he said, shrugging one shoulder a little. "I've learned that in treating hybrids, a gentler approach is best."

Connor frowned in thought for a moment. "You said you've tried separating them and they reacted violently. What if there is some kind of field limit or limit of influence? You said Ethan is the alpha and the others…" he said, not knowing their names. He looked at them and their names appeared in his HUD. "Roy Emerson and Sheila Tran. What if you removed one of them? Transported them to the other side of the hangar? If that's not far enough, I can have the shuttle refueled and we can fly one of them out of here."

He was grasping for a solution in a subject he wasn't an

expert in, but he hated seeing Ethan like this. When Cynergy had turned Ethan into a Vemus hybrid, he'd been concerned that Ethan would become a Vemus, that somehow it would happen. He'd been wrong about that. Thoughts of Cynergy caused a pang in his chest. He liked her, and she was good for Ethan. They complemented each other. He hoped she wasn't dead, and that Ethan wouldn't have to deal with that kind of loss.

"I'm considering it, but I want to consult our records and the other hybrids here. Right now, I know it causes them pain."

"Yeah, but will it kill them, or will it hurt until they each assert control over themselves?" he asked and paused for a moment. "What if keeping them in proximity like this is making things worse?"

Harris regarded him calmly. "Those are all good questions, General Gates. I'm going to do everything I can to help them. Please believe me. I need you to give me some time to figure out the best way to do that."

It was a dismissal, and Connor didn't want to go. He clenched his jaw for a moment, giving in to his frustration, but then let it go. This was not the time for bullheadedness. Let the experts do their job.

Connor heaved a sigh and nodded. "I'm going to get some air. Then I'll come back."

Harris nodded in approval. "That's a good idea. I will alert you the moment I have something concrete to share."

Connor left the isolation unit and Bentley followed him.

"General, if you don't mind I'd like to stay by your side, unless you have orders for me?" Bentley asked.

Connor considered it for a few moments. "I do have something I need you to do. I want you to check on the surviving hybrids. They're the key here. I also want to speak with Wade Walsh."

Bentley looked across the hangar for a moment. "They're probably going through quarantine checks. I'll gather them."

"Good. I'll follow up with you in an hour," Connor said.

Bentley saluted him and left.

Several tables had been set up, and Connor went to one that was away from the others. He brought up the holoscreen and set his privacy to maximum, then initiated a comlink to Major Arvad.

The video comlink established with Arvad in his ready-room near the bridge.

"What's the status of the ship?" Connor asked.

"I've had damage assessment teams going through the ship, checking the impacted systems. In every case so far, the issues are with sensor malfunction."

Connor frowned, instincts pushing him to a conclusion. "That's a bit convenient."

Arvad nodded. "That's what I thought as well. A couple of sensors in unrelated systems could malfunction and be replaced, but this seems intentional."

Connor glanced around. No one could hear their conversation, but he wanted to check anyway. "Sabotage?"

Arvad grimaced. "General, I vouch for everyone on this ship. This impacted multiple systems, and to consider that this is the work of a group of saboteurs is unthinkable. What would be their motivation? This is the last mission before we head home."

Connor nodded. "I agree with your logic, but I still suspect foul play. Probably not by anyone on the ship but have your security detail review access logs for the impacted systems and make sure there isn't anything out of place." He paused for a moment, considering. "There is a timeline of events that we need to put together. I suspect they escalate as time goes on, but we need to prove it. Assuming there *is* an escalation and this isn't a cascade of failures building on itself, it means that whoever was causing these sensor failures was basing their actions on ours."

Arvad frowned, dark eyebrows squished together, eyes intent. "Reacting to us? But that means they'd have to be here among us or had somehow infiltrated our systems without being detected."

Connor nodded. "We need to look beyond the ship. In the absence of evidence, we need to consider the possibility that there is another ship out there that we can't detect. I can think of only one group we know of that has those kinds of capabilities."

Arvad blinked, then looked away for a moment. "The Phantoms."

He tipped his head to the side. "You got it. The alternative is another advanced alien race that we haven't encountered yet. I still tilt toward the Phantoms because they're familiar with our technology. They deciphered the probes and sent them to Earth, targeting precise locations in the star system. It wasn't random. If they can do that, then why couldn't they cause our internal sensors to fail so they could manipulate events?"

"Why would they do that? Assuming it *is* them, what's their motivation for doing it in the first place?"

"I wish I knew. If they wanted to interact with us, why not initiate contact in a more diplomatic way?"

Arvad arched an eyebrow. "I've only read about first contact. These events don't fit in with what's recorded in the archives."

Connor chuckled. "I was there, and the two times it happened occurred completely differently. But those were different circumstances. Let's see if we can find out what we're actually dealing with," Connor said.

For the next hour, they brought in the team leads from CIC and put together a timeline of events. Doing this kind of forensic reconstruction was something Connor had always excelled at, and those skills had helped him survive more times than he cared to admit. It also helped him anticipate weaknesses in their defensive posture. Beyond the obvious escalation, it wasn't clear what the goal was for the cascade of failures on the ship's monitoring sensors of both critical and non-critical systems.

Arvad looked at Connor with a thoughtful expression, as if he had an idea to share. "If I was going to make a wager, I'd say that someone was keeping our pilots from reaching the hangar. Meaning that our ability to launch a rescue mission for the away team was impacted. They were trapped."

"Why weren't they already in the hangar? They should've maintained a readiness status for the duration of the mission on the planet," Connor said.

Arvad looked away from the camera for a moment. "You're right. This was during a duty shift change, but the relief team was on their way and running late. Could be a coincidence. It just depends on how suspicious of seemingly innocuous events we want to be."

"I want to know why those pilots were late. I don't care how minute the reason is. Did they lose track of time? Did they ignore the automated alerts that should've informed them they were running late? Or was it a series of unfortunate events that stacked up to delay them?" Connor replied.

"We'll find out," Arvad said and paused for a moment, considering. "This is a leap, but in keeping with the Phantom theory, have you considered that they wanted to see what our response would be? Perhaps they were measuring our performance, seeing how we overcame the interference."

Connor leaned back and rubbed his chin for a second. "It's not a bad theory, but I don't like the thought that someone could monitor us like that. I was able to make it to the hangar and take the shuttle, so it seems there was a line of impact that delayed them between the crew quarters and the hangar. But I was in Main Engineering when this happened."

Arvad nodded. "After you left on the shuttle, the escalations seemed to slow down. We still had the damaged sensors, but no new systems were impacted. So maybe they were interested in you, sir."

Connor leaned forward, bridging his hands in front of his chin. The Phantoms could've been monitoring them for longer than they'd been in this star system. That would give them time enough to observe the command structure. He let those thoughts go because it felt like he was spinning around, making way too many assumptions. "I don't know if we can prove or disprove that, so it's an unsolved variable. All we know is that despite the obstacles, we were still able to launch a rescue mission. Then things calmed down. That's the long and short of it."

Some of the enemies he'd faced had taken particular interest in him. Sometimes it was because of his proximity to critical events. Were the Phantoms really interested in him? Of all people, why would they focus on him? There was no way for him to answer that question, and until he actually met one of these Phantoms, he would never know.

"Another idea put forth by Captain Kershaw," Arvad said, "is that the sensors failed because of a manufacturing defect. They're fabricated in batches. He's checking into whether the failures occurred for a particular group of sensors based on their manufacturing specs."

Connor smiled with half his mouth. "Good idea. Honestly, I prefer that explanation to considering an adversary that we can't see or detect who has unfettered access to our systems." A notification appeared on his holoscreen, and he dismissed it. He looked at Arvad. "Stay on it. I'm going to meet with the surviving hybrids and try to get some answers."

"Yes, General," Arvad said.

Connor closed his holoscreen and ended the privacy mode that blocked out the sounds coming from the hangar. As he stood, he spotted Lieutenant Bentley waiting nearby with a group of people.

He walked over to them, and the CDF soldiers saluted him while the civilians waited.

"General Gates, these are the people you wanted to speak with," Bentley said, and gestured toward the man next to him. "And this is Wade Walsh, salvage expert."

Wade Walsh was as tall as Connor, but with narrower shoulders. Most spacers were taller, due to the fact that they'd spent most of their lives in lower gravity than the standard 1 G maintained by artificial gravity fields.

"Wade Walsh, good. I'm hoping we can go over what happened down there," Connor said.

"Of course, General Gates," Wade said and proceeded to go over the events that had transpired on the planet.

It was obvious that Wade was accustomed to reporting events to the CDF because he kept his recounting of them straight and to the point. There was no embellishment, which Connor appreciated. He'd likely learned this by serving with Ethan for the past year.

"Cynergy left a team to try to retrieve the probe's data core, and we set out to look at what the recon drone found," Walsh said. "We thought it was part of the massive structure that the CDF team was investigating. It was an entrance of sorts, like a door. There was some kind of ambient lighting, so we thought there was something powering it."

Connor frowned and glanced at Bentley. "First I've heard of that," he said and looked at Walsh. "Are you sure it wasn't a form of bioluminescence?"

Walsh looked away. "Maybe. We never got a chance to find out." He looked away, wincing. Then shook his head a little. "Sorry, it's just a headache. It's been happening since we got back."

"Did you tell the doctors about it?" Bentley asked.

Walsh nodded. "Yeah, just a little dehydrated. I've drunk that cocktail they make us do after missions. It comes in waves." He shifted in his seat, rolling his shoulders and looking as if he was trying to relieve some tension.

Connor saw some of the other people doing the same, as if they were all uncomfortable at the same time.

"Damn headaches. Should've gone away by now," Walsh said and closed his eyes. He began rubbing the sides of his head.

Bentley was about to speak and then stopped.

Connor looked around at the others. They'd changed. Their skin darkened as they embraced their hybrid nature. The change was sudden, and it usually brought a sense of exhilaration to them, but not this time. They looked agitated and a little disoriented.

Connor spun toward the isolation center, remembering how Ethan and the other hybrids there were linked, then looked back at the group. "Walsh, stand up. All of you get up. You need to get away from here."

Connor pulled Walsh to his feet. The others tried to stand, looking unsteady on their feet. Bentley shouted for help, and several soldiers joined them.

"Take them back across the hangar. Have the doctors check them," Connor said.

He ran toward the isolation center and heard screaming from inside. The two soldiers posted outside followed him in.

Connor raced through the corridor and saw that it was Ethan

and the other hybrids who were screaming. Harris was inside, sprawled on the floor, looking dazed.

Connor ran toward the door and gestured for the soldier to open it, then hastened inside and went straight to Harris. Ethan screamed, and it sounded animalistic. He jerked against his restraints so hard that the bed would've toppled over if it hadn't been secured to the floor.

Connor turned toward Harris. "What happened?"

Harris blinked. "I gave them the revival cocktail to slowly bring them out of sedation. I gave it first to Sheila Tran, and she calmed down, her vital signs taking on their own rhythm. Then I did the same to Roy Emerson. But when I did the same for Ethan, this happened. He knocked me across the room."

Connor's eyes widened. If it hadn't been for the restraints, Harris could've died from the force of the blow. Ethan was the source. Somehow, he was affecting the others.

"You need to sedate him. He's affecting the other hybrids. Not just them, but others outside. Sedate him!"

Connor helped Harris to his feet, and Harris brought up his personal holoscreen. As the drugs flooded Ethan's system, his body sank to the bed, going limp. His head hung down and to the side. Connor went over, retrieving the pillow from the floor, and slipped it behind Ethan's head. His skin felt hot, as if he had a fever.

"He's burning up," Connor said.

Harris was checking Sheila. She'd relaxed into a barely conscious stupor. Harris looked at Connor. "Body temperature is within normal range for hybrids. They can control their body temperature to extremes, depending on the environment."

He moved away from Sheila and checked on Roy. Then he turned toward Connor. "Ethan is in an extreme state of heightened hybridization. According to the accounts we have, if he remains in this state, his physiological identity could shift, and this will become the new normal for him. They do this in extreme circumstances, mainly for survival…"

Connor stared at him. "But what?"

Harris looked around uncertainly for a moment, and then his shoulders slumped as he met Connor's gaze. "I don't think I can help him. The records for hybrids are spotty at best. There are accounts, but it's not like they took detailed reports and recorded vital signs. They were just trying to survive. We don't even understand how they can sync together. Sometimes it's a physiological response when they're in proximity to one another. Other times it's based on sub-vocalizations. Uh, sounds they make. Unique rhythms."

"There has to be something you can do for him. Don't tell me you're giving up, Doctor!"

Connor saw the hopelessness in Harris's gaze. He had the look of a man who had exhausted his options and hit a wall.

"I'm sorry, General Gates. Ethan has become a danger to himself and others. I need to put him in an isolation capsule."

Connor clenched his teeth. "No."

Harris met his gaze. "Look at them. They're dying. I don't know how much longer they can keep this up. The only link I've got to their wellbeing is that Ethan has somehow caught them up in whatever is happening to him."

Connor stepped toward him, exhaling through his teeth.

Harris backed up a few steps. "General Gates, please!"

Connor stopped. He needed to be strong. He turned toward Ethan. "You want to keep him sedated and put him in a barometric chamber to cut him off from the others?"

Harris nodded. "It's the only way to destabilize the hold he has on them. I'll re-sedate the others and put Ethan in the capsule, then slowly bring the others out of it. I'm hoping this will help break his hold over them."

"What about Ethan?"

Harris's hands came to rest at his sides. "I don't know. I want to have a better answer for you, but I don't. I just…don't."

Connor inhaled a deep breath. They couldn't help Ethan. He couldn't help Ethan, and the only person he suspected could was missing or dead.

# CHAPTER 21

Connor sat alone in the cockpit of the shuttle. Remnants of a meal he hadn't really tasted were on a tray on the copilot's seat. He needed the calories.

The secondary hangar wasn't the largest space to begin with, and all the quarantine equipment and temporary living space didn't leave much room. He'd gone into the shuttle so he could speak privately with his wife.

Lenora looked at him through the video comlink. She was four light-years away aboard the *Reliant*. "So, Ethan broke the isolation capsule?"

Connor nodded. "Yeah. Harris thinks he's becoming immune to sedation."

Lenora's eyebrows drew up in concern. "That's not good."

He slowly shook his head. "Vemus can't be sedated either. There's only one way to stop them."

"Connor," Lenora said, tenderly, "Ethan is not a Vemus."

He raised his gaze to hers. "Our son is locked in a cage

within a cage. Since the capsule failed, they put him in a box. I had no choice but to let them. I tried to speak to him, but he wouldn't even look at me."

"I know. I saw the recording of it."

"I don't know how to help him. I mean, I feel like there's something of him that's still in there, but I don't know how to reach him."

"What about the other hybrids?"

"Distance helps, but they're affected too—increased agitation, violent outbursts… Reminds me of a cornered animal. I don't understand how Ethan could still be doing this. Physically, he's cut off from everyone. He's in a mobile airlock, essentially."

"Even after all this time, we're still learning more about the hybrids," she said and looked away for a moment. "What about Cynergy and the others?"

Connor shook his head. "We've got recon drones searching the area. The two other survey teams have completed their missions on the other side of the planet. No Vemus activity and no civilization remnants, aquatic or otherwise. We have them on standby."

"That's something, at least. Are you going to order them to search for the missing team?"

"Not if the recon drones can't find anything. I really hate to say it, but there is no indication that anyone from the missing team is alive."

Lenora pressed her lips together as she pushed a strand of auburn hair behind her ear.

"I've reviewed the combat suit cams with the help of the ship's computer, isolating the hybrids. They fight the alien Vemus, but at the same time there seems to be confusion on both sides. Look at these incidences of it," Connor said and shared what he'd found.

Short clips from both combat suit and EVA suit cameras came to prominence. They watched in silence and then Lenora made a swiping motion, clearing the video clips.

"I see what you mean. I just don't know what to make of it. What if Cynergy is still alive?"

"It's a long shot at best, but okay, let's assume that she is," Connor said.

"She and Ethan have a strong bond, even by hybrid standards. They can share information, learn things together. It's fascinating, but what if the reason Ethan is in his current state is because he's trying to hold on to something? What if he's trying to hold on to her?"

Connor blinked. He hadn't considered it like that. "There's too much distance between them. How could they still be connected? How would that work?"

"I don't know. I don't even know if it's possible, but what if it is somehow, and Ethan is caught up in it?" Lenora said, looking away from the camera for a moment. "Now that I've had the thought, I can't let it go."

She was just as tenacious as he was when he had an idea that kept pushing to the forefront of his mind. He shoved his doubts aside and considered it. "If she's dead, there might not be anything we can do to help him."

Lenora frowned. "I don't understand what you mean."

"You said what if Ethan and Cynergy are still connected through their bond? There is no precedent for it. On the flip side, what if this is a remnant of that bond, and Ethan is stuck in some kind of loop because he can't reconcile the bond anymore? Does that make sense?"

She folded her arms across her abdomen with a thoughtful frown. "Yes," she said slowly. "You'll need to prove it."

"What do you want me to do? Go back in there and show him a picture of Cynergy and hope for the best?"

"Do you have a better idea? If you do, I'd love to hear it."

Connor sighed, giving her a guilty look. "Sorry."

Her expression softened. "Me, too. I know you're doing everything you can, and you're pushing people to squeeze out every last idea they may have. I know you."

He shook his head. "It hasn't paid off."

A message from Doctor Harris appeared on the holoscreen. He read it and looked at Lenora. "Sheila Tran and Roy Emerson's vitals are weakening. The only explanation Harris can come up with is that their bodies are giving out. Separating them from Ethan reduced what was happening, but there must be something else going on."

He balled his hands into fists and shook his head. "What are we doing out here, Lenora? We knew the Vemus probe was of extraterrestrial origin and that there was the possibility of finding more of them on other planets. We assumed that since the hybrids had resisted the Vemus contagion on Earth, they were resistant to an alien version of it. Please tell me that we're not that foolish. Did we just..." He stopped speaking. He might've already said too much, but the doubts were gnawing away at him, and the memory of his son sealed in a cage was locked in, as if he couldn't look away.

"We're explorers, Connor. All of us. It's in us to push the boundaries, to go where no one else has ever been, and shine a light in the dark places, but there are no guarantees. Go to him, Connor. Make him listen to you," she said. "But keep this comlink active! I want to see him. Maybe together we can figure out a way to reach him."

His first instinct was to shield her from the bad things. It was that same protective instinct that drove him to put himself between danger and the ones he loved. It wasn't because he thought Lenora couldn't handle it. She could, but he did worry about the cost.

"Okay, I'll initiate the comlink once I'm at the isolation chamber," Connor said.

Lenora gazed at him. "Be careful."

The edges of his lips twitched a little. "Always."

He severed the comlink and left the shuttle. While he walked, he sent a quick message to Harris that he was going into the isolation chamber. He didn't get a response.

Connor crossed the hangar. The survivors looked as if they were bracing themselves right before a collision. More than a few people looked in his direction—some with hope and others with uncertainty. It felt as if there was a clock counting down, except that none of them knew how much time they had left. They were quarantined, and too many hands were idle.

Connor strode toward the isolation center, and the soldiers on duty both saluted him. He walked inside. The configuration of the inner chambers had changed. Sheila and Roy were at the far side of the unit. Connor glanced inside their rooms as he walked past. They lay on a bed with restraints holding them in place. He turned down a corridor and went into an airlock. Once he cycled through it, he spotted Harris waiting for him.

There were two soldiers nearby, watching them.

Connor looked at Harris. "I'm going in there," he said and looked at the soldiers. "Alone."

"General Gates, I don't recommend you do that. Ethan's behavior is completely unpredictable. He could hurt you," Harris said and stepped closer to him. "He could kill you. You may not want to see it, but the potential is there."

Connor looked through the window at the inner chamber. Ethan was locked in a cell, hardly moving at all.

He stepped toward the door as he turned toward the others. "No matter what happens, you don't open that door," he said to the soldiers. "That's an order."

"Understood, General Gates," one of the soldiers said.

Harris's mouth opened with an unspoken question, but then he shook his head. "General Gates, please. Give me more time. I know I can come up with something. There are protocols we haven't tried yet."

Connor shook his head. "I can't. The others are dying. Eventually, Ethan is going to die if we don't do something. Even if nothing comes of this, I'm not going to let my son die alone locked up in a cell."

Harris swallowed hard and nodded. "I'll be monitoring from out here."

Connor regarded him for a moment and softened his gaze a little. It wasn't Harris's fault that he couldn't figure out a way to help Ethan. Connor knew how he felt. He opened a comlink to Lenora.

"Are you ready?" he asked.

"Wait, data comlink is connecting. Okay, it's there. I can see," Lenora said.

Harris frowned in confusion, and Connor explained what he was doing.

He walked to the door and opened it. Once he stepped through, the door's locking mechanism activated, and the indicator light above went from green to red.

Across the room was a cell. Connor peered at Ethan. He was strapped to a chair behind an airlock door.

Connor looked at the window. "Are the environments linked?"

"They're linked, General," Harris replied.

Connor walked to the airlock door and opened it, then

stepped through and stopped. Ethan raised his head, eyes half closed as if being roused from sleep. Connor glanced at the holoscreen nearby that showed Ethan's heart rate. It was elevated, as if he was exerting himself.

He heard Lenora inhale a breath. It sounded soft, almost delicate. "Oh, Connor, look at him."

"I know," he said.

Connor walked toward the cell door and opened it. It clanged as it reached the end of its run, and Connor stepped inside.

Ethan opened his eyes. They were bright green, almost gleaming, and his skin was black.

"I'm going to remove the restraints," Connor said.

He imagined Harris having a fit, but no warnings came over the speakers in the isolation room.

Connor kept his movements slow as he released the restraints from Ethan's legs, torso, and arms. Then he stepped back, giving Ethan room.

Ethan shot to his feet, darting out of the cell in a sudden burst. The strength and speed displayed were still shocking, even though he was expecting it.

"Ethan," Connor said.

His son ignored him. He went toward the door and stopped, as if he somehow knew it was locked.

"Where do you want to go?" he asked.

Ethan surveyed the room, as if searching for another door.

Connor brought up his personal holoscreen and activated it. An image of Cynergy appeared. He played a video of them while they were recording a message to send to Lenora. They'd just had dinner together.

Ethan spun around, eyes fixed on the screen.

"That's it," Lenora said. "Talk to him."

While Connor thought about what to say, Ethan stopped looking at the image of Cynergy. The video snippet played on a loop a few times and stopped.

"We don't know where she is," Connor said. "She was lost during the fighting."

"His heart rate is spiking," Lenora said.

Their comlink session allowed her access to the data feeds in the room.

Ethan spun around again with a snarl.

Connor brought up several images. Some were of the ship and their home on New Earth, and others were of all of them together. The last was of the landing zone on the nearby planet.

He called out to his son. "Look at it. I know you can hear me."

Ethan walked to the side away from the door, which didn't make sense to him.

Connor closed the distance, and he heard Lenora gasp. Ethan spun toward him and grabbed his arms. Connor grabbed his to stabilize himself. There was no way he could overpower him. Instead, he used Ethan's strength against him and maneuvered him toward the holoscreen.

"Look!" Connor shouted.

Ethan bellowed as he lifted Connor off his feet and slammed him against the wall.

Connor clenched his teeth for a second. "What are you going to do? She's not here."

Ethan winced as if in pain and dropped Connor. He wobbled on his feet, his breath coming in ragged gasps. His shoulders hunched to the side, and he looked at the images as if seeing them for the first time. Then he snarled as he raced toward the holoscreen but passed through it and stumbled.

"Connor," Lenora said, "instead of stills, try a live feed from the recon drone that's scouting the area now. He might notice something we don't."

He did as she asked. The other images all disappeared and several video feeds from the recon drones scouting the attack site appeared.

Ethan stared at the video feeds, studying them intently. He moved slowly toward them. This was the most engaged Connor had seen him since his return. The left-most feed showed a bird's-eye view as the drone slowly patrolled over the area. Movement tracked below and Ethan stepped toward it, blocking Connor's view.

Connor stepped to the side and gasped. Someone was running. The recon drone's computer system flew toward them. It wasn't an alien; it was a survivor, but the drone was too far away to identify who it was. They ran down a path, disappearing from view. Then a group of alien Vemus raced after them.

Ethan snarled. Connor put the recon drone in attack mode, and it flew at the alien Vemus.

Recon drones had no weapons systems but could be used as either a blunt instrument or as a means to distract the enemy. The drone swooped down, flying right over the alien Vemus. It reached the cliff edge and slowed as it tried to find where the survivor had gone. It circled around the area, and Connor saw the survivor being dragged from view. It looked like a man. Then the video feed went offline.

Ethan spun toward Connor.

"It's gone. The drone was destroyed," Connor said.

Ethan drew himself up and stared down at Connor. He spread his arms wide and stalked toward him. Connor backed up, guiding Ethan toward the cell.

Ethan lunged toward him, and Connor stepped out of the way, shoving his son back into the cell. The door slid shut, and

Ethan howled in frustration. He grabbed the bars tightly, thick muscles straining, but the battle steel wouldn't yield, not even to a hybrid.

Ethan slammed his fists against it, and a dull metallic thud sounded.

"Are you all right?" Lenora asked.

Connor pressed his ribs to see if there was a sore spot, but there wasn't any. His MPS had absorbed the blow, protecting him.

"I'm fine," he said and then hastened toward the door.

"Where are you going?"

"Didn't you see it? There are survivors down there," Connor said and looked over at the observation window. "Harris, did you record that?"

"Yes, we got it," Harris replied.

Connor nodded and felt as if some of his tension had been released. "Get Major Arvad down here. We're going back to the planet. I'm taking Ethan and the others back down. It's the only shot they have."

Harris frowned. "Taking him down there could further compromise him. They're in a heightened state of hybridization, and the stress of being down there could make it permanent."

Connor heard Lenora sigh explosively, muttering a curse. He glanced at his son for a moment and then at Harris. "You can help, or you can get out of the way. This is going to happen."

The door unlocked, and Connor went through it. He looked at Lenora on his HUD. "I've got to go."

"Go," she replied. "I'll let the others know."

Connor looked at Harris. "Prep them for transport. I know Ethan is resisting sedation, but is there anything you can do?"

Harris frowned. "What exactly do you need?"

"I just need him to get down to the planet without tearing the shuttle apart."

Harris looked away for a moment. "Give me some time to come up with a solution."

"Okay, but I need to be able to reverse any sedation when we reach the planet."

Harris nodded. "Understood."

# CHAPTER 22

Connor walked out of the isolation area and back into the hangar. His mind was racing, and the beginnings of a plan were already taking shape in his mind. He walked across the hangar to a common area where most of the people were gathered. Nearby, cots had been set up for people to use.

Lieutenant Bentley noticed him first and came over. "General Gates," he said and saluted.

Connor gave him a nod and turned toward the common area. "Challengers!" he said, using the nickname Ethan had given them. "That's what you call yourselves. Your unofficial designation."

A large portion of the survivors were from the CDF and the rest were made up of spacers and field scientists. They stood and began coming over to hear what Connor had to say.

"A survivor was spotted down on the planet. They were being chased by the alien Vemus," Connor said, and let them digest that for a moment.

"General, I volunteer to be on the away team," Lieutenant Bentley said.

"Thank you, Lieutenant," Connor said.

Others began raising questions.

"We don't know how many of our people are alive, but we're not going to leave them behind."

"What about us?" Wade Walsh asked.

Connor regarded him for a moment. "I can't make you go, if that's what you're asking."

Wade glanced at the two hybrids at his side and then shook his head. "I'm not asking to be left behind, sir. None of us are. We're asking to be allowed to come with you."

Bentley came over to Connor's side. "Sir, there have been concerns raised about the risks involved in bringing hybrids back down to the planet." He paused for a moment. "We hoped we'd be going back there to find the other team."

Connor nodded and looked at Wade. "I'm bringing Ethan, Sheila, and Ray with me. They're suffering the worst of it. Going back to the planet may seem like the easy decision to make, but you are vulnerable. I've seen evidence of it from the combat suit recordings."

"We'll be better prepared for it this time," Wade said.

Connor gave him a pointed look. "How?"

"It's worse if we're exposed to the atmosphere, like Captain Gates was. For most of us, it was just shocking, not compelling. We were still in control. Encountering the alien Vemus was just something we hadn't expected," Wade said.

Connor bobbed his head once. "I believe you," he said, and looked at the other hybrids. "The video evidence confirms it."

"General Gates," Lieutenant Bentley said, "how does that explain what happened to Ethan and the others?"

"The doctors believe Ethan is the cause. It has to do with the bond he shares with Cynergy, and the synchronization that hybrids are capable of. I don't know the ins and outs of it. All I know is that time is running out for them," Connor said, gesturing across the hangar where the isolation chamber was. "And time is running out for the people we left behind."

"What about the quarantine, General Gates?" Sergeant Wilson asked.

"We're already following quarantine protocols. The doctors haven't found anything that indicates any of us are infected with a variant of the Vemus contagion," Connor said.

A group of people came through the airlock that isolated the hangar bay from the rest of the ship. They wore quarantine suits that protected them from others just in case the doctors were wrong.

Major Caleb Arvad strode over to them at a quick pace. "I just heard, sir. The *Reliant* is forty-six hours out and is the closest ship to give us assistance."

Connor nodded. "That's too much time. We can't wait for support from the other ships. What we've got here is what we've got to work with."

"Then that shuttle is all we've got to work with. The other two are on the planet," Arvad said.

They'd lost two shuttles in the surprise attack.

"Excuse me, sirs," Wade Walsh said, "what about the *Mariner*? We left it on the planet."

"Recon drones are unable to locate it. All tracking signals are offline. We're assuming it's unreachable," Arvad replied and looked at Connor. "I have a couple of ideas about the alien Vemus."

Connor smiled. "So do I. We need to restock the shuttle. No frontal assault, but we need more recon drones." He paused for a moment, considering.

"What about attack drones? Might help even the odds a little," Arvad said.

Attack drones were based on advanced Krake technology. They were two meters in length with an elongated, bronze-colored head. They achieved temperatures similar to that of a main sequence star and could penetrate the armor of a CDF warship. Only powerful gravitational fields could protect a ship from them. Attack drones could cause serious damage, but they'd risk harming the survivors on the planet because they were difficult to control. Those drones weren't precision weapons capable of carrying out surgical strikes; they were used for causing wanton destruction.

Connor gave Arvad a knowing look. "I think we'll take a few of those. We'll need a full combat deployment kit."

Arvad looked at the soldiers in quarantine. "We've got armament for the soldiers here, but not enough for the spacers. They'll have light combat armor."

Over the next hour, supplies made their way to the hangar bay. Technically, the hangar bay was still a quarantine zone, but that didn't impede the delivery of equipment. Connor and Arvad discussed whether it would be worth the time to bring the other teams back but decided against it. They didn't have the time.

Connor would lead the assault team. With the additional weapons and combat suit heavies, there wouldn't be much room for the survivors when they found them. They'd have to depend on the other teams to fit whatever survivors they were able to rescue.

There were too many unknowns but not enough to prevent them from returning to the planet. Connor watched as the portable airlock cell was loaded onto the shuttle. Ethan was inside, while Sheila and Ray were sedated inside a medical capsule.

Connor walked onto the shuttle, and Lieutenant Bentley followed him.

"Wish we could bring more people with us," Bentley said.

Connor nodded. They'd had more volunteers than they could use, so they'd limited participation to CDF soldiers and hybrids who had combat training. "More people, more equipment, better weapons, or technology that hasn't been invented yet. The list could go on and on."

Major Arvad insisted that they take pilots with them. This would free Connor to command the mission. He thought about his last conversation with Ethan. Connor missed the missions sometimes. He glanced at the mobile airlock in the cargo hold, wondering what Ethan was thinking. Could he string together coherent thoughts? He had to believe that his son was still there. There were times when Connor was reassured of it, but other times, he questioned whether he was doing the right thing. He'd spoken to Lenora about it, and she agreed with him that bringing Ethan to the planet was their best chance at saving him and finding the others.

What if they were wrong? What if Ethan was just too far gone and bringing him back to the planet was the surefire way of watching his son die at the hands of the Vemus…alien or otherwise? The Vemus had extracted a heavy toll on humanity.

Connor inhaled deeply and steeled his resolve. The decision had been made, and he wasn't about to second-guess himself now. He pushed the doubts out of his mind. They had no place in there anymore.

Connor and Bentley walked to the tech workstation that had been set up. He recognized the man sitting there.

"Hash," Connor said.

Hash started to stand, but Connor gestured for him to remain seated.

"General Gates, I was just checking on the status of the drones in storage," he said and frowned for a moment. "Had no idea that exterior storage compartments could be added to these shuttles."

The combat shuttle had some flexibility in its armament and configuration. They needed more recon drones, as they would scout the area for them before they even set down.

"Only two of them," Connor said.

"They're online and ready to deploy as soon as we enter the planet's atmosphere."

Connor nodded. "Good. Get them in as fast as possible. Maybe we'll get lucky and hit the ground running."

"Will do, sir," Hash said.

Connor and Bentley walked down the loading ramp.

"Combat suit staging area is over here, General," Bentley said.

The staging area was next to the shuttle. There were a pair of NexStar combat suits waiting for them. They were series sevens, and Connor frowned a little.

"Have you used this series before, sir?" Bentley asked.

"You don't want to know."

Bentley chuckled. "I hear the series nines are quite the upgrade."

Connor nodded. "They are."

They'd put the expeditionary force together outfitted with the current stockpile, using older equipment. It was nothing veteran soldiers weren't accustomed to working with, but it did take civilians by surprise that not everyone got to use the latest and greatest equipment. It took time to build and to replace the current equipment that still had functionality left.

Connor stepped inside the combat suit and it closed in around him, feeling like an old friend he hadn't seen in a very long time. Authentication included his personal preferences, and the suit adjusted accordingly. The combat suit went through automated checks and his neural implants interfaced with the suit's computer.

He retracted the helmet, which folded in on itself in a compartment on his upper back. He extended his arms and raised his legs. The combat suit performed flawlessly.

Bentley looked over at him from his own combat suit. "When was the last time you wore a series seven?"

Connor thought about it for a second. "Actually, haven't used a seven. Had extensive use of a six, though. You could say I've pushed my fair share of combat suits to the limit."

Bentley stared at him for a moment, looking as if he wanted to say something.

"Don't worry about it, Lieutenant Bentley. If you get into trouble, I'll make sure you get back home safe," Connor said.

Bentley blinked a few times, then rolled his eyes a little. "Yes, sir," he said.

Connor walked up the loading ramp, with Bentley following behind.

The other soldiers gathered around them.

"You all know the mission. This is a rescue of the missing team. We know that at least one of them survived, which raises the probability that more may have. Our enemy has vastly superior numbers, which is nothing new when you consider the history of the CDF," Connor said.

More than a few soldiers chuckled at the mention of that. The CDF had been outnumbered in every war it had ever fought.

"We survive by studying the enemy and adapting our tactics to meet the threat we're facing. The Vemus of Old Earth were directed by an alpha. Studying the alien Vemus attack pattern indicates that there is also a hive mentality to how they behave. However, they seem to also follow a pre-programed script. They'll kill us if they get the chance, and it seems they'll capture hybrids if the opportunity presents itself. That's the long and short of it. Since we can expect that once the alien Vemus engage they will never retreat, we'll try to misdirect them—get them to chase a few red herrings to take some of the pressure off. That's what the two other shuttles will do while we penetrate the interior of that ship."

Sergeant Wilson raised his hand, and Connor gestured for him to speak. "What if there are no survivors, sir?" he asked, his expression grim.

"Then we'll leave and blow this place to kingdom come," Connor replied.

Wilson nodded with a gleeful smile. In Connor's experience, demolition experts walked a bit on the reckless side. At least he was in good company.

## CHAPTER 23

The combat shuttle left the *Challenger*'s secondary hangar behind. It had taken longer than Connor expected. They'd had to establish another quarantine location and move the people who were staying behind to that location while mission prep was occurring. Connor couldn't fault the ship's crew. As fast as the temporary quarantine measures had been put in place, the crew disassembled and moved them. It hadn't occurred to anyone that another mission would be launched from the secondary hangar. At least the shuttle had been more or less prepped and was flight-ready.

Captain Hank Carver stood at Connor's side, along with Deacon and Cole from his protective detail. Lieutenant Bentley and Wade Walsh joined them.

Carver eyed Connor with a bit of suspicion in his gaze. "I don't like the look in your eyes, General Gates. I feel like I'm being sized up for reassignment."

Connor smiled. Carver had guessed what was going to happen. "Then you know why I need to do it."

Carver lifted his chin toward Bentley. "Lieutenant Bentley is a fine young officer, and all of Ethan's reports support that fact, sir."

Bentley frowned a little as he glanced at them but remained wisely silent.

Connor regarded Carver for a moment and saw that the leader of his protective detail had a stubborn glint in his eyes. "I'm putting you in charge of these men as my second. Lieutenant Bentley will report to you for the duration of this mission."

Captain Carver narrowed his gaze. "Meaning no disrespect, sir, but I cannot comply with that order as it conflicts with my primary objective."

Walsh frowned as he watched them. "What's going on?"

Connor's muscles tensed, and his gaze narrowed slightly. "Hank, these men need you," he said, ignoring Walsh's question.

Walsh cleared his throat. "Excuse me. Why do I feel like I'm watching some kind of pissing match?" He looked at Carver. "Isn't he your superior officer? Don't you need to do what he says?"

Carver smiled a little. "General Gates is my superior, but I don't report to him. My command comes under the purview of Senior General Nathan Hayes, and my primary objective is to protect General Gates, even from himself, should the need arise." He looked at Connor. "General, I remind you of article—"

"Enough, Captain," Connor said, putting steel in his voice. He knew the regulations about to be quoted to him. "These men need leadership."

"With all due respect, sir, they have you," Carver replied.

"Are you going to make me say it?" Connor asked.

Carver considered it for a few seconds. "General, I will

follow any legal order you give me, except the one that leaves a loophole for you to separate yourself from the rest of us."

"The chain of command will be established."

"It *is* established. As long as we're all together, the chain of command will remain intact."

"Not good enough. These men need someone to look to in case something happens to me."

Carver locked gazes with Connor. "Nothing is going to happen to you without it going through me, Lieutenant Deacon, or Sergeant Cole first."

Connor's frustration with the damn regs Nathan had put together all those years ago was rising. It was Nathan's guarantee that officers serving in the Protective Services Battalion couldn't simply be ordered away by the officer they were protecting.

Connor exhaled a breath. "Fine," he said and looked at the others. "Deacon, Cole, you'll stay at my side for the duration. Captain Carver, you'll liaise with Lieutenant Bentley's platoon, acting as the primary source of contact for the duration of this mission. Is that understood?"

A flash of annoyance played over Carver's face. Connor could play the regulations game with the best of them, and he knew that this was an order he couldn't refuse. After recognizing that he'd been outmaneuvered, he stood up straight and gave Connor a salute. "Understood, General Gates."

Lieutenant Bentley looked uncomfortable, as if he'd been caught in the middle of a location he had no business being in.

"Captain Carver," Bentley said, "I can update you as to the status of the platoon."

Carver nearly scowled at Bentley, but his expression stopped short of open hostility. Connor watched them impassively.

The two stepped to the side and began speaking quietly.

Connor walked over to where Hash and Specialist Lasky had

set up a tech workspace. Semitranslucent amber-colored holoscreens were arrayed in front of them.

Lasky began to stand, but Connor gestured for him to remain seated.

"What's your status?"

"General, the drones are online and waiting for launch as soon as we clear the atmosphere," Lasky replied. He brought up a high-res image of the area. "We've got them separated into groups with assigned priorities. The drones will network the existing remaining drones in the area, which should cut our search grid down to the unexplored areas."

Connor studied the map for a few moments. "We'll need to revisit the ambush sites, both from the extraction point and from where the missing team was taken."

Lasky nodded. "Yes, sir. I mean, we've accounted for that, but…" he paused and glanced at Hash, giving him a meaningful look.

"Sir," Hash began, "misdirection and reconnaissance are the key here, so I advised that the initial survey should ignore the ambush sites for the first pass. I'm hoping to get the enemy to show themselves. This will allow us to coordinate with the two other shuttles to lure the enemy away, freeing our drones to investigate the sites we're really interested in."

Connor looked at the young hybrid for a few moments. "Sounds like you've done something like this before."

Hash smiled a little, but the worry was still there. "I've been on plenty of missions playing hide-and-seek with remnant Vemus forces. Granted that these are alien Vemus, but I still think it's our best shot at maximizing chances of finding the others."

He knew that Hash was a lifetime spacer and Vemus hybrid, brought up on old space stations. Hybrids were a tight-knit group that were more like family than a bunch of people who happened to be thrown together by circumstances.

"Good, let's hope it works," Connor said.

The shuttle descended through the atmosphere, and the pilot chose speed as the high priority. They shot toward the mission area.

"Recon drones, away," Lasky said.

Connor watched the holoscreen at the mini-command center. There were sub-windows that showed the drones speeding ahead of the shuttle. Groups broke off, heading toward their objectives. Two more icons appeared on the plot, showing the shuttles commanded by Lieutenants Washburn and Rosen. They'd been on the other side of the planet when the ambush occurred.

The operation was about to begin, and he hoped they reached the others in time. No amount of planning could disguise the fact that this operation was a shot in the dark. They had evidence of a single survivor who had been alive over four hours ago.

Connor resisted the urge to glance at the shuttle's cargo area where Ethan waited in a mobile airlock. He had no protection of any kind. They'd included an MPS suit disguised as a regular ship suit, but Ethan hadn't touched it. Connor wasn't sure if Ethan even realized they'd left the ship. The mobile airlock was functioning as a prison cell and was in full lockdown. This was his last shot at helping Ethan.

Connor inhaled and sighed. Either his son was going to die during this confrontation with the alien Vemus, or he was somehow going to pull through it. The key to it was finding Cynergy and the rest of the team. How they were would directly affect how Ethan and the other hybrids with them were going to be. Would all the hybrids become like Ethan, stuck in a heightened embrace of their hybrid nature, or would they be able to resist it? Their ability to coordinate and communicate without speaking was a strength, but it was being used against them. To the best of his knowledge, no one, not even the hybrids, had anticipated something like this happening, which made him question whether Ethan was a victim of it or the perpetrator of it. Neither thought sat well with Connor, despite his thoughts tilting toward Ethan's condition being a combination of the two, with Ethan being both a victim and a perpetrator. Yet, if they were right and Ethan was perpetrating this behavior because of his reluctance to let go of his link with Cynergy, could Connor really blame him? Could anyone? Maybe to some degree or another, but Connor didn't think Ethan had the wherewithal to understand the effect his abilities were having on the other hybrids. How much of what they were able to do was instinctual? Sure, they might train to enhance their abilities, but at the onset, those abilities were instinctual. Couple all that and throw in the unknown variable of alien Vemus and the current situation wasn't so farfetched.

Connor looked at the video feed from the drones as the shuttle flew high above the area. The weather-worn landscape of dark, frozen sand almost appeared like low-lying mountains or very large foothills, desolate and artificial, as if some kind of calamity had covered the alien city. But learning there was a species here that was aquatic in nature lent weight to the possibility that this city had perhaps been constructed underwater. This entire civilization could have come to being primarily underwater.

The drones flew over the area without the alien Vemus appearing until they began to map out several winding ravines. Even then, it was mostly a scouting force sent to investigate.

"They're not buying the ruse," Carver said.

"Not yet," Connor said.

The drones covered a three-kilometer area, mapping it and searching for signs of recent activity. Several undisturbed rockslides showed in an area north of their position.

"They don't look recent, but with the temperature changes, appearances can be misleading," Specialist Lasky said.

"Time to send the drones inside," Connor said.

There had been more than a few dull thumps from Ethan's cell.

Carver looked at Connor. "They seem reluctant to chase the drones, sir. Maybe we need to step it up and really give them something to chase."

"You mean live bait," Connor replied.

Carver bobbed his head once. "It worked with the ryklars all those years ago."

Ryklars were genetically modified super-predators that had been brought to New Earth a long time ago. They had the beginnings of an early civilization, but they were extremely dangerous to most other species on the planet. The Colonial Security Council quietly authorized a program where the CDF lured them through a gateway to another universe. They'd been sent to a planet that had no intelligent life on it and was a close match to New Earth's planetary ecology. The program involved using CDF soldiers in combat suits enticing the dangerous predators to chase them. Combat suits enabled the wearer to move at speeds that rivaled ground vehicles, especially on rough terrain.

"Not a bad idea," Connor said. "Have Lieutenants Washburn and Rosen drop off a scout team with a planned egress point. See if the alien Vemus will take the bait."

"Yes, sir," Carver said, and told Bentley to coordinate with the other shuttles.

The plan was only authorized for CDF soldiers in full

combat suits capable of navigating the icy terrain. Three-person fire teams were dropped off at designated locations. They would navigate to another extraction point.

Hash glanced at Connor. "These ravines are mazes. What if they get cut off?"

"Then they'll ascend to the top of the ravine and the shuttles will fly to them," Connor replied.

Hash frowned a little but didn't push the issue.

There was a vast tunnel network under the surface that the alien Vemus could use to traverse the area unseen.

Connor watched the holoscreen. Eight fire teams on the ground were making their way to another part of the grid, hoping to lure the alien Vemus away from the previous ambush sites.

"Have recon drone groups seven and nine go into stealth mode and move into the target area," Connor said.

"Yes, General," Specialist Lasky replied.

Connor knew the shuttle's computer systems were being utilized beyond their capabilities. They could carry some of the load, but the bulk of the computing power came from a subspace comlink to the *Challenger*. It was a delicate balance of resources, but Connor didn't want to depend solely on the ship's computing core because of what had happened earlier with the sensor failures. There was someone else operating out here—every instinct in his gut pushed him to that idea—so he had to keep in mind that they were being watched and that their computing systems were compromised. What he couldn't figure out was what their motivation could be.

Connor looked over at Lieutenant Bentley, who was watching another set of holoscreens. "Any power sources detected below?"

Bentley shook his head. "Not yet, sir. We didn't detect

anything until we were well below the surface. Could be that our scanners can't penetrate deep enough to detect anything."

Connor nodded.

It wasn't long before the alien Vemus began investigating the CDF scouts moving through the area. They used their weapons, firing on the alien Vemus and pausing long enough to get them to commit before running away.

The alien Vemus made good use of their vast tunnel network as they began appearing ahead of the scout teams, scaling up from the bottom of the ravines. The alien Vemus had thick, black tentacles that helped propel them up at alarming speeds. The shuttles operated like mini-command centers, providing valuable intel to the soldiers on the ground as they navigated their way through the ravines.

"General Gates," Hash said, "I've got drones at the ambush site where the team was taken. Looks clear. No sign of the enemy."

Connor checked the feeds himself and then nodded. He looked at Carver. "Have the pilot take us in."

Orders were relayed, and the soldiers on the shuttle switched to their own individual life support as helmets were engaged.

"Into the belly of the beast we go," Hash said.

Connor appreciated the sentiment. It felt like an accurate description of what they were about to do.

## CHAPTER 24

The shuttle flew down into the frozen ravine. Heavy crosswinds attempted to push the ship into jagged walls of ice, black sand, and rock, but the pilot deftly navigated to the landing zone. The shuttle hovered over the ground for a few moments and then the pilot committed, setting it down.

Connor waited to give the order, watching the video feeds from the recon drones in the area. Vemus tactics tilted toward overwhelming force in place of clever tactics, and everything he'd seen of the alien Vemus showed they applied the same strategy.

"Clear," Connor said.

Captain Carver began shouting orders, and the loading ramp of the shuttle lowered to the ground. CDF soldiers quickly descended, spreading out to form a defensive perimeter.

The mobile airlock was next to go down the ramp, floating on counter-grav emitters.

Connor heard Bentley speaking to a medic by the two medical capsules, and he walked over.

"What's wrong?" Connor asked.

Corporal Stef Brooks gestured toward the capsules that contained Roy Emerson and Sheila Tran. "General Gates, I'm unable to revive them." Connor glanced at the small holoscreens on the capsules showing the status of the occupants inside. "I've started the revival cocktail and can confirm it was administered, but they remain incapacitated. Their vitals are such that they've gone into some kind of hibernation."

Connor frowned and glanced down the loading ramp. He heard the insistent thumping of Ethan's fists on the airlock that was just out of view. "Okay, they stay here for now. Remain on the shuttle and coordinate with Dr. Harris or Dr. Williams. Maybe they can help."

"Yes, General Gates," Corporal Brooks replied, looking relieved.

Connor walked down the loading ramp and headed over to the mobile airlock. Carver glanced at the shuttle as the ramp was closing.

"What about the others, sir?" Carver asked.

"They're in hibernation and we can't take the time to figure out how to revive them," Connor said.

The shuttle's engines increased, and it lifted into the air.

Carver glanced at the shuttle for a second and then at Connor. "I'd say it made little sense, but none of this does."

"Yeah," Connor replied as he walked over to the mobile airlock unit.

He noticed some of the soldiers taking in the dreary, semi-frozen state of their surroundings. He cataloged the landscape in his brain and took a good look around. He'd visited so many different worlds that visiting a new one felt like putting on something old and familiar.

Sleet began to fall, sometimes pelting the dark sand beneath their armored feet. The ravine walls followed artificial angles at some places, especially the higher it went. Open plateaus looked like steps that only a behemoth could climb. The whole thing resembled remnant ruins that his mind could only attribute to the alien race that had once thrived there. It wasn't a landscape, although that was part of it. Large tunnels hinted at a dark interior network that almost taunted him with its secrets, but most of all, this planet reminded him of a vast graveyard. He'd been to enough dying planets to know the signs.

Connor turned toward the window of the mobile airlock. Ethan's bright green eyes stared at him, and the unique hybrid patterns nearly stood out from his dark skin. A soldier stood near the controls, and Connor told him to open it.

A brief hiss sounded as the airlock door opened, and Ethan stepped out. He went a short distance away from the airlock and paused. At some point during their descent, he'd put on the MPS suit but didn't engage the helmet, leaving both his head and his hands exposed to the frigid temperatures. His hands were larger and the skin more robust, as if there were extra layers insulating it. Ethan's facial features were more pronounced, with a thicker brow and a sharper angle to his cheekbones and chin.

Connor's eyes widened as he took in the sight of his son, and something cold settled into the pit of his stomach. He'd never seen his son embrace his hybrid nature to such a degree before, and he wasn't sure if it was because Ethan had previously spared him or this was a result of exposure to the alien Vemus.

The soldiers watched Ethan as he raised his chin into the air. Connor could tell that he wasn't breathing, and by the way he cocked his head to the side, he appeared to be listening intently.

Carver gestured toward the airlock. "Should I have the shuttle retrieve it on their next pass?"

"Negative," Connor said, unsure why he did. He didn't know

what was going to happen, whether they'd find the other team or if Ethan would return to normal, but either way he doubted they'd need the mobile airlock. He wasn't sure if their egress point would be anywhere near here.

"We might need it for the survivors," Connor said.

Carver delayed for a second and then said. "Yes, sir."

Ethan moved forward with a jolt of energy, then halted. He slowly turned, as if he was detecting something the rest of them were incapable of hearing.

"Walsh," Connor said, "can you tell what he's sensing?"

"He's trying to detect his link to Cynergy, but either it's very faint or something is interfering with it," Walsh replied.

Connor looked at the hybrid, who wore a combat suit. "Are you able to sense anything?"

"Not like he can, sir. He's attuned to it. Maybe after we move closer to wherever they've been taken."

In a sudden burst, Ethan shot toward one of the corridors ahead of them and quickly disappeared.

The platoon of soldiers began following. A scout force led the way and several recon drones kept pace with Ethan.

Connor moved to the rear of the platoon, Deacon and Cole keeping pace with him. They went quickly through the narrow corridor. Their combat suits had adapted to the icy conditions, and small spikes extended from their armored boots. By the time Connor covered the same ground, it was well worn, with large gouges cut through it.

He glanced over at Walsh for a second, wanting to ask him if he detected anything but decided not to. Walsh would tell him if he did.

The tunnel widened as they reached an open area, and Ethan sprinted across, moving at speeds that rivaled CDF combat suits.

Eventually, he outpaced the scout group and they lost sight of him.

"General," Captain Carver said, "it's too reckless to keep at it like this. We need to move slower, not at such a breakneck speed."

He was right, and Connor knew it. "Understood. Keep the drones on him."

They slowed their pace to something more manageable, but Connor had a video feed on his HUD that showed where Ethan was.

They went down a tunnel that took them deeper underground and eventually opened into a cavern. Gray light came from high above them, and Connor realized they must be at the bottom of a very narrow ravine.

"That's it over there," Bentley said. "It has to be part of the ship we found."

He gestured across the cavern to the left side. Ethan had run by it without giving it a backward glance.

Connor looked at the metallic walls that appeared as if they'd been frozen in a liquified viscosity. It reminded him of the exoskeletal material that the Vemus produced but different at the same time. It was similar to materials for building, but its application wasn't the same at all. This was metallic, and its dull gleam reflected from the lights of their helmets.

Complex patterns adorned the metallic walls that drew Connor's gaze toward an area where two long protrusions formed an arch that could also be a doorway, but the way was blocked by more metallic material.

"General Gates," Walsh said. "That's a doorway. We found a similar one before. There could be Vemus on the other side of that door."

Connor peered at it, searching for some kind of control interface, but there wasn't one. "Did the other one open?"

"Yes, it happened as the ambush started. We had already been attacked, but I'm positive I saw the doorway open," Walsh said.

Bentley turned toward him. "General, we detected a power source before, but that area was unfinished."

They skirted the doorway as they headed into a shallow tunnel leading to another, larger cavern. More of the alien ship was exposed. Its purplish metallic sheen reflected the dim lighting.

Ethan was several hundred meters ahead of them. He ran close to the ship, as if searching for a way inside. The ground sloped downward, and Ethan disappeared from view as he ran underneath it.

The platoon headed toward Ethan.

"General, I'm able to detect the alien Vemus," Walsh said. "Subsonic frequency, but there is a rhythm to it."

Several of the other hybrids confirmed it.

The scouts reached the area where Ethan had gone and waited for the rest of the platoon to catch up. The ground sloped at a sharp angle, as if the earth had given way a long time ago. Connor ordered the scouts ahead, and they went underneath the ship.

Connor looked at the hull above him. It was built in the same manner as the rest of what they'd seen. They spotted fissures up ahead, a patchwork of broken ground about half a meter wide, and Connor saw more of the hull below.

"Are we inside the ship?" Carver asked.

"Can't be. We never entered it," Connor said.

"Are we sure this is a ship? We could be walking between two levels of some kind of building," Walsh said.

"Unless this was a giant dock for a ship," Carver said.

A small light pierced the distance. The area ahead curved from right to left, and the walls seemed to close in as the path narrowed. The video feed from the recon drone showed a massive cavern ahead. There was some kind of light source far below.

They reached the edge of the cavern and a path wound along the outside, descending far into the depths. Ethan had gone ahead, not slowing down one bit.

"How long can he go on like this?" Carver asked.

"He told me he could hold his breath for two hours," Connor replied.

"Two hours!" Carver said. "Even while exerting himself?"

"Not sure—" Connor began to reply when the ground shifted to the side and he stumbled.

One moment he was falling into Deacon, but then there was a shift and he was flying through the air. He hit the ground, nearly dropping his rifle. The surrounding area was completely dark, and he stood in a pool of light put out by his helmet.

"Carver?" Connor said. The active comlink status switched to red. He was cut off.

Connor spun around, holding his weapon, aiming it. There was no one around him. He was completely alone.

Connor shouted, expecting to hear an echo, but there wasn't one. It was as if he was in a soundproof room. He glanced at the ground. It was black, almost semitransparent. There were tiny orbs of light at a distance, and the ground was smooth.

He exhaled explosively as he tried to reach the others. This made little sense. One moment he'd been in the middle of the platoon, surrounded, and now he was alone. He glanced above. Had he fallen into the cavern? If he had, he ought to be able to spot the other soldiers, and he should also be able to reach them through comlink.

His heart thundered in his chest, and he took several shallow breaths. The times he'd been isolated had been times he'd been in the most danger. Could the alien Vemus have done this to him? They'd only begun to detect them. Did they have the technology to teleport him somewhere else?

Connor shook his head. "Keep it together."

He said it aloud because hearing his own voice in the vast sea of darkness was better than giving in to fear. He still had his weapon, and his combat suit had plenty of power, so life support wouldn't fail.

Connor slowly spun around, and his footsteps caused a shimmer of dull light to ripple across the floor. He froze, face tight with a frown. Then he raised one foot and tapped the ground. A muffled "boing" sound came from the ground, and a small wave of light rippled away as if he'd thrown a rock into a calm lake.

"What the heck is going on!" Connor said.

He considered shouting for help but then dismissed the colossally stupid idea. If the alien Vemus had done this to him, he wasn't about to give away his position by shouting, "Here I am!"

He replayed his last moments with the others in his mind. He hadn't tripped...the ground had felt slippery for a moment and *then* he had tripped. He was stumbling into Deacon, and at the last second, he fell to the ground. It was as if he'd been dropped out of nowhere. He looked around. He had to be in some kind of chamber. He peered at the ground and could still see tiny shimmering lights far beneath his feet.

Connor squatted and tapped the ground with his hand. A smaller shimmer of light rolled away from him. The ground seemed to give ever so slightly, as if it was stretched tightly over something.

A spiral of pale light appeared off to the side. It was slightly distorted, as if he was seeing it through a lens that had a curve to it. It slithered through the area like a snake coming around. An orb brightened at the end and turned sharply toward him. There was a moment of resistance as it pushed through some kind of invisible barrier and spilled onto the floor.

Connor backed up, lifting his rifle but not quite pointing it at his visitor.

The light gathered around the orb, and it was as if it had substance as it expanded, taking on a shape of some kind. It didn't look like any Vemus he'd ever seen, alien or otherwise. This was something different.

The being was outlined in a pale light that brightened at select intervals, but the shape hadn't fully formed yet. Connor had the impression he was being evaluated and had absolutely no idea what to do next.

---

"Where is General Gates?" Captain Carver asked.

Deacon jerked around as if struck. "He was right behind me."

They both looked at Cole, who swore.

"Don't say it!" Carver warned.

"He was right in front of me. He was right there," Cole said, gesturing with the end of his rifle.

Carver brought up his holoscreen, and their combat suits showed their locations. Ethan's tracker had him farther away, making his way down the cavern, but General Gates's combat suit was gone.

Deacon peered at the ground where General Gates had stood. He started a scan with his combat suit computer and waited for the analysis to finish. "Scan shows that he was standing right here and then slipped. The tracks stop right here," he said, gesturing to the ground.

Carver walked over and tentatively stepped into the area as if testing for some kind of trap. When nothing happened, he stomped his foot down. The ground was as hard as it had been before.

Carver swung his gaze toward Deacon and Cole. "All you had to do was keep an eye on him."

"We were," Deacon replied.

"Oh, yeah? Then where the heck is he?"

"I can't help it if he disappeared out of thin air. Stop sounding as if this was my fault," Deacon shot back.

Lieutenant Bentley cleared his throat. "Are you sure he didn't slip away somehow?"

Carver blinked a few times. Connor wasn't above taking matters into his own hands, but slipping away? He looked at Deacon. "Do you know if his suit had stealth capabilities?"

Deacon considered for a few moments. "Doubtful. These combat suits are series sevens, standard combat suit configuration, so no, I don't think he slipped away from us."

Cole raised his gaze, searching above them, and Carver followed his gaze. There wasn't anything there.

"He couldn't have used his suit jets without anyone noticing," Carver said.

"Just checking, Captain," Cole said.

Lieutenant Bentley cleared his throat. "What do we do now?"

The edge of the cavern was thirty meters away. There was no way Connor had gone over the edge.

The other soldiers looked at him, waiting for him to give them an order. Carver gritted his teeth. He'd just lost the greatest general in the history of the CDF, a man he'd give his life to protect.

"I can't raise General Gates over comlink," Deacon said.

"Spread out and search the area," Carver said. He could do that much, at least.

They had to spare a few moments for that, but if they couldn't find Connor, he'd have no choice but to report this to the ship and keep following Ethan. It's what Connor would've wanted, but he hated to do it.

As Carver looked around, he kept trying to figure out how Connor had been taken from among them. He tried to force an answer from his mind, but none came. There was simply no explanation for it, and that bothered him more than he cared to admit, but he had to focus.

"It could be the alien Vemus," Deacon said quietly when their search for Connor came up empty.

Carver wasn't sure about that and said so. They couldn't afford to stay there. There wasn't any hidden place that Connor could've been taken to. Their only option was either to go back the way they'd come, which would go against Connor's orders, or keep pushing forward, hoping Ethan would lead them to the missing team. Neither of those options would help Connor.

"We keep going," Carver said.

Deacon and Cole shared a grim look, and a tense silence settled over the CDF platoon as they trekked into the dark cavern.

# CHAPTER 25

A shadow moved inside the sphere of light, and Connor couldn't look away. He recalled the other times he'd encountered a new alien being and lowered his rifle. The sphere was made of shadows and starlight on a clear night. It elongated to form a pillar, and when the end contacted the ground, it sent ripples of light toward him.

Connor glanced down at his feet, watching the ripples pass by him but didn't register any kind of force behind them. The first-contact protocols he'd helped write came to the forefront of his mind. They'd been augmented over the years because of their experience encountering new life-forms. At the top of the list was to make every effort not to provoke them so the encounter didn't become hostile. He frowned a little, knowing how the previous encounters with both the Ovarrow and the Krake had turned out. He supposed he could lump the Vemus into that pool, but it also didn't quite fit. He wasn't even sure that the column of light was an actual alien.

Connor made the faceplate of his helmet translucent. His

mouth had gone dry, and he worked up some saliva so he could speak. "Hello." He waited a few moments for a response but didn't get one. "Did you bring me here?"

The pillar of light was over two meters wide and three meters tall. It wasn't excessively bright, but there was a luminescence to it. There was a slight pulse along the edges, and it seemed to contract, becoming smaller. Either something dark moved inside, or it was a trick of the light, and Connor couldn't decide which it could be.

After waiting for a full minute, he turned away and looked above him, thinking he observed a slight curvature that felt kind of like being inside a vast holotheater, used throughout the colony for education and entertainment purposes. In the dark, it presented the night sky and other phenomena. This place was starting to remind him of that.

A slight play of the light drew Connor's attention back to the pillar. Tiny pulses sent waves across it, building in momentum and intensity, and then a flat calm took hold of it.

"Biological entity," a voice said. It was male and had a pleasant tone that carried a slight basso tone at the edges, as if they were communicating through a speaker. "Human. Male. Designation, Connor Gates."

Connor blinked. The fact that the voice spoke perfect English without any sort of accent and that it knew his name nearly paralyzed his mind with shock.

"Surprise registered. Understandable. I will wait a short duration."

Connor licked his lips as he worked his mouth, then exhaled softly. "Uh, hello. You already know my name. Who are you?"

The pillar of light continued to contract, shrinking down to a size near Connor's own height. "Perplexed response. You refer to us as Phantoms. Therefore, you may refer to me as Phantom."

Connor bit his lower lip for a second. "Yeah," he drawled. "That's because we didn't know what to call you. Surely you have a name? A way to identify yourself?"

"I do, but it is not appropriate for this exchange. It would be unpronounceable by your means of communication. Therefore, to assist in this exchange, I agree to be referred to by the name you've already assigned to us."

Connor considered it for a few moments. He'd spoken in the singular until the end when he'd indicated there were more of them.

"Okay, Phantom," Connor replied, feeling slightly foolish.

"Do not be afraid. The designation is an apt description for beings that are unknowable by your current technological capabilities."

That was the first time he'd ever had an alien try to set him at ease and establish who was the dominant force here. It didn't strike him as arrogant but more of a statement of fact. He decided to reserve judgement until later.

"I don't want to offend you," Connor said.

"No offense has been noted. I've been expecting this encounter for quite some time."

"You've been watching us?"

"Affirmative."

"For how long?"

"Perception of time is different for us, but to put it in terms you might understand, then it is safe to say we've observed your species since the beginning," Phantom said.

Connor frowned for a second. "Since the beginning of what?"

The pillar shimmered and seemed to collapse on itself, becoming a humanoid figure of shadow framed in lines of starlight. There were vague impressions of facial features that appeared impassive.

Phantom stepped toward him and gestured with a glowing hand. "Since we encountered your interstellar probe swarm. That is how you referred to them, yes?"

Connor nodded. The atmospheric readout on his HUD indicated that Phantom had a temperature of absolute zero. Yet, he was a being of some kind of energy.

"Yes, that's correct," Connor said finally.

Phantom gestured away from them. "Shall we walk? It is known to us that you prefer movement in times of stress."

Connor gritted his teeth a little, annoyed that Phantom seemed to know so much about him.

"Detecting an increase in body temperature commensurate with agitation," Phantom said and peered at Connor for a long moment. "You do not like that we've observed you."

It wasn't a question. Phantom's statement indicated that he was sharing his thoughts as they occurred.

"No, I don't like it. Some could call it an invasion of privacy."

"Privacy? Invasion? These are aggressive terms that can elicit an aggressive response. Is it your desire to do this?"

Connor's mouth opened a little. Then he shook his head as he considered his response. "You were watching us without our knowledge. Does this seem like appropriate behavior toward someone you haven't officially communicated with before?"

"Question is irrelevant."

Irrelevant? Was it a dismissal, or was it another statement of fact that he didn't understand?

"How is it irrelevant? Do you understand how privacy works?"

"Your behaviors change depending on the company of others

and their level of influence on the individual. I am familiar with the concept, both its advantages and limitations."

More than a few questions came to Connor's mind while he considered his response. Any of them could take this conversation off in several directions, so he considered his options.

"Is privacy something you experience?" Connor asked.

Phantom's head tilted to the side, looking pleased. "Intuitive inquiry. We have no privacy because we've moved beyond it. All are part. All are one."

"All are one? Are you an individual or many?"

"Yes," Phantom replied.

He should've expected that answer. "Okay, let's try it like this. I'm Connor Gates, a human being and a colonial citizen. First and foremost, I am Connor."

"We have individuality *and* are part of a whole. Your term for this is society."

"How do you know so much about us?"

"We've observed you."

Connor blew out a breath, inwardly telling himself to take it one step at a time. "How?"

"We deciphered the computing language that governed the interstellar probes and then observed the status of your species in your origin star system. Analysis of records in various archive systems, both partially and completely intact, indicates a rich history. However, archives were incomplete based on fragmented data. It left us with many questions. Eventually, we traveled to the New Earth star system." Phantom paused, anticipating a response.

Connor clamped his mouth shut. Sometimes the best answers came from someone willing to fill up the silence by speaking.

"The data repositories for your species were much more

complete there, but it led us to another anomaly—the species of Bhaneteran, a race called Ovarrow, whose historical records contain the barest fragments of a peculiar conflict with another species known as the Krake."

"How are you able to access our computer systems?"

"The information is accessible."

"Yes, but how do you access it?"

"By interfacing with your storage medium."

"How much data were you able to see?"

"All of it."

Connor blinked a few times and regarded Phantom. "All of it? Are you sure?" he asked, thinking about the secure data archives preserved in hardened security facilities.

"To a degree of accuracy with absolute certainty. If you wish, I can show you what we've discovered."

"Okay, show me," Connor replied.

Phantom gestured above and the dark sky flickered. A schematic representation of the New Earth star system appeared. They weren't true images, but a line drawing in three dimensions of the planets.

"This shows the arrival of the Ark and the subsequent beginnings of your colony," Phantom said.

The video focused on New Earth, showing an accurate depiction of the Ark orbiting the planet. Connor had seen this before. Every colonist had.

A series of images flashed across the sky, showing various stages of the colony as it was built and later expanded throughout the star system. The condensed colonial history was almost too much for him to watch. It was like being confronted with thousands of screens, each one demanding his attention to the finest detail, but it was too much for him to even consider.

"Stress levels rising. Cease data share."

The images disappeared.

"Updating preferences for future interactions," Phantom said.

"I'm fine," Connor said. "It's just a lot to take in."

"Perfectly understandable. There are limits to your physiology that you haven't overcome yet."

There it was again, another comment about their limitations, and yet it was just a statement of fact. Sometimes, things were said to observe the reaction of the other person, and Connor wondered if that was happening here.

"Okay, you've proven that authorization isn't an obstacle for you. Some of that data is confidential. How did you access it?"

"As I've previously stated, we accessed your data on the storage mediums themselves and not through the framework your species has created as a means of interacting with it. You might consider this a bypass of your security measures, but that would be incorrect since we never touched those measures. They were irrelevant to us."

"I understand. Why bother with security when you can just access whatever you want? Doesn't explain how you do it, though."

Phantom was silent for a long moment. "You're limited in how you interact with the surrounding space. You move *in* space, instead of moving *through* it."

Connor felt like he was spinning around in circles. "That doesn't make any sense," he said and paused. "You directly access our data storage and do what, then? Copy the data? Read it? How is it that we can't detect it?"

"A copy of the data is transferred to us for analysis. It's much quicker, so it's no surprise that you are unable to detect it."

"How fast?"

"Faster than your fastest ships can fly."

The Infinity drive allowed them to travel hundreds of kilometers faster than light. Could they really access data faster than that? Connor considered asking Phantom to prove it but decided not to.

"Where am I?"

"A meeting place created for us," Phantom said, gesturing toward Connor and then at himself.

"Why?"

"You've suspected our presence and you're at a crossroads. Our meeting was inevitable."

"What do you mean, we're at a crossroads?"

The edges of Phantoms' lips lifted. "You're very deliberate with your questions. Careful not to go too far; otherwise, it might influence my response."

"Yours is not the first species I've had first contact with."

"You speak truth. You have an abundance of influence with your species. It has been observed for some time by your own records."

Connor didn't respond right away. He had a feeling that this entire encounter was more important than a mere conversation between two species. There was some kind of reckoning, a judgement, or a weighing. He just wasn't sure what he was being measured against. They already seemed to know so much. What else did they want to know?

"Is that why you brought me here?"

Phantoms' expression became blank. "Yes."

Connor glanced around, still uncertain where he was, but he needed to get back. He needed to help Ethan. He imagined the others would be searching for him.

"You could've spoken to me anytime. Why now? What is it you hope to learn from me?"

"Not just you, but I understand your question."

"Who are you?"

"We've already covered this."

"Fine, then *what* are you? Is this you?" Connor asked, gesturing toward the humanoid being of light. "Do you look like us?"

"No, we don't. This form is to set you at ease."

"Or to lull me into a false sense of confidence. I don't like being manipulated."

"That statement is accurate. Your records indicate as much."

Connor shook his head. "All right, that needs to stop. You've made it abundantly clear you've accessed all kinds of records and you know so much about me, but something must be lacking. Why else would you bring me here? So, tell me. What happens now?"

"Exposure of information you deem sensitive has made you agitated. This response was not unanticipated. I understand that complete transparency is perhaps a foreign concept to you."

Connor chuckled a little. "Not foreign, just invasive, and not the best means to make this interaction worthwhile."

He was becoming impatient and felt like he was being toyed with. The Krake had been supremely arrogant as well, but this was something different, something more, and unlike the Krake.

"As I've said before, you are at a crossroads."

"I heard you. Are you telling me that you can predict the future?"

A ripple of light cascaded from Phantom's forehead, almost as if there'd been some kind of disruption.

Connor arched an eyebrow. "Are you all knowing? If you can access any information system you want, then surely you must be all knowing. If that's the case, why are we even here? What could I possibly have to offer someone like you?"

"We are not all knowing. We exist. We do not see across

what you perceive as time. Therefore, we are not all knowing, but there is a purpose to this visit. Your visitation, as it were."

Finally, a different kind of response that wasn't packed with double meanings and ambiguity. "Where do you exist? What do you look like?"

"We exist right here. Our appearance can be whatever we choose to be."

"So, you don't have an appearance? You just mimic others?"

"Incorrect, but in your current state, it will be impossible for you to conceive our true form."

Connor looked away for a moment. "What if I don't believe you?"

"Since that is a hypothetical question, I would seek to dissuade you of that belief. However, your probing questions are noted."

"I guess I'll just have to take your word for it," Connor said and leveled his gaze at Phantom. "Was it your interference on the ship? Did you manipulate our internal sensors for critical systems?"

"Yes."

"Why?"

"We wanted to observe your response."

Connor gritted his teeth. "Lives were lost because of it. You delayed our ability to launch a rescue mission."

"That is incorrect. The attack on your people had already occurred. You were able to overcome the obstacles."

Connor exhaled forcefully through his nose. "Just wanted to see me in action? Didn't you access all our data? It's all there, the parts that we were able to record through two wars and other skirmishes. There is plenty there."

"We wanted to know if you were still capable of doing those

things, which led to the level of influence you exert among your species."

"I'm not here to amuse you. If this is all you want, then send me back."

"No."

Connor waited a few moments. Then he turned away from the Phantom and strode away. He'd only gone a short distance when his feet wouldn't move. He looked down at them, and they were stuck to the ground, rooted in small pools of light.

"You cannot leave," Phantom said.

"So, I'm a prisoner then? You brought me here to hold me captive?"

"Your agitation has increased."

"You think! My son is on that planet, and so are a lot of other people. They're outnumbered by the alien Vemus, so forgive me if I don't relish the thought of staying here and speaking with you."

The pool of light at his feet went out and he could move again. He stumbled a little and turned around.

"Your request for forgiveness has been noted."

Connor frowned. It had been a figure of speech, but he didn't see the point of alerting Phantom to that.

"What are you? Are you able to explain to me what you are in terms I can understand?"

Phantom walked toward him. "I am a construct designed for species interaction."

His eyebrows squeezed together. "So, you're a machine?"

"Not as you know them," Phantom said and paused for a moment. "You use personal communication devices. Does that mean the person you're speaking with through a comlink is a machine?"

Connor cleared his throat. "No, I suppose not. So, you're a communication…agent?"

He'd almost said "device" but that was too simplistic.

"That description is acceptable. Now that you understand, we can finally begin this interaction in earnest."

Connor frowned. "Haven't we already started?"

"That was merely introductions."

As fascinating as this was, he knew things were happening on the planet, and he had to get back to the others. He needed to help Ethan, but how could he escape? He glanced around. Was he even still on the planet? Phantom had said this was a meeting place created for their interaction. He shook his head.

Connor sighed, resigned to the fact that he couldn't leave. "What do you want with me? And don't repeat that bit about being at a crossroads. It doesn't explain anything."

"On the contrary, it explains everything. However, to facilitate a harmonious exchange, I will simplify it even further. I'm here to present you with a choice—a choice that you must make before we can go any further."

Connor pressed his lips together in thought for a second. "What kind of choice?" he asked and shook his head. "I'm not authorized to make concessions on behalf of our leadership."

"Irrelevant. You're here, and they are not. A choice must be made."

Connor swallowed hard. Although Phantom's tone was even, it carried a weight that dragged at him. He stared at Phantom for a long moment, feeling unprepared, but in battle you leaned on experience and, to a certain extent, luck. He hoped he was lucky today, but if not, then so be it.

"Okay, tell me about this choice."

## CHAPTER 26

Captain Hank Carver glanced at the video feed of the recon drone they'd left behind to monitor the area where Connor had disappeared. Deacon and Cole had insisted on staying behind, hoping Connor would return, but he'd denied their request. They weren't happy about it, but they couldn't countermand his orders. An overwhelming attack force would make short work of two soldiers who insisted on trying to make sense of what was incomprehensible to them.

A recon drone hovered in a slow spin above the area where Connor had disappeared, set to alert them if Connor returned or the alien Vemus were detected.

Carver had always been an on-point kind of soldier and sometimes logical to a fault, and he didn't often encounter anything that defied that logic. There was an explanation for Connor's disappearance, even if he couldn't figure out what it was. Despite what others thought, Connor hadn't sneaked away from them. It made little sense. Why would he sneak away to follow Ethan when they were already tracking Ethan? This made him believe that, somehow, someone had abducted Connor, and that thought had become a certainty in his mind. But, again, what could he do about it? There were no clues for him to piece together. One moment, Connor was there, and the next, he was gone. Carver never liked mysteries, preferring rational explanations for things. However, leaving the area where Connor had disappeared felt much like abandoning his post. It went against his nature.

Exhaling softly, Carver dismissed the video feed. He'd receive an alert if something was detected or if Connor suddenly reappeared. His report of Connor's disappearance had been sent back to the ship. He'd hoped that Major Arvad would re-task the other platoons to back them up in their search for Connor, but he hadn't. He was sticking to the plan that both he and Connor had come up with. Arvad had told him to use the recon drones to find Connor, but the priority was to rescue the missing team. Carver knew it was the right call, but he still hated it, just like this entire place. Everything about it felt wrong, and if they stayed here too long, they were going to die. He'd made himself a grim promise that he'd take down as many of the alien Vemus as possible if it was time for him to leave the living.

The CDF platoon left the cavern behind, following the tunnel Ethan had gone down earlier.

"I wonder how he picks a direction," Deacon said.

"He's sensing the alien Vemus," Carver replied.

"Yeah, but what exactly, and why can't we detect it?"

The clatter of falling pebbles sounded from up ahead, and they slowed down. Deep under the ground, the temperature was warmer than it had been closer to the surface. There was still plenty of ice and mud with some rock mixed in, but the tunnels had more of an artificial look to them. Despite not finding any construction equipment, the tunnels looked as if they'd been bored out with large machines.

The farther they went, the more cautious they became. They'd sent recon drones ahead, but some of the connecting tunnels went on for a long way. They didn't have time to map it all out. Ethan was following the alien ship, or at least they thought it was a ship. Carver was beginning to think it was a connecting structure or some kind of docking place for a ship, but he was at a loss as to why there were so many tunnels. There should've been a purpose to them.

As quietly as possible, the CDF soldiers kept going.

"Looks like he's unsure again," Deacon said.

Carver brought up the video feed of the recon drone that monitored Ethan. They were catching up to him.

"Let's close the distance," Carver said, and the platoon began moving faster.

---

Ethan came to a stop near the structure, and his mind registered that it had been built by the alien Vemus. His connection to Cynergy was becoming stronger, but it was changing. *She* was changing, and so were the others. He could barely sense them through Cynergy. He detected their subsonic rhythms, but they were being drowned out by the alien Vemus.

Ethan knew he was in danger of his hybrid nature creating irrevocable changes to his physiology. The thought was there, but he knew he couldn't do anything about it because so much was unclear to him. He held on to his connection with Cynergy, which was part of him, but he also recalled his father trying to communicate with him. Those memories were like a disjointed dream whose meaning remained on the fringes of his thoughts.

The alien Vemus were beginning to make sense to him, and he knew their behavior had purpose. He also knew he should be afraid of becoming too familiar with them because it meant that the alien Vemus were affecting him somehow and he couldn't retreat from it, not when he was so close to finding Cynergy and the truth about the Vemus. He'd sensed some commonalities ever since that first encounter. There must be another Vemus probe here—the catalyst for everything that had happened on this planet. They were building a ship, and even in his current state, he could guess as to why they needed to build it.

He stood before an opening in the ship. The metallic walls had ribbons of ice building up where water ran down. He could sense the alien Vemus. They were somehow tied to the ship, almost like there was a melding between the two that he couldn't understand.

Beyond the opening was a dimly lit corridor. He knew he was drawing closer to the alien Vemus. There must be an alpha in there. He recalled his experience with the Vemus probe on Earth and the powerful compulsion it had had on him and the other hybrids. Cynergy had resisted it then, but now he could feel her slipping away.

Ethan stepped into the corridor and placed his hand on the wall. It was cold, but he also felt a slight surge of energy from it as his perception of the area expanded down the corridor. It felt like he was plugged into a ship's computer system, except his connection wasn't limited to data communications. It was as if the entire ship was a huge sensor or communication hub. It drew him in, immersing him in so many ways he couldn't understand that it was overwhelming. Ethan focused his attention on the others, using them to anchor his mind, but he was still adrift in a vast ocean of data. Among it all was a pulse of recognition. It sent shockwaves through him, and he jerked his hand away from the wall.

He clutched his fist to his chest and felt a momentary urge to gasp but quickly asserted control over himself. He didn't need to breathe right then, even though doing so would allow him to produce more hemoglobin in his blood, which helped him maintain oxygen. He had to remember to breathe but knew he couldn't breathe on this planet. The atmosphere was toxic. If he somehow reverted from his hybrid form, the frigid temperatures would make quick work of his frail human structure.

Ethan stared at his hand, remembering what he'd felt. Cynergy was there, as were the others. They were being held prisoner by the alien Vemus, who were trying to understand what the hybrids were, as if they couldn't decide whether they were enemies or comrades to be embraced. The process was absorbing the prisoners into a collective as part of the protocols that must be from the Vemus probe that had come to this planet.

He set off at a run. They weren't far, but he was running out of time.

# CHAPTER 27

Phantom regarded Connor for a few moments, and he wondered what the alien was pondering.

"A choice. You were going to tell me about a choice," Connor said.

"I haven't forgotten. It would be impossible for me to do so," Phantom said. "Your species has faced many choices during its existence. I am reconciling the archival knowledge of your species with recent data gathered."

"It's simple. Our species was almost exterminated twice. Those kinds of things tend to have an impact on how we behave."

"Indeed, it does. Your sacrifices have led to greater wisdom, seldom observed in rising species. We're interested in you for a number of reasons."

"Such as?"

"Numerous anomalies detected on the planet you call New Earth and in the star system itself," Phantom said.

Connor could take a really good guess as to what Phantom

was implying, but he wasn't going to volunteer any information. "Okay."

"You've gone beyond the confines of the universe, and yet you still traverse *in* space instead of *through* it."

Connor frowned. This wasn't the first time this had been mentioned. "I don't understand what you mean by that."

"Interesting and perplexing at the same time, but I must move on."

"Wait!"

"You've traveled beyond this universe," Phantom continued, ignoring him. "There is evidence of it in the form of scars."

Phantom was referring to the space gates and their use during the Krake War. Connor had been unaware of any scarring. Their most advanced sensors hadn't detected it, and he wondered how *they* could.

"Yes, we've done it, but the technology wasn't ours."

"As your archives indicate, but you've limited its use. Why?"

"We have," Connor said, not seeing the point in denying it. "The Krake are gone. We only use the Space Gates in a limited capacity to ensure they won't return."

Phantom looked away from Connor for a few moments. "But why limit its use?"

"Because we don't need it anymore, and we don't fully understand the implications of its long-term use. We used it because it was necessary, but that time has passed. Sometimes it's better that certain doors remain closed."

"Does fear drive this?"

Connor shook his head at first, denying it, but then reconsidered and nodded. "The technology led to the annihilation of so many Ovarrow, and the Krake's understanding of it was limited. We are rightfully cautious as to whether we use it. The Krake sought to use it to understand why their existence was limited to their own universe. It consumed them. We decided that there was too much temptation associated with continued exploration of alternate universes. That was agreed upon with the Ovarrow we encountered on other worlds, and the use of the technology is limited to monitoring for a resurgence in Krake activity."

"But you could use this technology elsewhere."

Connor frowned, feeling like he was being tested. "The risks far outweigh the potential for reward. As you've already stated, there are consequences for its use. We're not aware of any scarring, which further emphasizes that the decision to limit and eventually abandon the use of the Space Gates is the right decision." He paused for a moment, glancing at the clock on his internal HUD. Too much time had passed. Carver and the others must've moved on by now, and who knew where Ethan was. "Is this all you want to know about? I want to go back. I *need* to go back."

"We'll get to that," Phantom said and turned away from him, as if he was pondering his next question.

Connor looked around, trying to find a way to leave. He'd tried before and Phantom had stopped him. Maybe if he—

"Why do you build alliances between species?" Phantom asked.

Connor blinked in surprise. "You want an alliance with us?"

"No."

"Why are you asking me all these questions? What's the point of this? I don't have time to get into a philosophical discussion. Did you really bring me here to ask me why we build alliances between species? Isn't it easy to figure out? You have access to all our data, don't you? Don't we build alliances among ourselves? The reason is simple. It has to do with a common morality and mutual cooperation, so we not only survive but we thrive."

"Yes, we've seen this in other species, but your species is so young. It's rare enough that a species survives long enough to explore the galaxy, and yet your species has done so and gone beyond. We've observed your efforts to assist those of your species who reside on the planet of your origin. Your efforts to build harmony have not gone unnoticed. You've inspired the Ovarrow to abandon their flawed practices and join you."

"That wasn't an easy or seamless effort. There are still challenges for us and for them."

"Change on such a vast scale is seldom easy. You work toward harmonious prosperity built on common morality. We've seen these practices crumble from unrelenting extremes disguised as tolerance of practices and behaviors considered to be at odds with a moral code. We've observed that in your archives as well. We've seen species who espouse anarchy in these extremes, using them as a means to enslave. Those civilizations are of a consuming nature, dangerous to others for a time, but ultimately they are doomed. The human species has struggled with this—these illogical pursuits that lead to destruction. You're attempting to build a union that will allow other species to join. We wonder how this union will survive when you encounter a species with superior intellect and technological base."

"We already have encountered species with those qualities. We're still here, and they aren't."

"Through clever tactics and the fact that the superior species in question didn't know where to find us, nor did they view us as a credible threat to their existence."

Connor frowned. "You're quoting me?"

"It was part of your assessment delivered to the Colonial Security Council. It's admirable that you seek to create a union that invites others to be part of it, but how will you handle the illogical pursuits of destructive philosophies?"

"The same way we do now, by discussing the problem."

"And if a consensus cannot be reached?"

"Then they would be invited to leave."

"And if they won't?"

Connor regarded Phantom for a moment, sensing another philosophical trap. "I've been down these philosophically uncharted territories before. There are many variables to consider, making even a high-level discussion like this appear anything like realistic. I think you want to know whether we'll use force to establish order. The answer to that is yes. However, a peaceful resolution or a breaking of the union would be better than open war."

Phantom seemed to consider this for a few moments. "We would like to see your species thrive."

"Does that mean you'll help us?"

Phantom was quiet, and the silence stretched between them. "As I've said before, only a few species survive to attempt what you've done. Divisions are inevitable. Morality is questioned and reaffirmed. You've admitted that use of force is not outside the realm of possibilities, but its use affects everyone. We've seen this cause unions to eventually disappear."

Connor shook his head. "The galaxy is a big place, and as you've pointed out, we have the ability to explore it."

"And we arrive at the root of the problem. You seek the Vemus."

Connor's gaze narrowed. "What do you know about them?"

"That you should abandon searching for them. Rebuild your civilization. Take your current technological base and expand it beyond what you believe to be possible."

"Sounds good. Why don't you let me get on with it then?"

"Because you are at a crossroads, and the decision you make now will have the greatest impact on your species' ability to survive."

Phantom's statement of fact seemed to penetrate Connor's mind, making him wonder what his motivations were. He was so certain of what he was saying.

"You are a protector, but your son is a seeker of knowledge. He pursues the Vemus because he's been touched by them."

"What's wrong with that?"

"The Vemus are beyond you."

"How?"

"There isn't enough time for me to explain it to you, but if you pursue the Vemus, you will be consumed."

"How do you know this?"

"We've seen it before."

"Why don't you do something about it then?"

"The Vemus don't affect us. We are apart from this and from you," Phantom said, gesturing around them.

"Okay, put yourself in our position. What should we do?"

"You should use your weapons to destroy this place and abandon your exploration efforts for a time. You've explored enough star systems that you could expand and thrive. Give yourself time to rebuild."

Connor regarded Phantom for a few moments. "Do you know where the Vemus are? The source of the probes being sent out?"

"It is beyond you."

It was the second time Phantom had said it, and part of him rebelled against it. It was just in his nature. "Yeah, but are they beyond you?"

"That question is irrelevant—"

"It is entirely relevant," Connor said, cutting him off. "You want us to destroy this place and stop exploring. I asked if the Vemus were beyond your abilities to stop, and you keep putting me off. Why won't you answer the question?"

"We don't seek to stop the Vemus."

Connor backed away from Phantom, biting back a snarl. "I think we're done here."

"You're not in a position to end this visitation."

Connor clenched his teeth and tightened his grip on his rifle. "If you want this place destroyed, why don't *you* do it? You could take control of our ship and fire our weapons, so why don't you?"

"It is not for us to do. We are travelers moving through the cosmos."

"Oh, so you just show up, shake things up a bit, and then leave? What aren't you telling me?"

"You're aware of the ship on the planet, yes?"

He must be referring to the alien Vemus structure that they thought was one massive ship. "Yes, we're aware of it."

"It was built by the Vemus here by following the instructions of their probe. Your exploration of this planet has started something that will begin a cascade of events, but you have this opportunity to prevent it by destroying this place."

Connor just wanted to get out of there. Speaking to Phantom was almost pointless. "As soon as we rescue our people, we'll leave and destroy this place." He wasn't sure he'd give the order to destroy what they'd found, but he wanted to get their people off the planet.

"That will not work. Even now, your son has made his way to the alpha. Like the others, he will be absorbed into the collective. Then, knowledge of your species will pass to the Vemus. They'll attack your ship and later your entire species."

"I already said we would destroy it."

"Then do so now. Open a comlink to your ship and order the attack."

Connor's eyes widened. Phantom wanted him to order the attack now while everyone was still on the planet. "No." He shook his head. "Not with our people on the planet."

Phantom leaned toward him. "Sacrifice is required. I know you're familiar with this concept."

"My son is there, so is his wife, and so are a lot of other people. I'm not going to order the attack that will kill them."

"What if I told you that your son will no longer be recognizable to you?"

"Doesn't matter. You've read all our records, and you supposedly know everything about me, so you should know that I will never abandon my son. Not for anything, and certainly not for you!"

"But this small sacrifice will give you a thousand years. A small price to pay for what will affect billions of lives that would come of this future."

Connor drew himself up, shoulders stiff and muscles tightening. "A small sacrifice, you say, the cost of which is unacceptable."

"But to those—"

"They aren't here! Future generations are not here. But the people on that planet are here now and don't want to die. I will not execute them for you."

"Not for us. I've already told you we exist in a place beyond you."

"So you've said. Good for you," Connor replied, not hiding the contempt he had for Phantom. "I've encountered species who were so sure of their superiority that they underestimated us. You told me that the Vemus are beyond us, but you won't help us. If you won't help us, then get out of the way and we'll forge our own path. At the end of the day, what do you really care? The Vemus aren't a threat to you."

"This is a mistake."

"Not from where I'm standing," Connor said.

He turned and strode away from Phantom. The ground began to glow under his feet, and Connor leaped into the air. Combat suit thrusters pushed him upward for a few seconds until he slowed down, but an unseen force took hold of him and pushed him back toward the ground where Phantom waited.

Phantom reached toward him, almost imploringly.

Connor's feet touched the ground, and he pointed his weapon at the alien. "This has gone on long enough."

He didn't think his weapon could hurt Phantom, but it was all he had.

The ground became dark and the tiny bits of light beneath it suddenly disappeared.

"You hold the future of everything in your hands, but what would others do if offered the same choice?"

"They're not here. You chose me."

"Perhaps I will seek them out."

Connor fired his weapon, and darts made from their strongest metallic alloys slammed into Phantom. Bits of shadow and light burst behind him, and Phantom staggered back. Connor moved forward, firing his weapon, and the construct that had been Phantom formed a pool of shadow and light on the ground.

"Let me go!" Connor shouted.

He stopped firing his weapon and backed away from the pool, expecting some kind of retaliation. He thought Phantom would reform, but the pool of light expanded on the ground.

Connor jerked around and ran away from it. Soon, the light

came from all around him and went overhead, showing the dome he'd suspected had been there earlier, and it overtook him.

The ground disappeared beneath his feet, and he just sank. There was a flash of light, and then he was in an abyss. He spotted something far beneath his feet, and he was falling toward it, fast. Several pools showing something like a video feed that were over two meters across. Connor peered at them and saw the bridge of the *Challenger*. Major Arvad sat in the command chair, and he was speaking to someone else. Another pool showed the cavern he'd been in when Phantom had taken him. It was overrun by alien Vemus.

Connor turned toward another pool, which showed CDF soldiers taking cover and battling the alien Vemus. There was a flash of light, and for a second Connor saw Phantom standing among the soldiers. They acted as if they were unaware of him.

Connor hovered in the air, but it didn't feel like he was dangling. If he leaned to the right, he moved in that direction. Another pool appeared a short distance away, and Connor moved toward it. His suit jets helped to steady him in the low-gravity environment.

The pool was dark, and Connor peered at its depths. This had to be the one he wanted, the way to Ethan. Sounds of weapons fire came from the other pool, and flashes of light brightened the area around it for a few seconds. Silence followed, and then more weapons fire. The soldiers were fighting for their lives, and Connor felt a longing to join them. But something inside him hesitated, and he swung toward the dark pool where a scene slowly came into focus. It was another cavern, and something immense was in the middle of it. It was a swirling mass, with tentacles as thick as a combat shuttle coming out of it in a dense web of flesh and darkness.

It had to be the alien Vemus alpha. The Vemus functioned

like an intelligent hive. Even though human scientists had modified the Vemus pathogen, it still retained the foundational instructions that compelled the Vemus to spread and create an alpha. Like Old Earth, the aliens of this world had lost their fight with the Vemus. There were none of them left, only the alpha and its minions, and since the alpha was there, Ethan and the others must also be there. That meant that this was where he needed to go.

More sounds of fighting erupted from the other pool, and Connor glanced at it. The pool in the distance that had shown the *Challenger*'s bridge was also there. He could hear Major Arvad giving orders as they helped coordinate the away team.

Connor gritted his teeth as he remained on the brink. Pieces of the conversation with Phantom kept repeating in his mind, like a warning and a dark promise. What if Phantom was right? What if this was his chance to give humanity a chance to thrive? Connor frowned as he considered it. Had Phantom given him any reason to trust him? He pondered that for a few moments. Phantom had shown him that he knew about New Earth and their history, but knowledge didn't mean he should trust him.

More weapons fired, and the sound of it made him wince. Was he wrong? Even though he couldn't decide whether to trust Phantom, or whoever was controlling the construct, he still had a decision to make. It seemed that all the paths were open to him. He doubted that Phantom would make these avenues available to him if they weren't routes he could take, each with implications that might affect not only his future but everyone's future.

Why would they do this? Was it to torture him?

He shook his head. They wanted to learn about him. What would he do? For some reason, they'd put the choice in his hands. They could've taken control of this entire situation, at least it appeared to be that way, but Connor wasn't so sure.

Phantom had expressed reluctance to do that, but was it reluctance, or was it that they couldn't do anything like that? They were observers but had chosen to intervene.

A sudden realization blazed in his mind, and his eyes widened. He clenched his teeth and inhaled a deep breath. Three choices, three outcomes, three groups who needed his help, but only one stood out far above all the rest.

Connor gripped his rifle and plunged toward the pool.

He'd made his choice, and he'd live with it. Everyone else could question it later, but there was only one choice he *could* make.

# CHAPTER 28

Connor hit the pool and then everything sped up. One moment he was somewhere else, and the next he was hurtling toward the ground of the cavern where the Alpha sat in the distance.

He angled forward and the suit jets spun him around, bringing his feet under him. With a final burst of energy slowing his descent, Connor hit the ground and stumbled, getting his feet under him.

Multiple comlinks hit his combat suit simultaneously. He spun around, having trouble getting his bearings. Each movement seemed slow, as if he was waking up from a deep sleep. Connor shook his head and blew out several breaths, trying to get his bearings.

The cavern was a wide expanse, and covered metallic channels led straight toward the dark mass at the center. Mists gathered overhead, blocking Connor's view of the top of the cavern. Tracks of light appeared beyond the mist, soft, as if there wasn't enough power to pierce the fog. A breeze blew in from overhead, scattering the fog and revealing wide-open cracks that the sunlight tried to penetrate. Then the fog returned, blocking it. He wasn't in a cavern at all; it was a large crater.

He looked around, seeing that the vast impact site was encased in an icy sheath that had made it appear like a cavern. Was this where the Vemus probe had come from? Had it crashed here, or had it been brought here? Taking the state of the entire planet into consideration left him with the opinion that Old Earth and humanity had prevented an even worse fate than the one this planet had suffered. He'd seen the aftermath and all the destruction. The cost was insurmountable—Old Earth had survivors, whereas this planet had none.

He brought up his holoscreen and searched for Ethan's locator. A new waypoint became active. Ethan wasn't far, but he was toward the Alpha.

He had to run. If the Alpha hadn't detected his presence, an alien Vemus scout would at any moment. The ground sloped toward the center, and he slipped a little on the frozen terrain. He saw more of the metallic structure, which seemed to fill the area, and the sight of it pulled memories from his mind—dark memories of an NA Alliance warship encased in Vemus exoskeletal material and the remnant forces fighting to take them. Memories of close friends who had died were coaxed from his mind, and Connor's throat thickened. He couldn't let it distract him, and he tried to ignore them—ignore the dead so he could focus on the living. His son was down there, along with the others fighting for their lives, but old memories brought old wounds that stirred in his mind.

Connor pushed forward, running quicker than he ought to, knowing that the Alpha would be protected. It had to be.

He thought he saw something move in the fog as it thinned in certain areas and gathered in others. He ran down a narrow path between two metallic shafts, appearing much like the giant tentacles leading to the Alpha.

A screeching bellow sounded from nearby, startling him. He began to stumble, but his combat suit computer helped steady him, keeping him on his feet.

An alien Vemus scrambled atop the shafts, moving like an agile spider committed to pouncing on its prey. A dome-shaped head jutted toward him, and a wide mouth opened, revealing large, cruel teeth that were stained gray. Connor stared at it, unable to take his eyes off the creature. Powerful arms and legs propelled the beast toward him, assisted by thick tentacles in a swirling mass of death. Its head locked onto him, and even though Connor couldn't see the creature's eyes, it somehow tracked him. It was almost twice his size and was gaining on him.

Connor leaped into the air, twisting as he brought up his rifle and fired. High-density slugs pelted the alien Vemus, causing it to stumble. Combat suit jets kept Connor aloft longer than the creature expected, and it scrambled to reach him.

Connor switched his ammunition configuration to incendiary, and high-heat darts blazed a path of red, striking the alien Vemus right below the neckline. It screeched in pain that became a shallow groan.

Connor hit the side of a shaft and bounced off it as he crashed. Tumbling to the ground, he felt something grab him, tossing him against the wall as if he didn't weigh anything.

A warning flashed on his HUD, and his combat suit computer drew his attention to the alien Vemus. Connor staggered to his feet and fired his weapon in a multi-round burst.

The alien Vemus moved at blinding speeds that he had trouble tracking, even with his combat suit helping him. The creature scrambled up the shaft and launched its body overhead, barreling toward him. Connor dove away, barely clearing the creature before it pounced. Seeing an opening, he fired his weapon at its back, and the creature cried out in excruciating pain.

Finally!

The creature jerked away, its limbs and tentacles flailing.

Connor swung his weapon back, aiming for the area where the alien Vemus was on its back that he'd hit before. It was a weakness. It had hurt it, and now he was going to hurt it some more. Gritting his teeth, he chased the fleeing creature. Several of its tentacles dragged behind it. Connor leaped into the air, firing his weapon at the creature's back in a spray of ammunition.

The alien Vemus howled in pain and collapsed as if its limbs had been cut off. Several of the tentacles dragged its body forward, but slowly stopped moving.

Connor landed on the ground near it, keeping his weapon pointed at the alien Vemus in case it was trying to lure him closer. But he didn't need to take a closer look. If these were anything like what he'd fought before, the creature wasn't dead. It would recover, but he had to reach the others.

Connor leaped atop the metallic shaft and slipped toward the edge. On the other side was a steep drop-off of about forty meters. He quickly backed away from the edge and ran toward the waypoint. Once he felt safe enough to drop down to the ground, he did and continued running.

A comlink from Carver appeared on his HUD, and Connor acknowledged it.

"General Gates! We're making our way to you. We've made contact with the enemy. Have you found him yet?"

Connor appreciated the fact that Captain Hank Carver knew when to get down to business rather than ask questions that could wait until later.

"I'm almost to them."

A few moments of silence passed.

"We lost you, sir."

"I know, Hank. It wasn't planned, but I'm back…" Connor's voice trailed off as he reached the waypoint.

The metallic shaft rose away from the ground as it continued to slope. Underneath it was an exoskeletal mound the size of a combat shuttle. It looked as if it had grown out of the ground, and the top of it was attached to the metallic shaft above. Exoskeletal materials merged with the metallic shaft as if they were the same. At the bottom of the mound were partially formed pods with roots attached to the missing survey team. It penetrated their EVA suits, and Connor spotted some of it in their helmets. He circled around the mound as painful memories attempted to crush his resolve. He tried to blink them away, but he kept seeing the strained look on his old friend Will Reisman's face as the Vemus exoskeletal material penetrated his combat suit, forcing him to become one of them.

He groaned in disgust, and his heart thundered in his chest.

"General Gates, what is it?" Carver asked.

"No, no, no," Connor said as he circled the mound and stopped.

Ethan knelt in front of Cynergy. Both his hands disappeared among the pod's tentacles that surrounded her shoulders. They'd also snaked around his arms, and several surrounded his middle.

Connor couldn't recognize Cynergy. It was her EVA suit computer that identified her. The pod covered her helmet as if it were slowly consuming her. He glanced at the rest of the survey team, and they were in a similar state. They had all embraced their hybrid nature. Their skin was black, and the patchwork of their skin held a purplish hue even in the dim light.

Connor turned back to Ethan. The muscles of his back looked as if they were straining. His body composition had changed to the point where his son looked more humanoid than an actual person. His skin was thick and rubbery, but with the markings of a hybrid.

Connor leaned toward his son and Ethan's face was squinched together as if he were in pain. He wasn't breathing. Connor glanced at the time and almost two hours had passed since they'd arrived. This was the upper limit to even Ethan's ability to hold his breath.

Connor opened the storage compartment of his combat suit and withdrew an emergency breather apparatus. He placed it on Ethan's face, and it expanded to frame his face, sealing it in. A mixture of oxygen was made available. Connor silently urged his son to breathe. He needed to start breathing.

A few moments went by, and Ethan didn't move. Then, the muscles on his back expanded as Ethan sucked in a deep breath. Connor watched his son breathe several times, giving him a moment's relief.

"Ethan, can you hear me?"

He didn't respond. There was no indication at all that he heard him.

"General Gates, what's happening?" Carver asked again.

"I found them," Connor replied, trying to remove the tentacles from Ethan. They were tough and adhesive. "They're covered with something from the Alpha."

"Are they being absorbed?"

Connor glanced at the others. "I'm not sure. If they were, it should've happened by now. This has to be something else. I'm going to try to free them."

"Can you wait until we reach you? We're on our way to you. ETA ten minutes."

Connor ignored him and tore the thick tentacles off Ethan's middle. They kept getting tangled, even as he pulled them free of the pod. Becoming frustrated, Connor pulled out his combat knife and began slashing them around Ethan's hands.

Ethan cried out in pain, and Connor thought he'd accidentally cut into his hand, but he hadn't. Frowning, he pulled the tentacles away and saw that they were attached to each of Ethan's fingers, encompassing his whole hands. He jerked his hands away and felt bile creep up his throat.

He sheathed his knife and brought up his weapon with a snarl. He was about to shoot when the entire survey team began shuddering violently. The pods grew in size, and there was a dim glow inside each of them. Connor saw shadows move inside them as if something was alive. Then the metallic shaft began to glow with an ethereal light, and the other shafts began to glow, too. A cracking sound came from overhead and several frozen chunks of ice crashed to the ground.

Connor looked up and saw large groups of alien Vemus climbing along the ceiling. Then they dropped to the ground. He brought up his weapon and began firing.

"They're here!" Connor said.

"We're minutes away. Can you hold out?"

Connor gritted his teeth and fired his weapon at the enemy, but there were too many of them. They landed on the ground and ran toward him, bellowing.

Connor leaped atop the mound, seeking higher ground. He'd make his stand there. That lasted all of a second and a half when his feet began sinking into the mound. It was trying to absorb him. Connor jumped up and was barely able to free himself.

Cursing, he looked for another vantage point, but they all took him away from the survey team. Muttering a curse, he went to stand behind Ethan and changed the configuration of his ammunition to use a larger and heavier round. He'd deplete his ammunition faster, but at least he'd gain more stopping power.

Connor moved several meters away from the others and cast a furtive glance at Ethan. Then, the horde of alien Vemus descended on him.

He'd been a soldier all his life, and there were just some things he excelled at to the detriment of his enemies. He brought up his weapon, waiting for the enemy to close in, and at the last moment, he leaped into the air, firing his weapon at the weak spots on their backs, sending them sprawling as the nerve endings connecting to their spines were severed.

His combat suit jets could keep him in the air for fifteen seconds before he'd need to come down to allow them to recycle. He made the best use of those precious seconds, and the bodies began to pile up beneath him. Maneuvering jets pushed him back, and the alien Vemus came toward him as if they were of one mind.

They wanted him gone, and an idea sprang to his mind. Connor leaped into the air again, his suit jets sending him in a long arc. The alien Vemus followed him, almost as if they didn't care what stood in their way. They exhibited similar behavior to the Vemus he'd encountered during the war, except those employed weapons. These Vemus were a step beyond a very dangerous predator.

He aimed his weapon at the Alpha and fired a few rounds in its direction. Though the Alpha was several hundred meters away, his attack sent the Vemus soldiers into a fury, as if he'd kicked the nest of the nastiest hornets in all creation.

Vemus soldiers came from all around, and they were of a singular purpose. They wanted to kill him.

Connor saw Ethan and the others in the distance. Exoskeletal material began covering Ethan again. Gritting his teeth, Connor ran back toward the others. Several Vemus fighters lunged toward him, and as he fired his weapon, several darts hit the metallic exoskeleton, making a loud clang that echoed throughout the cavern. A bright flash pulsed through the shaft, and Connor was suddenly knocked sideways.

He grunted as an alien Vemus grabbed his helmet. He shoved the business end of his rifle into the creature's middle, firing his weapon on full auto. It jerked back, screeching, but it wouldn't let go of him. He'd pushed off from the ground, dragging the alien Vemus with him, when another one grabbed his torso, slamming him to the ground.

The creature reared up, vicious-looking claws fully extended, ready to tear him to pieces. Suddenly, a barrage of weapons fire came from overhead, splitting the creature's head almost in two, and twin mag cannons from an attack drone unleashed its payload into the Vemus fighters.

Connor twisted out of the creature's grasp and scrambled toward his son.

Several CDF attack drones flew overhead, firing their mag cannons. The Vemus fighters focused their attention on the drones, giving Connor a few moments to breathe.

"General, I'm looking at the survey team," Carver said.

Connor looked around for them but couldn't find anyone. "Where are you?"

"En route. I have the video feed from the drones, and it doesn't look good. Sir, are you sure they can be rescued?"

Connor heard the implications in Carver's tone, but it wasn't something he wanted to admit.

He looked at his son's chest covered by the exoskeletal material. Snarling, Connor charged toward it, firing his weapon at its connective sections. Something let out a loud groan, as if coming from some unseen giant, but he couldn't tell where the source was.

"Sir, you have to get out of there."

"No, Captain. Get your people to safety, then have the ship obliterate this place," Connor replied.

The survey team, including Ethan, all convulsed as if there was an electric current going through their bodies.

"Sir!" Carver said. "General, I'm not leaving you behind."

"Go, Hank. That's an order."

"Shove it, General."

"I'm not leaving my son," Connor said. Even as he said it, he remembered the other son he'd left behind. He had fought and died because of the Vemus.

Not another one!

He fired his weapon at the exoskeletal material on full auto, and it tore huge swaths of it until his ammunition block was expended. Roaring, Connor drew his combat knife and slashed at it.

"Damn it, Ethan," he shouted as he cut through it, freeing one of his hands.

Ethan's hand sank to his side and became smaller, returning to its regular size, and Connor stared at it for a few seconds. Ethan's skin returned to normal for a few moments, but then it blackened and the hybrid markings reappeared.

A group of alien Vemus bellowed from nearby. Connor spun, rifle ready, until he realized it was empty. A dozen creatures ran toward him from atop the metallic shafts. Connor pulled out a grenade and threw it at the rushing Vemus.

The force of the explosion pushed him back and blew the creatures apart, scattering parts of their bodies.

More came. They leaped atop the shaft, hundreds of them, and they all charged toward him at once.

He'd only had the one grenade, and the only weapon he had left now was a combat knife. Running away wasn't an option. He would never abandon his son. An ache seized his heart as he thought of Lenora and then Lauren, along with the grandchild he'd never get to meet.

"Run, General!" Carver shouted.

"It's over," Connor said and hastened back to Ethan.

Connor reached out with an armored fist and sent the command for it to open, exposing his skin to the frigid temperatures. He reached out and grabbed Ethan's hand. It was cold, almost limp, as if he were dying.

Connor gritted his teeth. "I'm here, son. I'm not going to leave you."

Loud screeches pierced the air and seemed to crawl up his back, as if the alien Vemus were right behind him, and he heard their guttural pants as they careened toward him. He looked over his shoulder as hundreds of Vemus came for him. Too many. He wasn't going to survive this.

Connor lowered his gaze and turned back toward his son, waiting for death.

Several bright flashes come from overhead. A sizzling, hissing sound darted right past him, and he was momentarily blinded. Connor blinked several times and looked behind him. A grisly mess of the remains of Vemus bodies splattered the ground and both sides of the metallic shafts as a bright sphere darted away from them. Connor's eyes widened.

Overhead, several more specialized attack drones buzzed by, darting in different directions. They burned almost as hot as a main sequence star and were among the most destructive weapons in the CDF arsenal.

"Four attack drones in the air, General," Carver said between gasps. "Watch your head. They'll provide cover, but they can't distinguish you from the enemy."

Connor blew out a breath as the attack drones, burning with

a harsh yellow light, blazed overhead, the heat from which was affecting the mists, causing even them to retreat.

"Copy that," Connor replied. "Task one to attack the shafts."

He watched as one of the attack drones changed course and swooped toward the shafts. These attack drones could burn through every kind of armor, even the battle steel of a CDF warship. The only defense against them was powerful artificial gravitational fields, and the alien Vemus had none.

His son's hand twitched and suddenly became warm. Connor squeezed Ethan's hand, and an answering grip was returned.

Ethan was aware of him.

Connor watched as the skin of Ethan's hand and arm returned to its normal skin tone, but it stopped near his shoulder. He kept his grip on Ethan's hand, hoping it would somehow convey that he wasn't alone.

"Come back to me, Ethan," Connor whispered. "Free the rest of them and come back. You're stronger than they are. Fight it. You must fight it. I know you're still in there. Do what you've gotta do, so we can get the hell out of here."

## CHAPTER 29

Ethan's thoughts had become a river rushing over rocks, powerful and turbulent. The Alpha assessed them, as if it wasn't sure how to understand them. It was stuck between destroying them and making them part of its ever-expanding hive.

He'd found Cynergy and the others. He could sense them among millions of others who all served a singular purpose. Cynergy had sensed his presence, but she was weakening. Her response was sluggish, as were the others on the survey team.

He could feel the alien Vemus and the will of the Alpha as it doggedly carried on with its purpose. It was simple to decipher what it wanted—consume, build, and fulfill the instructions that were the cornerstone of its entire existence. The culmination was to return. The Alpha inquired of him if he had the information that was missing from it.

Ethan tried to ignore its pleadings and then demands as he sought to draw Cynergy back from it. The Alpha was trying to absorb the others, make them part of it so it could unlock what it needed to complete its cycle.

Several of the others were gone. There was nothing left of them. They were part of the Alpha, given a place in its order of operations. Vemus hybrids could sense each other, and Ethan tried to communicate with the lost, but there was no answer to his rallying cry. The first to respond to him was Cynergy. She resisted the Alpha and her connection to Ethan strengthened her resolve, but she was so tired. She all but begged that he let her go, but he would never do that. He distracted her by bringing their connection to the rest of the survey team to the forefront of their minds. Cynergy was loyal to her team and him directing her towards them brought forth a maternal instinct that was uniquely feminine. It came from nurturing, bonding, supporting, and love. But it wasn't enough. The Alpha was too strong. It was like a drop of water trying to resist a hurricane, so Ethan shifted his focus. He had to, because to do otherwise meant losing everything.

Ethan sought the Alpha. He opened himself up, taking in the subsonic waves unique to the alien Vemus, letting it draw him in, and part of him worried he was going too far. His own hybrid nature began to adapt, coming into alignment with the alien Vemus.

The Alpha wasn't an intelligence unto itself. It followed a set of instructions, much like the DNA of all living things has a set of instructions that, when followed, produced harmony. The Alpha sought harmony, and it regarded the world as disharmony. It was so much different from the Vemus he'd encountered in the Old Earth star system. They were starving husks, left behind, unable to completely die. The alien Vemus were different, vibrant, which made him wonder if this was how the Vemus had been at the beginning of their attack on Old Earth.

The Alpha sought materials to fulfill its task of building. They couldn't finish the ship, and it was compelling Ethan to help it. The Alpha had gleaned intelligence about humanity from the hybrids that had succumbed to it. Between that and the learnings from its hive-bearers, it knew that they had the resources necessary to complete its mission.

Ethan understood its mission. He felt his hybrid nature change as the information exchange occurred, and he found himself wanting to comply. Somewhere inside of his mind, he shouted a denial, but the voice was so small that he could ignore it. He understood why Cynergy and the others were so divided. They wanted to surrender and at the same time were resistant to the idea.

A jolt rushed through him, zapping his thoughts, waking him from near oblivion. He felt as if he'd snapped awake before he was ready, his mind desperately trying to make sense of everything around him. His hand felt like a frozen block. Numbness traveled up to his forearm where there was sharp pain.

Then a voice tugged at him. It sounded muffled but familiar, and he sought it out. The voice was insistent and carried with it an authority that he recognized. The frozen numbness retreated down his arm, and he heard his father whispering to him.

*I'm not going to leave you, Ethan. You must fight this.*

He had to fight. He had to resist the Alpha, but it had the answers, and he couldn't force it to reveal them to him. The origins of the Vemus were within his grasp. If only he could…

Cynergy's presence strengthened. He felt her resistance becoming stronger as she pulled back from the Alpha.

The Alpha wailed in pain, and its desperation increased as it sought to return to harmony. Somehow, the Alpha was dying. Ethan could detect its many wounds. Something burned it, severing it from the ship and its minions. Cut off, they would descend into oblivion, lifeless and purposeless. The knowledge of it sent out a wave of sadness from the Alpha.

It was dying.

Ethan felt its presence diminish and he searched for knowledge of the Vemus. What was the next step for it? Spread, grow, thrive, build, and then return? He had to know, but the Alpha was fading. Ethan demanded the knowledge, and something seemed to switch inside the Alpha.

Through the tentacles that connected them to the subsonic rhythm, it turned on Ethan, seeking to dominate, it's one last bid for what it perceived as harmony. Ethan fought it, retreating into his core, anchoring his mind in the thing that would shelter him from the onslaught.

Enemy. The Vemus in all forms were the enemy, but he could never escape them. They were part of him and all hybrids.

Ethan turned inward, focusing on his connection to Cynergy and the other hybrids. Their bond strengthened, forming a solid resistance to the Alpha. Their cooperative bond was stronger than its indomitable will. In the end, the hybrids had something the Alpha could never have. For all its power, it was a slave, and for all its adaptations and knowledge within, it had no choice but to follow the orders given to it. It had a singular purpose, but the hybrids were free.

The Alpha's hold on them fractured and then disintegrated into nothingness.

He was free.

They were free.

## CHAPTER 30

The CDF soldiers formed a perimeter around Connor and the hybrids trapped by the alien Vemus. The central structure that supported the Alpha had been destroyed by the attack drones. Fires burned throughout the cavern, and it was melting the ice. Chunks of ice continued to fall from the top of the crater, allowing more sunlight to come through.

Ethan started to rise, losing his balance a little, and Connor steadied him on his feet. The exoskeletal pods fell to the ground like lifeless husks, and the tentacles that surrounded the hybrids loosened, allowing them to escape.

Connor watched as Ethan swayed on his feet, looking lost. Cynergy collapsed to the ground and was followed by the other hybrids. The helmets of their EVA suits were damaged and leaking oxygen.

"Quick!" Connor yelled. "We need emergency breathers down here. Quickly, before they suffocate!"

Each combat suit had an emergency breather in the event that the suit was damaged or the occupant had to take it off.

Several soldiers collected their breathers and attached them to the surviving members of the survey team. After getting some much-needed oxygen, they sank to the ground, incoherent and barely responsive.

Ethan knelt by Cynergy's side, and took off his own breather, giving it to her. The breather quickly adjusted to her face. After a few moments, she tiredly looked up at him with relief.

Ethan smiled down at her, mouthing reassuring words to her.

Captain Carver tossed Connor a breather and he gave it to Ethan, who nodded his thanks and put it on.

Carver came over to Connor. "They stopped attacking once the Alpha was destroyed," he said, looking grimly pleased.

A massive fire burned several hundred meters away, consuming what was left of the Alpha. The attack drones circled above, bright and constant, waiting for targeting orders. The surviving alien Vemus fighters were in disarray and had scattered.

Connor surveyed the death and destruction. Thousands of alien Vemus had been killed in such a short amount of time, and the remains of them could be found throughout the crater. Their bodies had either been cut in half or were missing large portions that were impossible for even a Vemus to regenerate. He frowned, considering. Perhaps not impossible, but it would take them a long time.

"Without the Alpha, they don't know how to fight. They'll revert to a pre-alpha state," Connor said.

Carver heaved a long sigh. "I don't care what the reason is. I'm just glad they stopped." He glanced above them. "I think we can get a combat shuttle in here and start the evacuation."

Carver was right, they shouldn't stay there. There was no way to know if and when the remnant fighters would change their minds and attack them.

Connor looked at the mound. There were six people who hadn't made it. Their bodies were dark gray, as if the melanin in their skin had been leached out of them.

He looked at Ethan and gestured toward them. "Are they dead?"

Ethan nodded. "They were already dead when I got here. They held out as long as they could."

"How do you know what happened to them?"

"The others told me," Ethan said and paused for a moment. "They, uh, surrendered to the Alpha."

"Surrendered?"

Ethan frowned. "I'm trying to figure out the right way to say it. They couldn't resist any longer, but the Alpha wouldn't completely accept them. I'm sorry. I'm still trying to make sense of this myself."

Connor nodded grimly and looked at Carver. "We take them with us."

"Uh, wait," Ethan said, and Connor frowned. Ethan glanced at their fallen comrades for a second. "We need to take precautions. Quarantine protocols. They might be..." his voice trailed off for a moment. "We just need to be sure, okay?"

Connor regarded his son thoughtfully for a few seconds. "We'll take every precaution."

Ethan was worried. This experience had shaken him up, but he was alive. They'd figure out the rest later on.

"How did you free them?" Connor asked.

Ethan was about to reply when Cynergy sat up. She looked disoriented and confused.

"The Alpha, is it—" she began.

"It's dead," Ethan replied. "It's gone. We're going to be okay."

They stared into each other's eyes and something unspoken

passed between them. Some of it was relief, but Connor also saw concern and fear. What had it been like for them?

A combat shuttle discharged its weapons, and a huge chunk of ice broke away from the roof. It wasn't enough to extinguish the fires, but steam did rise from where the ice fell.

There was nowhere for the combat shuttle to land, so it hovered in the air. Sentinel attack drones flew nearby, and soldiers kept watch in case the alien Vemus fighters returned.

It took time for them to retrieve their dead. They'd been individually sealed in carriers designed for hauling bio containment.

Carver took charge of getting everyone else aboard the shuttle. Eventually, it was Connor's turn to board.

Carver arched an eyebrow. "Unless you want to stay, sir?"

Connor shook his head. "No thanks. I don't ever want to set foot here again."

Connor grabbed the tether from the shuttle, and it quickly hauled him up. Once he was aboard, he made his way toward Ethan and Cynergy. Both looked exhausted.

Ethan gave him a tired smile as Connor sat next to him. "I heard you, you know." He tipped his head to the side. "Down there."

Connor eyed him for a moment. He hadn't been sure, but he hoped Ethan had heard him.

Ethan swallowed hard, staring intently at Connor. "You pulled me from the brink. I don't know," he paused and glanced at Cynergy's sleeping form, "I don't know if I would've been able to save them otherwise."

Connor frowned. "The brink of what?" he asked quietly.

Ethan looked away. "I'm not sure. I'm still trying to make sense of it all."

"The Alpha?"

Ethan nodded a little. "It's more complicated than that. I was trying to figure out what it wanted. It's all chaotic. I'm just not sure."

"Take your time," Connor urged.

Ethan exhaled a long breath, fogging the breather for a second. "I can't seem to get my brain to focus on anything. I just need to be still."

"You're past exhaustion, Ethan. Just rest. We can sort it out later on."

The shuttle doors closed and the atmosphere cycled so they could remove helmets and breathers alike.

Ethan blinked a few times and rubbed tired eyes. Then he raised his gaze toward Connor. "Dad, I don't know what happened. I should. Part of being like us is that we need to understand how it works." He pressed his lips together for a second. "Being a hybrid, but something…" He shook his head.

All the hybrids had changed back into their regular human forms. That had to mean something. "We'll figure it out, Ethan. We'll figure it out. All of us."

Ethan slowly nodded. "Okay."

"Get some sleep."

Ethan leaned back, eyes closed, and Connor stood to walk toward the workstation near the cockpit.

Carver and Bentley were there together, speaking quietly.

Carver looked at Connor. "How is he?"

"He's out of it. Exhausted. Trying to make sense of what happened. How are the other teams?"

"The other shuttles report they've made their last extraction. All teams are accounted for."

"Casualties?" Connor asked.

Carver and Bentley shared a quick look. "Some, but not nearly as many as it could've been."

Connor looked at Bentley. "Can you get me a comlink to the ship?"

"Yes, sir," Bentley said.

A few moments later, Major Arvad was on the holoscreen. "I'm glad you made it, General Gates."

"Thanks," Connor replied. "Once the other shuttles are clear, I want that entire site vaporized. Authorization for the use of heavy weapons has been granted."

"Understood, General Gates," Arvad replied.

Connor severed the comlink.

"You're destroying the site?" Carver asked.

"Absolutely. I don't want to take any chances that something survived."

Carver frowned, looking toward the video feed on the nearby holoscreen.

"What's the matter?" Bentley asked.

"I just thought that maybe you'd want it studied more. Search for the Vemus probe," Carver said.

Connor shook his head, thinking about some of the things Phantom had said about the Vemus being beyond their abilities to deal with. "We've got all we're going to get from this place. It's nothing but a tomb."

Bentley blew out a breath, looking as if he'd just received a gift. "I'm so glad to hear you say that, sir. I was worried we'd have to go back down there, and honestly, I can't wait to get back to New Earth."

Carver chuckled tiredly, and then shrugged. "You'll get no argument from me."

Connor raised his eyebrows. "Is that right? All the insubordination is done now?"

Carver smiled. "You're alive, sir. That's my primary objective. I'll stand by my record."

Connor chuckled with a slight shake of his head. "You don't have to be so smug about it."

"Well, it doesn't happen that often. Rarely, even." Carver shrugged.

Bentley frowned. "What doesn't happen?" he asked, looking at each of them.

Carver leaned toward Bentley. "It's rare that our beloved General Gates makes a misstep."

Connor laughed. "Misstep my ass. You still commanded the platoon. You were just a pain about it."

"You mean referring to rules and regulations, sir?" Carver asked.

"Oh, you're really enjoying this. You know how it goes, though. Sometimes your next assignment is the one that gets you in the end."

Carver grinned. "General, I don't think you have any idea how many people warned me about this assignment."

"Did I live up to my reputation?"

Carver's expression became serious, some of the mirth leaving him. "Sir, I'd follow you right back down to that hellhole if you needed it done. But if I'd let you die down there, there would be hordes of people lined up to take a shot at yours truly. So honestly, I should be thanking you that you survived. Really, you've done me a huge favor."

Connor tipped his head to the side. "Until next time."

"So, you're not going to have me reassigned?"

"Not today, Captain."

"Excellent news, General Gates."

The shuttles flew to the ship, and Connor received confirmation that the site on the planet was an even bigger crater than what had been there before, deep enough to account for the vast tunnel network. He watched the video feed for a few minutes and then sighed.

He sat down, leaning back as best he could in a combat suit, and was soon asleep.

He'd learned long ago to grab a few winks when he could. Carver woke up as the shuttle was about to enter the secondary hangar bay.

"Back in quarantine," Carver said.

"Joy," Deacon replied dryly. "They'll probably have to reset the clock. We'll be here a few days." Connor eyed him and he shrugged. "It'll be downright cozy."

"Won't be that long, at least not for all of us," Connor said.

Deacon frowned. "Why is that, sir?"

"The *Reliant* was already en route here. Should be here in about a day. We'll transfer there after it arrives," Connor said and glanced at the hybrids. He noted that the people who'd been trapped by the Alpha were separate from the others. He wondered if they were avoiding them. "We won't be alone, either."

Carver and Deacon followed his gaze. His protective details, due to the nature of their work, often had an insider view of things that their military ranks would've prevented in ordinary circumstances.

"It's hard to tell if there will be any lasting effects from their exposure to the alien Vemus," Deacon said.

"I hope not, but until we know for sure, they will be watched," Connor said.

Carver cleared his throat. "Sir, what happened to you back there? You just disappeared without a trace. Then, somehow, you ended up ahead of us inside that crater."

"I had some help, and it wasn't planned," Connor said.

"What do we include in our mission reports? That you just disappeared?" Carver asked.

Connor nodded. "Report it exactly as you saw it. No need for secrecy. I'm still trying to piece it together myself."

Carver regarded him for a few moments, his gaze a little insistent.

"I had an encounter with the Phantoms," Connor said.

Carver blinked a few times, looking confused for a few seconds. "You mean the aliens that…" He stopped speaking. It was too crowded to discuss this in the shuttle.

"Yes," Connor said.

"They picked a heck of a time to make contact."

According to Phantom, they'd done quite a bit of watching them on this entire mission, but he wasn't going to share that with Carver and Deacon. "Yeah, you could say that again."

He could tell that both Carver and Deacon had more questions but were experienced enough not to ask, trusting that Connor would keep them informed.

Connor felt weariness seeping into his bones. He needed real sleep and a hot meal. He hadn't realized how hungry he was and couldn't remember the last time he'd eaten anything.

The shuttle entered the hangar, and they began decontamination protocols all over again. They'd have to go through all isolation protocols, medical exams, and the whole bit, but Connor didn't mind it so much. At least this time they hadn't left anyone behind. It had cost lives to rescue the others, but that was part of the risks of doing what they did. However, that truth didn't make the cost any easier to bear.

Over the next few hours, they went through decontamination protocols and medical examinations, and had gotten a meal. Then many of them slept. The hybrids that had been affected by Ethan were completely normal now. Mission debrief would come, but what many doctors had told Connor over the years was that rest was the best medicine.

# CHAPTER 31

Twelve hours later and way more refreshed, Connor met with both Doctor Charlie Harris and Doctor Cassie Williams. They looked tired around the eyes, and a few yawns were barely stifled.

Dr. Williams glanced at Connor's hand. "How's it doing?"

"It's fine now. The stinging aches are gone," he replied.

Exposing his hand to a frigid and harsh alien atmosphere had damaged the skin on the back of his hand. When he'd released Ethan's hand, his combat suit had administered medical treatment that protected him until he returned to the ship. The pain increased after they'd gotten back. At first, he'd dismissed it as a dull ache, but he'd been wrong about it. But the pain was now nothing but a memory.

Connor looked at Dr. Harris. "How are they?"

"The hybrids who were exposed to the Vemus Alpha the longest have peculiar readings from their biochips. We'll need to monitor them. They'll also need extra food for the next week or so to fuel their recovery."

"What do you mean by peculiar?" Connor asked.

"Outside of their norms. It's not one major red flag per se but a bunch of small variances that are a bit curious. We think it's because of their exposure to the Vemus Alpha," Dr. Harris replied, paused for a moment, and then said, "We're in uncharted territory."

"Are they compromised? Should I be concerned?"

"Are they a security threat?" Dr. Harris said and pressed his lips together. "I wish I could give you a definitive answer to that. Honestly, I don't know." He held up his hand. "Now, before you get irritated with my answer, please let me explain. They were able to communicate with the Vemus Alpha, like two factions from different hives interacting. There is an acknowledgment that they are like cousins—I'm putting this in the simplest terms —but it's much more complicated than this. I'm not saying that hybrids and these alien Vemus are the same, but there are similarities I need to acknowledge."

"Understood," Connor replied.

"Hybrids can affect one another, and how much depends on the individual. That much we know. So, the precedence is set with that."

"I need to know whether it changed them permanently. Do they have something of the alien Vemus in them now?" Connor asked.

"What I've observed doesn't support that, but what we must keep in mind is that they've had an alien encounter. We need to observe and monitor them until we're comfortable that there is nothing actually wrong with them. After that, I'm afraid we'll just have to wait and see."

Connor bobbed his head in understanding. "I doubt all the monitoring will come as a shock."

"I'm told that you'll be transferring back to the *Reliant*?"

"That's right. We'll complete quarantine protocols there."

Dr. Harris nodded. "I'll make sure all our records are transferred to the team on the *Reliant*. However, there is one more thing."

"Yes?"

"You've also had an alien encounter. I've reviewed your preliminary report," Dr. Harris said and eyed Connor for a moment. "It's a little sparse."

"It's preliminary," Connor replied evenly.

"You encountered some kind of being made of light and shadow. They teleported you somewhere else, if it was teleportation. You went through a question-and-answer interview, and then you left. Just like that?"

"That's the long and short of it."

Dr. Harris blinked, looking unconvinced.

"I'm not sure how else to explain it. One moment, I was with the other soldiers, and the next, I was somewhere else. I'll put more details in the report."

"I understand that, but you've got to admit that it seems kinda fanciful."

Connor raised his eyebrows. "Do you think I'm making it up?"

Dr. Harris shook his head, giving him a determined expression. "No, of course not. But could it have been some kind of illusion?" He shrugged.

Connor shook his head. "Not a chance. An illusion wouldn't allow me to travel to another part of the alien complex."

He hadn't included that he'd had three options for returning from wherever Phantom had taken him—one of them being the bridge of the ship, which was orbiting the planet. He had no explanation for that.

"Is there anything in my biochip that indicates an issue with my memory?" Connor asked.

"No, your brain is fine. Completely normal and in line with previous activity. It means that you're either fine or you're convinced that what happened to you is the actual truth."

"That's because it *is* the truth. I understand you want more details. That'll come if it's appropriate."

Harris's eyebrows peaked. "General, I'm trying to help you. I'm not trying to worry you or anything like that. I hope you realize that."

Connor believed him. "I know. I just think I need time to get it straight in my head."

He had something even more reliable than his memory of the incident, but he wanted to review it before alerting the doctors that there was a recording of the entire incident captured on his combat suit.

Connor regarded both doctors for a moment. "Is there anything physically wrong with me?"

"Physically, you're in excellent shape," Dr. Williams said. "I doubt this comes as a surprise. The most pressing issue is one of rest and de-stressing from this entire ordeal. Give your mind time to make sense and evaluate what this entire experience has been. The tendency I've seen among soldiers is to lock away those experiences, which has the appearance of working for a while. However, stress has a way of rearing its head eventually. Again, I'm not telling you anything you don't already know."

Connor smiled knowingly. "I'm more open to it now than when I was a lot younger."

She nodded. "I'm concerned about the hybrids, in particular. As a demographic, they're slow to trust—with good reason, given their history. They will be under a lot of scrutiny until trust is re-established."

Connor frowned. "Trust?"

"Yes, and it's not just a matter of trust of the people in their immediate vicinity or up the chain of command. It's also among themselves. Until now, their experiences when encountering Vemus have been separation. The Vemus we know are the enemy. I think they expected future encounters with the Vemus to be similar, and this experience wasn't entirely like that."

Connor considered it for a few moments. The hybrids he knew were vehemently against the Vemus. They were the enemy. But, because hybrids were different, they also had more to prove, both to themselves and to others—that they weren't vulnerable to the Vemus. The fact that they were a hybrid of both humans and Vemus was a strength for them. It was part of their identity. If that confidence had been upended because of this experience, it could have repercussions down the line that they couldn't entirely anticipate.

Connor sighed, thinking about Ethan. "They're worried, and they have every right to be. I'd rather they were cautious than pretend everything is fine."

"Awareness and understanding are good things, but it's up to the individual. Some will need reassurance, while others will need time. We all deal with things in our own way," Dr. Williams said. She spoke with quiet confidence and had a natural, soothing presence.

"I'm open to suggestions," Connor said.

"It's a blessing that we will soon return to New Earth. It'll give everyone time to work through things, and in some cases, regain their confidence."

Connor glanced at Harris for a second and then looked at Williams. "Is that all?"

She smiled a little. "A lighter training schedule for a week or two would go a long way toward helping."

"Okay, I'll take those things into consideration," he replied and eyed her for a moment. "Speaking of rest, both of you look like you could use some yourselves."

Harris grinned. "The very next thing on our list."

"We won't be far, so if anything comes up we'll be here," Williams said.

Connor smiled, appreciating their dedication. "We'll be fine. Go get some rest."

They left the office space outside one of the exam rooms, and Connor received a text message from Major Caleb Arvad.

Connor walked over to the meeting area that connected the quarantine spaces to the free zones.

"I'm glad to see you up and around, General Gates," Arvad said.

"Feeling better than yesterday."

Arvad nodded. "A couple of updates for you, sir. The *Reliant* will be here in about ten hours, and we'll transfer you back there for the remainder of the quarantine period. Reconnaissance drones show that there is no more alien Vemus activity detected on the planet, so unless there's an additional hive hiding somewhere, I think we can close the book on this planet."

"We still need to update our star charts so this planet remains under quarantine. I don't want any other missions coming back here for the foreseeable future."

Arvad frowned. "What about investigating the alien race who inhabited this planet?"

"We'll leave a monitoring station there, equipped with surveillance tech that can report if anything changes with the planet. Given its state, I'd hardly classify it as a potential colony site. I also didn't think the other survey teams found any indication of survivors."

Since the planet had been attacked by the Vemus, the only reference to the original species was "survivors."

"They're aquatic and could, therefore, be hiding in the depths of the vast oceans here. We're not equipped to explore those depths."

Connor nodded. "The monitoring stations are our best option. It'll allow us to keep tabs on this planet. If we're wrong and the alien Vemus survived somehow, another mission will return to finish the job."

Arvad nodded but looked unconvinced.

Connor arched an eyebrow. "Doubts?"

He shrugged and then shook his head. "I just wish we understood them better. The probes and why the Vemus do this in the first place. Why wipe out entire civilizations. I don't see the point of it. It goes against everything we've been taught. Civilizations go to war with each other over resources, but that's not happening here. How many other planets, or alien civilizations for that matter, are even now waging a war for their own survival against the Vemus? As we keep exploring, I'm wondering how many more worlds will be like what we found here."

"Yeah," Connor sighed. "If we don't keep exploring, we'll remain ignorant, and I don't know if that's the best course of action."

Arvad nodded. "It's not an easy question."

"No, it's not. But it's not up to us, either. This is something we'll need consensus on as exploration policy is established moving forward."

"Thank you, sir," Arvad said, and Connor lowered his chin once. "We did investigate further into the sensor failures on the ship. We don't have…" He paused for a second, "a smoking gun —I think that's the saying—but we have a pretty decent theory of how our internal sensors failed the way they did. The investigating team reviewed the design specifications for the sensors. There is some evidence that suggests the sensors experienced a sudden and powerful gravitational anomaly. It only affected the sensors themselves and not the surrounding areas. This further supports the theory that these failures were intentional. I'm unable to find a link to the Phantoms, but given your experience on the planet, I think it's safe to assume that they had a hand in this."

"Agreed."

"But it is worrisome that we're completely vulnerable to them. Based on what we know from the design specs for sensor failure, they could've caused severe damage anywhere on the ship. What can we do to prevent that?"

"I wish I had answers for you, but I just don't know. Our experience using artificial gravity fields requires the use of massive amounts of energy. Something like that would've been detected."

"A review of active scan data revealed a momentary mass anomaly near the planet. It didn't last long, and then it was gone."

"Can you show me?" Connor asked.

A holoscreen became active. "The general shape is that of a sphere, but as you can see, it's quite large."

Connor peered intently at the screen. "It moved toward the planet?"

Arvad nodded. "I had them triple check the data and later sent a team to manually inspect our sensor array. There is nothing wrong with either of those systems. The data is good."

"So, we have this mass anomaly that appears to move toward the planet and disappears. Too bad we didn't have another ship monitoring the other side of the planet."

Arvad frowned. "Are you suggesting that it moved *through* the planet?"

"It's possible."

"Yeah, but look at the size of it. This should've caused massive amounts of damage to the planet, but it didn't. Maybe they used the planet's gravity to speed them on their way."

Connor considered it for a moment and then nodded. "That's possible."

He didn't believe it, especially not after his experience with Phantom, but he also couldn't come up with a good reason for them revealing their presence like that. There were too many unanswered questions where the Phantoms were concerned.

"General," Arvad said, "I just wanted to convey my appreciation for allowing both me and my crew to work so closely with you. The experience is valuable beyond measure. I've learned a lot."

"You're an outstanding officer. The obstacles faced were enough to trip anyone up, despite their experience. We've all come out on the other side of it a little smarter and wiser than we were before. Have you given any thought to whether you'll push for another exploration rotation?"

Arvad smiled appreciatively. "I'm not sure. It'll depend on the mission goals. I'm looking forward to returning to New Earth. It's been a while since I've been home. A year is a long time, and before that I did a rotation on Old Earth. Also, it's not like there's a lack of volunteers waiting for their turn at exploring the deep dark."

"I'm looking forward to returning to New Earth, too. My wife can't wait to get back either. But there is something to be said about venturing where no one has ever been before."

Arvad smiled. "It's the stuff dreams are made of and one of

the reasons I'm here. I'm hoping we'll have a quiet trip back home."

Connor grinned. "We can always tempt fate if you want."

"No thanks, sir," Arvad said quickly.

Connor's gaze narrowed, and Arvad looked guilty.

"Something you'd like to say?" Connor asked.

"No, General. I just want a smooth trip home, and I look forward to some much-needed downtime."

"Until you get bored."

Arvad laughed and tipped his head to the side. "Isn't that the way it always is, sir?"

They spent a few more minutes going over the ship's status and then Arvad left. Many people wondered about Connor's experience on the planet. He'd disappeared from among a platoon full of soldiers, then reappeared in another location entirely. Speculation would always abound.

A message from Ethan appeared on his HUD.

::*Join us for lunch?*::

::*On my way.*::

Connor left the meeting space and went over to the mobile mess hall. Ethan and Cynergy sat at a table, and there was a covered tray of food for him.

Connor sat down. "Thanks," he said.

"There weren't a lot of options, so I grabbed what I thought you'd like," Ethan said.

Cynergy had a triple portion of food and was eating ravenously. Connor was a little surprised she could consume so much in one sitting, even with a high metabolism.

Ethan had a double portion.

Connor finished his meal of meatloaf, mashed potatoes, and a salad, and chased it down with water. "Did you get enough food?"

Cynergy looked up guiltily. "I can't seem to eat enough. Harris said it will calm down in a week or so."

"How are you feeling?" Connor asked.

She still looked extremely tired and had only perked up while eating.

"I don't know. I'm tired. I remember being captured," she said, her eyes becoming fearful for a moment. "Then I…I couldn't get away." She closed her eyes. "Davis escaped. I remember that. I don't know how he escaped. It's like we were drugged. I can't think of another way to describe it. My memory is spotty at best."

Connor gave her a sympathetic look. "Hopefully, you just need some time. You're beyond lucky to be alive."

"You can say that again," Ethan agreed.

Connor looked at his son. "The same applies to you, too."

Ethan returned his gaze with a solemn look of his own. "I know."

"Can you explain what happened?"

"It's the bond," Cynergy said.

Ethan nodded. "That's right. It started off that way, but then something else happened." He looked away. "The attack. The interaction with the alien Vemus. I remember thinking that if I lost the bond, I wouldn't have found Cynergy again. It became instinctual and I couldn't function right. It's hard to explain."

"You were affecting other hybrids."

"I didn't know that was happening. I think it was instinctual for all of us."

Connor looked at Cynergy. "Were you aware of this? Could you sense Ethan when he was back on the ship?"

She frowned thoughtfully, then shook her head. "I can't remember. I don't think I could. We tried to stay united when the Alpha was deciding what to do with us. I think it was more perplexed by us than we were by it."

"Until it decided that we were the enemy," Ethan said.

Connor regarded both of them. Sometimes it seemed like there was a lot of communication happening that wasn't spoken, and he was on the outside. It wasn't that they were being rude; it was something innate and almost instinctual.

Ethan sighed, giving him a concerned look. "How much trouble are we in?"

Cynergy frowned. "Why would there be trouble? It's not like you could help what happened."

Connor had worried he'd have to bring it up.

"No, there will be fallout from this," Ethan said.

"I don't know if I'd call it trouble. We're going through everything to understand the hows and whys of what happened, which includes what happened to you. Do you even remember what happened on the ship?"

Ethan frowned for a second. "Some. I remember you."

"You were affecting the other hybrids. I don't just mean Roy Emerson and Sheila Tran."

"I didn't know that was happening."

"Then that means you were out of control. That can't happen. You hurt other people, Ethan."

Ethan winced, and his gaze sank to the table. "I don't know what to say."

"Neither do I," Connor replied and looked at both of them. "I understand the drive for what you did, but I feel like a line has been crossed. I'm not sure what it is or what the consequences will be."

"Are we going to be sidelined then?" Ethan asked.

"Until we understand exactly what happened. And take the fact that you're a hybrid out of the equation. If any senior ranking officer was so out of control that he put other lives at serious risk, how do you think they would be handled?"

"The worst case is that he'd be relieved of duty. That's assuming he didn't get anyone killed, including themselves. If it's not the worst-case scenario, their superior officer could reprimand him, but I don't think that applies here. So much of this was reactionary, and there were things happening that had never happened before."

"Those are important factors."

Cynergy cleared her throat. "Wouldn't special considerations apply here based on what hybrids are capable of doing?"

She put her hand on Ethan's.

"Of course," Connor replied and paused. "Cynergy, this isn't your fault. Or anyone else who was captured."

"I have to take responsibility," Ethan said.

"It'll be easier to do that when we better understand what happened. It seemed like you were stuck in a heightened state of hybridization, which I'm told is dangerous. The question that needs to be answered is whether you knowingly remained in that state, or was it involuntary? Meaning you were unaware of the harm you were causing."

Ethan frowned, looking uncertain. "I don't know. I wish I did. It might be both. It might've begun as something I was aware of, but at some point it went beyond that. If I'd known that what I was doing was hurting other people, I would've stopped, but I don't know how I can prove that."

"Hence, why we need to figure this out. It could be something that got out of control, but the fact that this all started after the alien Vemus showed up isn't going to be lost on anyone."

"I'll do whatever it takes," Ethan said. Cynergy squeezed his hand. "*We'll* do whatever it takes."

"You and the others will be going to the *Reliant* for a couple of weeks. We'll be in quarantine for a few days, and the rest of the time will be spent on evaluations."

"I figured. More lab space there," Ethan said.

"Among other things."

"Will we be able to return here after?" Cynergy asked.

"Assuming you're cleared and nothing else comes up."

Cynergy looked relieved. "Thank you for coming after us. Not leaving us behind."

Connor smiled. "I'm glad we were able to find you."

"What about what happened to you?" Ethan asked.

"The doctors say I'm fine."

"That's good. What did they say?"

"That we don't understand the Vemus and we should stop looking for them."

Ethan and Cynergy shared a look. "Please tell me we're not going to do that."

Connor pressed his lips together. "Do you want an honest answer?"

They nodded.

"I don't know. It's not up to me, either."

"Dad, when you learned about the Krake, you sought them out because we were all in danger. How is this any different?"

"We didn't have a choice. The invasion was on our doorstep. This is different. We don't *have* to search for the Vemus."

Ethan blinked. "So, we just ignore it? Leave it for some future generation to deal with?"

"Maybe," Connor said. He didn't like it, but it might be what they had to do.

"That just seems wrong."

"I understand that, but at the same time, there is something to be said for not bringing attention to us. When it comes to the Vemus, we really don't know exactly what we're dealing with."

"I don't want to give this up," Ethan said.

Connor regarded them for a moment, and they both gave him a determined look. They'd faced death, and while it had affected them, it hadn't dampened their determination to understand the Vemus.

"We don't have to decide anything right now, nor should we. What we all need is time and distance from it," Connor said.

Ethan inhaled a deep breath and sighed. Then he smiled a little. "I was thinking we needed a different ship. Better gear. Cyn's prototype drone has more than proven itself. I've got about fifty other things I could list off the top of my head," he said, stifling a yawn.

Cynergy yawned as well. Then Connor and the two of them shared a laugh.

Connor stood. "I'm going to get some sleep. Now that you've stuffed yourselves silly, I suggest you both do the same."

They stood, and Cynergy gave him a hug.

Ethan stared at him for a long moment. "I don't know what to say. I feel that saying 'thank you' falls far short of what I really mean. I wouldn't be here if it wasn't for you."

"*We* wouldn't be here if it wasn't for you," Cynergy said.

Connor's eyes tightened a little. If they'd died on that planet, he didn't know what he would've done. "Let's not make a habit of it. Okay?"

They smiled and gave him a nod.

Connor watched them go for a few seconds. They weren't going to give up searching for the Vemus, and he wasn't sure how he felt about it. He doubted he could stop them or the exploration initiative even if he wanted to, despite what the Phantoms thought. The thing that came with experience was knowing that taking time to make important decisions was much better than rushing into a course of action that might have long-term consequences. Though he was tired, sleep was going to have to wait. He had reports to prepare, and he needed to begin thinking about the Phantoms. He had to get it out of his head and written down so he could consider it. Maybe it would yield more insights than if it remained trapped in his head.

# CHAPTER 32

In the days that followed, the only privacy Ethan had with Cynergy was in their temporary cabin aboard the *Reliant*, which was certainly more comfortable than their temporary HAB unit on the *Challenger*'s secondary hangar. The days of rest provided just what they'd really needed, but now Ethan was getting restless.

The door to their small cabin opened and Cynergy walked in. Having come from the communal showers, she wore a white robe and shower shoes. She raked her fingers through her long blonde hair, and her gold wedding band glittered as she did.

"Have a good shower?" he asked.

She nodded, looking content. "Absolutely. I got the good one on the far right."

Cyn loved hot showers, and the stall on the far right had the most powerful jets, a tad below scalding. It left her pale skin a bit blotchy until she cooled off.

She eyed him for a moment. "I thought you had an evaluation this morning?"

They'd been on the *Reliant* for a few days, which came with daily evaluations that covered a wide range of objectives.

"It's the physical. Only medium level of exertion, though."

Cyn walked over to the dresser and paused. She let the robe fall a bit and looked at him over her bare shoulder. It was all the invitation he needed.

In addition to eating enough for three people because of her ravenous hunger while recovering from her experience with the Vemus Alpha, she—or rather they—were experiencing significantly increased sexual activity and desire for each other. At first, Ethan thought it was from the euphoria of having survived a terrible ordeal, but it hadn't stopped. They'd learned that the other hybrids were experiencing the same behaviors and urges.

Since they were still in quarantine and their biochips were being monitored, all their physical exertions were reported. The doctors monitoring them weren't concerned about their behavior because strong intimacy among married couples often showed more resilience, quicker healing, and a better overall mindset.

"I don't think we'll be here as long as we thought we were going to be," Ethan said.

"What makes you say that? I thought it was going to be three weeks."

"Me, too, but the protocol for quarantine is only a week unless there is evidence that supports more time is needed. I saw it in the latest update from Dr. Bennett."

"So, we'll be able to return to our ship?"

Ethan nodded. "By the next stopping point on our way back to New Earth."

"A week earlier than expected. Will they open access for us to use the common areas while we're here—after the quarantine protocols are lifted, that is?"

"No reason to expect not."

She inhaled a breath and sighed contentedly. "The past few years have spoiled me. I've gotten used to having a lot more space."

Ethan looked around their cabin and shrugged. "It's kinda cozy."

She rolled her eyes. "I keep wondering what's going to happen to you and your promotion."

Ethan had submitted all the documentation required for his application to be promoted to major. He needed the rank if he was ever going to command a ship. "I'm sure it'll go through. Can't pursue the Vemus if it doesn't."

Cyn eyed him for a moment. "The CDF isn't for me." She held up her hand, forestalling the comment on the tip of his tongue. "It isn't, and you know it. I'm a spacer. I'm fine with working with the CDF but as a civilian. Maybe one day we can explore the galaxy without having ties to the military."

Ethan snorted and shook his head. "Not us. Maybe future generations."

Cyn shrugged. "People adapt quicker than you think."

"There are science ships, but it's dangerous. I wouldn't want to venture out there without weapons to defend ourselves."

"Makes sense for places we've never been to, but what about the other places? Star systems we've tagged for future missions?"

Ethan shrugged. "Depends, I guess." He paused a moment, giving her an appraising look. "Do you still feel it?"

Cyn frowned, looking away, her eyes distant. She gave him a small nod. "It's not like it was, but I can't put it entirely from my mind."

Ethan had communicated with the Alpha, but Cyn and the others had been there much longer. She'd had nightmares about it, afraid she was being absorbed into the Vemus hive.

"What if it's part of me now?" she whispered.

Ethan reached across the table and held her hands. "I can remember every detail of what it felt like. I knew what the Alpha wanted. It needed to finish building the ship. The Vemus are out there. There are more worlds with probes on them. They must all contain a set of instructions that get unlocked as the Vemus develops."

"But each world is different. That means all the Vemus will be different."

"To a certain degree, but what if there are more like us? Hybrids. What if they're fighting the Vemus even now on some far-off world?"

Cyn's eyes narrowed with a flash of anger. She didn't like being vulnerable to anything. Not that anyone else did, but with her and many other hybrids it was different. They were able to not only resist the Vemus but also fight them and give insights about them that would've been impossible otherwise. But the alien Vemus had proved that for all their capabilities, hybrids could be just as vulnerable as any other species.

"I wish I could stop," she said.

"Stop what?"

She placed her hand on her chest. "I wish I could walk away from it. Divide our time between New Earth and Old Earth, but I can't. The Vemus are out there, and I feel like we have an obligation to search for them. Learn all we can." She looked away from him. "I feel like they're on their way to our homes even now. Little by little. World by world."

He knew exactly how she felt because it was in him, too. "I don't want to walk away from it. The answers are out there, Cyn. If we stop now, we'll remain ignorant of both the threats and potential alliances in the galaxy."

She arched a blonde eyebrow. "Isn't there a saying about ignorance and bliss?"

"Never heard that one."

"Do you have any idea how long it would take to travel across the galaxy?"

"A really long time, even with the I-Drive. But, we have to think in those terms. Eventually, we'll be able to. Should we wait until then to figure all this out?"

"Not when you put it like that."

"What we know for sure is that Vemus probes have gone to multiple planets. Possibly even many of them. We don't know why, but look at all the destruction it causes. All those lives. As it stands now, we're the only species to have survived their attack."

She gave him a long look. "Be careful, Ethan. The core of our drive must be exploration. Push too much with searching for the Vemus and you'll encounter more opposition."

"But we can't lose sight of it."

She sighed. "I keep thinking about your father. If it hadn't been for him, we wouldn't have made it."

He nodded. "I know. This has to be a joint effort. Can't be just hybrids, as unlikely as that sounds. That's not what I'd push for. I want multiple species in the crew."

"Crew? You're already planning on being awarded command of a ship?"

He shrugged. "I like to think ahead."

She stood and pulled him to his feet. "Time to go."

As she reached the door, Ethan spun her around and kissed her. He'd almost lost her, and himself. He needed to build a new team, because the next time he encountered the Vemus, his father might not be there to pull him out of the fire.

## CHAPTER 33

Connor left the quarantine area and Lenora waited for him just beyond the boundary. Though they'd spoken over vidcom, it just didn't compare to being there in person. Her long auburn hair was down the way he liked it, thick and vibrant. They hugged and she pulled him down for a long kiss. He'd long since moved on from limiting public displays of affection. Life could be much too short for that.

"I missed you, too," he said.

Colonel Oliver Martinez waited nearby and gave him a salute. "Welcome back, General Gates."

They shook hands.

He wasn't the only one to be released from quarantine, and they filed past the others, heading for the visitors' quarters. Carver stood nearby, almost unassuming as he waited. Since they'd been back aboard the *Reliant*, his protective detail had returned to individual shifts. Connor wasn't surprised that Carver was first in the rotation.

They walked through the ship and Martinez led them to

Connor's office. It was spacious, with a desk in the far corner and a long black couch along the wall. Across from the couch were several chairs.

He inhaled the familiar scent of his office, noting that the atmospheric settings had used his personal preferences, mimicking the spicy scents of several New Earth plants that grew around his home at Sanctuary.

Lenora inhaled deeply and smiled. "A little taste of home."

Martinez hovered just outside the door. "Would you like to push this meeting back? Give you both a chance to reunite?"

While Connor would've loved to spend some time alone with Lenora and was quite tempted to take Martinez up on his offer, he decided not to.

He shook his head. "No, there's something I'd like to discuss with both of you."

Lenora had been expecting it. She sat on the couch and crossed her legs. His gaze lingered on them for a second. Sometimes a month really could feel like a year.

She smiled up at him and gestured for him to sit next to her.

Martinez sat across from them.

"I wanted to talk to you both about the report," Connor said.

Martinez nodded. "The Phantoms picked you."

"And they could be listening to this conversation, and we wouldn't even know it," Lenora said.

"They could, but I don't think they are. The impression I got from them was that they were monitoring our progress over the course of the mission," Connor said.

"They can access any of our systems? Is there no way to secure our data from them?" Martinez asked.

"They knew a lot, and we'll need to review the recordings of the entire encounter, but they also made some mistakes."

"We can only go by your account, since they don't appear to be interested in anyone else," Lenora replied.

"What kind of mistakes?" Martinez asked.

"Just some assumptions during the course of the entire conversation."

"They might've been testing you," Lenora said. "You only gave us access to your report, so we have yet to review the data recorded by your combat suit."

"I haven't uploaded it to any of the computer systems," Connor said.

Lenora frowned. "You're carrying a data storage device."

He nodded and tapped his right front pocket.

"Why? What if it gets damaged?" she asked.

"I'm worried that they might seek to erase it, or worse, manipulate it."

Martinez pursed his lips for a moment. "And since you're carrying the only hard copy of the encounter, you think they can't do anything to it?"

Connor nodded. "They were able to pull the data from our archives. They wanted to learn our history."

"I understand that," Lenora said. "But why to do you think they'd manipulate the data?"

"Because I didn't do what they wanted me to."

"You mean when they told you to abandon everyone on the planet and destroy the site? Somehow, if they're so brilliant and have access to all our records, they should've known you'd never do that."

"That's just it. Why ask in the first place?" Martinez asked.

Connor glanced at Lenora. "Because if the circumstances were different, I might've made a different choice."

"That's debatable, one that I don't see the point in exploring,"

Lenora said. "I'm more concerned about their assertion that Ethan, Cyn, and the others are irrevocably changed."

"You're not going to like hearing this, but they might be right about that," Connor said. "There are enough people keeping an eye on the survivors that I don't think we're in any real danger. But the experience and the way hybrids can interact, I keep asking myself how could they not change? I just don't know what it means."

Martinez tipped his head to the side. "The reports of the hybrids in quarantine don't indicate that there are issues." He gave them a considering look. "I'm just going to go ahead and say it. What if whatever has happened to them knows enough to conceal itself until later?"

Lenora became stiff next to him. This next part she wasn't going to like at all.

"That's what I'm worried about. I've talked about it with Ethan and Cynergy. They're aware of the possibility that this could happen. That's why they've agreed to allow their biochips to be monitored after the quarantine period has ended."

Lenora blew out a long breath and shook her head. "At what point does it stop? All the monitoring and precautions? When does it stop for them? Why should they have to live with all this invasiveness? We've been down this road before when Ethan first became a hybrid. He cooperated at first, and then eventually pushed back on the invasiveness and mistrust. Why would the normal performance-monitoring guidelines be any different for them?"

Connor shared her frustration, but at the same time he knew it was necessary. "Because we're in uncharted territory. This is the first time hybrids have been vulnerable to the Vemus. The fact that the Alpha didn't know what to do about them is one of the reasons they're still alive."

"Well then, they can stop searching for the Vemus," Lenora said.

Connor looked at her with raised eyebrows. "He's not going to stop. Neither is she."

She crossed her arms, looking vulnerable. "Stubbornness is a Gates's family trait."

Connor grinned. "They get it from both sides of the family."

She snorted and leaned toward him, and he put his arm around her.

"I saw his application for promotion come in," Martinez said. "His writeup is clear about what his intentions are. He wants a ship and to be assigned to the expeditionary core. I don't see where his qualifications are lacking."

Lenora sat up and looked at Connor. "You don't seem surprised by this."

"I'm not. I urged him to do it. He'd already been in the process of doing it when I left the *Challenger*. Ethan and Cyn are going to do what they want. And they won't be alone." Connor looked at Martinez. "What do you think?"

He sighed. "You finally meet a Phantom and they tell you the Vemus are a problem that's too much for humanity? My gut reaction is that they don't know what we're capable of, but after that bravado fades, I wonder if they're right. Then, as more times passes, the question becomes whether we're the kind of species that does as they're told."

Connor smiled. Martinez was a good man. "Not likely, nor do we like being kept in the dark."

"I think you're misunderstanding them," Lenora said. "They were urging us to slow down. They didn't say that we should abandon exploration altogether."

"They were trying to manipulate us, so how can we trust anything they say? I'm all for being cautious, but I don't like knowing that the Vemus are out there. Maybe the Phantoms are right and we shouldn't seek them out. If that's what we learn, we can decide on that later, but to not even try to learn about them for ourselves would be negligent," Connor said.

Lenora regarded him for a few moments with a knowing look. Then she sighed with a slight shake of her head. "I was suddenly reminded of those early days of the colony."

"Yeah, but this is different. I have no intention of seeking the Vemus. It's time for someone else to lead that effort."

He looked at Martinez and his eyes widened.

"Me?" Martinez asked, surprised.

"You've got all the qualifications. I know I'm putting you on the spot, but give it some thought," Connor said.

"I will, sir."

Lenora smiled at Connor. "For a second, I thought I was going to have to convince you. Glad to see you're finally getting it."

It had taken him a while to admit to himself that it was time for others to take the helm, but he also wasn't convinced that the Phantoms were done with him. He smiled at Lenora. He didn't want to worry her, and there was always the possibility that he might be wrong. It had happened on occasion, but deep down he knew the score. He'd been right a heck of a lot more than he'd been wrong about these things, but those were tomorrow's worries.

## CHAPTER 34

Connor left Lauren and Isaac's house where their welcome-home celebration had occurred. He'd really missed Lauren, and with a swollen belly and pregnancy glow abounding, she'd never been more beautiful to him. It filled him with a fatherly pride that he couldn't quite explain.

Lenora stayed behind, and he sensed they needed some mother-daughter time.

It was late afternoon in the city called Sanctuary. The skies were clear and blue, and the temperature was warm. New Earth's rings stretched across the sky, nearing the horizon. He inhaled the fresh spring air, allowing it to fill his lungs, and sighed. He had been a long time away from home. As much as they tried to make their interstellar ships more like home, they fell far short of anything like standing on a planet. He'd lived longer on New Earth than Old Earth, and this was his home. He'd done his part, returning to Old Earth three years ago, and he doubted he'd ever go back there. This was where he intended to stay.

A reminder appeared on his wrist computer. There was to be

another welcome-home celebration, this one hosted by the Salty Soldier, and Connor smiled. He missed his old friend Juan Diaz. It would be good to see him again.

Connor climbed into the aircar and set off to visit another old friend. Meanwhile, his new protective detail was under the impression that he was still at Lauren's home. He needed some privacy for this, but they wouldn't be fooled for long.

Connor flew the aircar to a house on the hillside that was tucked among the trees, home to an old friend and the smartest man he'd ever known. He landed the car on the pad and stepped out.

He heard barking from behind the large house, and as he walked toward the front door, two huge dogs bolted from around the side of the house, galloping toward him. Long, pink tongues lolled in their mouths, tails wagging like giant windmills. Standing on all fours, their heads easily reached his chest.

Connor spread his arms wide and greeted the two guardians. It had been a long time since he'd seen them, but they still remembered him. They leaned against him while he scratched behind their ears and down their backs. "Where's he at?"

A man jogged around the side of the house, and stopped, eyes wide. "Connor!"

Connor smiled. "Hello, Noah!"

Noah Barker was older now, near his late fifties, but looked more like he was in his late twenties. He had short hair, an average frame, and was undeniably brilliant. Despite all the years they'd known each other, Connor still remembered the long-haired youth who rode with him on the shuttle for his very first trip to New Earth. Even then, his talent couldn't be contained, and he was already one of the most sought-after technical experts at the time. It was one of the reasons Connor had recruited him, but the good man Noah grew into was why they'd remained friends all these years.

Noah walked toward him. "It's really good to see you!"

"You, too, Noah. It's good to be back."

Noah smiled. "I thought I wouldn't see you until later on at Juan's place."

Connor glanced at the house. "Is anyone else here?"

Noah shook his head. "No, Kara just took the boys over to her mother's place."

They spoke about their families as Noah led him inside the house, and they ended up in a garden in the back.

Noah eyed him for a moment. "Why do I get the feeling this is more than a social call between old friends?"

Connor smiled. "That's because you know me so well," he said and proceeded to tell him about what happened.

When he was done, Noah bit his lower lip while he stared at Connor for a moment. "Sounds made up," he said, the edges of his eyes crinkling. "I know you're not making it up, but…wow, Connor. How many people know about this?"

"Not very many," Connor said and then placed a data cube on the table.

Noah glanced at it. "What's on it?"

"A recording of the encounter, but there are some precautions about looking at it."

"Such as?"

"Can't be on any networked system. Needs isolation."

Noah arched an eyebrow and looked at the cube again. "Why are you bringing this to me?"

"Isn't it obvious? I need your help." He watched Noah for a few seconds and then continued. "Something Phantom said has been banging around in my head the entire trip back. He said we move *in* space instead of *through* it. That it limits us. Any idea what that could mean?"

Noah frowned in thought and then rubbed his chin. He started to speak a couple of times and then shook his head. "Hmm, that's a tough one."

"I know. It's deceptively simple."

Noah stared at the data cube, brow furrowed in concentration. Then, he heaved a sigh. "I swear. Why do you always come to me with impossible tasks?"

"Because you're the best at it."

Noah chuckled, and Connor smiled.

"Seriously, does that make sense to you at all?"

Noah shook his head. "Not really…maybe a little…okay, more than a little, but that doesn't mean anything," he said and checked his wrist computer. "We should probably head out. Kara was going to meet me there, anyway."

Connor blinked in surprise. Where had the time gone?

Noah looked at him with raised eyebrows. "You didn't think I'd just pluck a solution off the top of my head? These things take time, *genius* takes time." He pressed his lips together with an accusatory look. "We do have time, right?"

Connor regarded him for a moment, feigning disappointment. "Well, *I'm* on a timetable here, Noah."

They laughed. It felt good, like it had been a while.

It was good to be home.

# AUTHOR NOTE

Thank you so much for reading. *Resurgence* is the 16th book in the First Colony series. This series has grown beyond what I'd originally conceived when I first started writing it in 2017, and it has been a welcome surprise and delight. Of the growing library of stories that I've written, First Colony has gotten by far the most response from readers. I'm humbled by all the feedback and the love for the characters. Stories for me start with a simply question: *What if...*

I sincerely hope you enjoyed this latest book. *Expedition Earth* (Book 14) began another series arc answering the question of what happened to Old Earth. *Resurgence* (Book 16) takes the next step in the journey, laying the foundation of what happens next. Exploration has been the heart of this series, and I look forward to writing more stories that challenge the characters simply by starting with the question: *What if...*

Thank you so much for reading my books. Please consider leaving a review for *Resurgence*.

**If you're looking for another series to read consider reading the Federation Chronicles. Learn more by visiting:**

https://kenlozito.com/federation-chronicles/

# ABOUT THE AUTHOR

I've written multiple science fiction and fantasy series. Books have been my way to escape everyday life since I was a teenager to my current ripe old(?) age. What started out as a love of stories has turned into a full-blown passion for writing them.

Overall, I'm just a fan of really good stories regardless of genre. I love the heroic tales, redemption stories, the last stand, or just a good old fashion adventure. Those are the types of stories I like to write. Stories with rich and interesting characters and then I put them into dangerous and sometimes morally gray situations.

My ultimate intent for writing stories is to provide fun escapism for readers. I write stories that I would like to read, and I hope you enjoy them as well.

If you have questions or comments about any of my works I would love to hear from you, even if it's only to drop by to say hello at KenLozito.com

Thanks again for reading *First Colony - Resurgence*

Don't be shy about emails, I love getting them, and try to respond to everyone.

# ALSO BY KEN LOZITO

### First Colony Series

Genesis

Nemesis

Legacy

Sanctuary

Discovery

Emergence

Vigilance

Fracture

Harbinger

Insurgent

Invasion

Impulse

Infinity

Expedition Earth

Fallen Earth

Resurgence

### Space Raiders Series

Space Raiders

Space Raiders - Forgotten Empire

Space Raiders - Dark Menace

**FEDERATION CHRONICLES**

ACHERON INHERITANCE

ACHERON SALVATION

ACHERON REDEMPTION

ACHERON RISING (PREQUEL NOVELLA)

**ASCENSION SERIES**

STAR SHROUD

STAR DIVIDE

STAR ALLIANCE

INFINITY'S EDGE

RISING FORCE

ASCENSION

**SAFANARION ORDER SERIES**

ROAD TO SHANDARA

ECHOES OF A GLORIED PAST

AMIDST THE RISING SHADOWS

HEIR OF SHANDARA

IF YOU WOULD LIKE TO BE NOTIFIED WHEN MY NEXT BOOK IS RELEASED VISIT KENLOZITO.COM

Made in United States
Orlando, FL
17 January 2025